DILLIGAF

A Life in Chapters

Iain Parke

GW00777104

bad-press.co.uk

Also by Iain Parke

The Liquidator

The Brethren MC Trilogy:

Heavy Duty People
Heavy Duty Attitude
Heavy Duty Trouble

The Iain Parke Papers:

Operation Bourbon – The First Chapter
Lord of the Isles – The Next Chapter

ISBN 978-0-9930261-0-2

bad-press.co.uk

iainparke@hotmail.com
Facebook: /Iain.Parke and /TheBrethrenTrilogy
Goodreads: /author/show/4400967.Iain_Parke
Pinterest: /iainparke
LinkedIn: /iainparke
Twitter: @iainparke

To Pat as ever for continuing to put up with me, and to my family

To all the writers who've gone before me and whose work I've plundered ruthlessly

And with thanks to Ed, for your generous interest and support – here's to a shitty wall!

First it's fun.

Then it's not.

Then it's hell.

Attributed to Dr John Cooper Clarke

Talking bikes and bikers

Whenever I mention I've been talking to outlaw bikers, I almost always find that people have an image of what they must be like to deal with.

Perhaps, reading this, you do too.

Hostility, an air of danger, and an intimidatingly aggressive attitude, probably from a big hulking bloke covered in tattoos and with a shaven head or wild straggling hair. Is that what you immediately envisage?

Well I'd be lying if I said that over the years I hadn't come across versions of this in a few of the bikers I've met.

But then, I'd be lying if I said I hadn't come across the same things from quite a few guys who aren't bikers as well in my time.

As a crime reporter, in my line of work whatever groups of blokes I mix with, from football fans to coppers, I'll always come across some who are suspicious, bordering on antagonistic, towards any outsiders who are seen to be poking their noses in where they don't belong.

So, as a journalist, it's often difficult to have the type of conversation I want to when talking in a group. People always act and talk differently in front of their mates, whereas on a one-to-one basis they can be a lot more open about what they're prepared to share and how they say it.

Given the press they get, you'd also have to grant outlaw bikers a reasonable degree of grounds to be suspicious about any journalist who wants to talk to them.

After all, journalists write for papers whose owners want to sell copies. They want good stories, the racier and juicier the better, and if that has only a passing resemblance to the truth, well so what? As long as the punters buy and keep on buying, the editors, street dealers that they are, will keep on peddling whatever it is that feeds their appetites and keeps them hooked.

Sex, violence, drugs, money, danger, depravity, a threat to society to give a visceral shudder of fear, outrage and a sneaking secret envious jealousy down a reader's spine, that's grade A product to an editor, to be cut, recut and moved out onto the streets in easy to swallow hits that just keeps their marks coming back for more.

And of course it's a self-perpetuating cycle. All journalists think people want to read is the outrageous stuff, so that's all they ever want to write about.

Then there's the books by rats and ex-undercover officers. Of course, they need to justify what they've done, so they focus on the crime, the drugs, the violence every time. All they want to see and present are the negatives so these are always front and centre.

They want to ignore the positives, the camaraderie, the family, the support, the opportunities that being in a club provides its members. Although it's noticeable how in some of the undercover cop's books you can see a recognition and respect for these values and loyalty, however sneaking or begrudging, coming through as the cops work their way into acceptance in their target clubs.

So is it any wonder that any biker who ever talks to a journalist thinks he is just asking to get burned?

Whatever they actually have to say, however articulate or otherwise they might be, they're simply too tempting a target for most media hacks who are just looking for their next quick hit.

The bikers aren't daft. They see the way the world works, they know how they're likely to be treated, and they factor it into what they'll say to whom. And so yes, it is sometimes difficult to get to talk to bikers and yes, they can often be wary of journalists and their agendas, and yes, it can therefore take quite some time to gain a level of trust.

But once you are talking on a one to one basis with a biker, well then it's usually nothing like the popular image might have you believe.

I've just been interviewing a long-standing patch-holder for example, a relatively senior individual within his club and the only way to describe him is as a real gent. He's pleasant, easy to talk to with a sense of humour and a willingness to range quite widely in what he'll discuss with me.

One of the things that comes across quite clearly in our conversations is his pride in his club and the values he believes they stand for, as well as a keenness to explain this to anyone who has a genuine interest in understanding. But in our discussions this has never been in a threatening way, even when it's touched on serious issues from club business and conflicts, right through to the deeply personal, which to me comes back to the old saying in the biker world about respect earning respect.

Becoming a patch-holder in any serious club is a serious business. It's something not to be undertaken lightly and something which, whatever you think about the clubs and their members, clearly requires an immense amount of dedication and effort. So, finally being awarded a patch and recognised as a club brother is something that gives a man a real feeling of achievement, of having made it into an elite.

And for some members the self-confidence this success brings, alongside the acceptance into membership of a brotherhood that will back them unquestioningly, translates into an easy self-assurance which affects every area of their life, and which actually makes them very easy to talk to.

Iain Parke interview in ▆▆▆▆ *Magazine*
Originally published in June 2009 shortly before his disappearance

It was Wednesday 18 April 2012 when the call to our offices came through at round ten past ten in the morning. The number was withheld.

'Hello bad-press, can we help...'

'Hi, are you the lot that publish Iain Parke's stuff?' the gruff sounding voice demanded directly, in what sounded like a slight Mancunian accent.

As his publishers we were in the process of sorting through his files and papers. He had left behind literally stacks of material, ranging from published extracts such as the one above, to folders containing transcripts of interviews and background he had gathered, and we were starting to try to make sense of it all.

This then was the process that would eventually lead to both the wide ranging revelations published in *Operation Bourbon* (2013) of a long running police operation to place an undercover officer high in the ranks of the Rebels MC in Scotland, but also the highly personal story of one biker's journey across the UK of *Lord of the Isles* (2014).

Given Iain's profile and the circumstances, someone making contact with us about him and his books wasn't unheard of. It didn't happen every day by any means, but often enough to be a normal part of business. As Iain's publishers we manage his old social media accounts on Twitter, Facebook and the like; in his absence we see it as just part of our job in continuing to promote his books on his behalf.

The only thing that was odd really, was to get a call.

Since his profile was relatively well established before he disappeared, his email accounts were pretty widely known, and as monitoring and managing them is part of the overall work we're doing, we're used to getting emails from readers addressed via his personal Hotmail address and through our bad-press.co.uk business account. Sometimes they were from people asking questions about his books, once in a blue moon they were writers offering a manuscript for us to look at, but mostly they were notes from readers just writing in to say how much they liked his stuff, which was always great to hear.

The one thing people didn't generally do, was call.

Whether it's because they know he's missing, or whether they prefer the anonymity of the internet, when people get in touch about Iain and his writing it's always, always, by email.

Or was, until that day.

The caller sounded tense, stressed, but in control.

'Yes, that's us, what can we do for you?'

'I've got some stuff for you.'

'Um, right, so what...?'

Our immediate assumption at this stage was that this was someone calling with a manuscript. As we've said, it had happened a few times already, people who'd read Iain's books and who wanted to send in

4

their own story to us in the belief, hope, that we would publish it for them and overnight turn them into bestselling authors. Ah, if only the publishing business was that easy. An assumption that the mystery voice's next comments seemed to bear out.

'This is something you're going to want to see... this is a thing where we can do each other a serious favour,' the voice said, with an intense earnestness that didn't sound as though it would brook any quibbling.

'OK, so what would that be?' we asked.

'Files, the straight shit,' came the voice.

'Files? What sort of files?'

'The sort people don't want published.'

In some ways that was going to make it easy, we thought. We're not a newspaper, we don't employ journalists to go and ferret things out. We're a publisher, which means we publish books, things that people have written with a beginning, a middle, not necessarily in that order, and hopefully, an end worth waiting for. What we don't do is put out the contents of some random collection of files, as we started to explain.

'I see, well, have you tried the press? You see we don't really...'

'Only they're the sort of files that you're going to be interested in,' he insisted.

'Why's that?' we asked warily.

'Because you're in it, that's why, your lot, that Parke bloke, every-thing, and I think you're going to wanna see what they're saying about you.'

'Why, whose files are these?' we wanted to know, we didn't like the sound of this and where it was going.

'Well take a wild stab at a guess,' the voice said sarcastically.

Which wasn't a reassuring turn of phrase in the circumstances, so we guessed it wasn't a very hard question really. There were only going to be a few organisations he could be referring to.

'The club?' we ventured.

'Uhuh, some of them...'

Some of them, we wondered, worried by this revelation. What does he mean *some of them*?

If he had club files then by implication he had to be, or at least to have been, a club member, a full patch. More than that, to get hold of any documents, particularly any sensitive ones, he'd have had to have held a fairly high rank, which meant an officer, so a secretary, treasurer, VP or even a P, at local charter or possibly national level. You have to appreciate how little we at bad-press actually knew about things in the club world at this point. After all, it was Iain who had developed his relationships with the club and its members and associates over the years, as well as amongst the police who were targeting the biker scene. He was the one who'd heard the stories, knew the faces, understood the history and culture. We were just his publishers and we didn't have any of those links, and given it was that closeness which had led to his disappearance, and the speculation about his death that continues to this day, we weren't generally too upset about it.

But if out mystery caller was coming from a club background, it did raise the question, who else did he have stuff from? We didn't have to wait long for an answer.

'The rest are from the plod...'

Which had a certain sense of inevitability. Who else would it be?

But in terms of questions in our minds at that point we had other things we wanted to ask. Aside from whatever it was that was in these files, assuming they existed and we weren't being fed a complete line, was: Who the hell it was calling us. What did he want? If he had files with some interesting dirt in them, why call us?

It all came back to the old five finger question. There was a moment of silence before we asked it.

'So why bring this to us? What's in this for you?'

'Simple, I want you to publish this shit.'

'Well, assuming we see it and there's something publishable...'

'There is, don't you worry about that...'

6

We overrode him, 'Well, so you say, but we'll need to see what you've got and make our own minds up about that, and you still haven't answered the question.'

'What question was that?' he wanted to know.

'Why? Why do you want it, whatever it is, published? And why us?' we insisted.

There was a moment of silence on the line.

'Well why you, that's easy,' he said eventually, with what sounded like a sigh. 'You'll have an interest in this once you've seen what I've got and so I know you'll want to publish it.'

'But how about you, why's this so important to you?' we pressed.

'Because I'm quite keen on staying alive,' he said, his voice edged with bitterness, 'and because getting this crap out there through someone who will definitely make it happen, is the only thing that's going to give me a chance of keeping that way.'

CHAPTER 1   THE CALL

Q What do you call a biker in a suit?

A The defendant.

Joke told to Iain Parke by one of his police contacts

The phone rang. The number was untraceable and the mobile was a burner anyway, pay as you go.

'I need a couple of pieces of work doing,' said the voice, without preamble.

'Sure, no problem.'

'Let's have a walk and talk when I'm back and I'll fill you in.'

'OK, let me know when and where.'

'Will do.'

And with that he was gone.

And with that it all kicked off.

*

'He's having a right fucking laugh here, isn't he?' muttered the junior Met officer disgustedly to no one in particular, 'Bulk Transport Logistics – Four Corners Of The World Limited? Who's he trying to kid?'

The two detectives and the Senior Rummage Officer from Customs, in his day glow yellow tabard, stood looking at the empty opened shipping container in the dockside warehouse, and neatly stacked rows of pallets and boxes arranged beside it, the product of their night's work.

'And it's all bears? You're sure of that are you?' The senior of the detectives asked, staring down at the clipboard in his hands and shaking his head at the manifest.

'Look, this is our job, sir,' said the Customs Officer bridling, but keeping his anger in check, the 'sir' almost, but not quite, a deliberate insult. 'This is what we do, take this sort of thing apart to find stuff.

And believe it or not, since we get a lot of it through here, A – we're actually quite bloody good at it and B – my team have checked everything twice.'

'Yeah, yeah, I know,' said the detective distractedly, glancing back down at the papers and then over to where the rest of the Customs team were now waiting. Someone had fetched steaming cups of coffee from the canteen which they were now drinking against the cold of the Felixstowe morning while they waited to see the coppers' next moves and their boss's response. As usual, while the professional courtesies were maintained between the two sides, the reality was there wasn't much love lost.

Quietly between themselves, the team all agreed it had been irritating to put all this effort into fossicking through the contents of the container throughout the night only to turn nothing up. For many of the team now lounging by the cases the feeling that they'd had their time wasted when it could have been spent tucked up in warm beds was made up for in part by the mental calculation of the overtime rate involved.

But even more satisfying in some ways had been the pleasure in watching the smug expressions slide remorselessly from the faces of the two coppers as the hours ticked by and it had become increasingly clear that, despite their zealous, know it all attitude, the plod were on a wild goose chase. The enjoyment of their obvious eventual discomfort and frustration was reward itself.

'And there's really nothing? Not inside any of them?'

'You're welcome to go through them yourself if you like,' the Customs Officer said in an exasperated tone, gesturing towards the stacked boxes, 'be my guest.'

Needless to say neither of the detectives moved a muscle.

'We've been going over this lot with a fine toothcomb for you for hours. Believe me, if there was something there, we'd have found it by now. My boys know what they're doing you know. We've unpacked every pallet and stuck them through the X-ray, nothing unusual. We've had the dogs go over them and there's not a sniff of anything dodgy. We've opened up some samples at random and taken them apart, and there's just what you'd expect to see when you dissect a teddy bear, stuffing. Take it from me, sir, there's nothing. No powder. No pills. Not even an aspirin.'

'Which is a pity since my head is killing me,' muttered the more junior detective, although whether this was supposed to be a joke neither of the others knew or cared enough about to find out.

'But there's got to be,' continued the senior one. 'How about something soaked into them? Some chemical maybe?'

The Customs Officer fixed him with a sceptical glare, 'Christ, you're grasping at straws here aren't you? Well we'll run tests back at the lab but no, there's no sign of any contamination on any of those we've looked at. No discolouration or matting of the fur or stuffing that suggests there's anything out of the ordinary. And before you ask, yes, we've looked at the eyes and scanned them specifically again in the X-ray machine, and unless the lab tells me different they're just the straightforward glass that you'd expect to see.'

As the two detectives glanced at each other the Customs Officer was starting to enjoy himself.

'No, what you have here, sir,' that 'sir' again in that making-an-effort-to-suffer-fools-at-least-politely tone, 'in my professional opinion, following our extensive and thorough review of all the available evidence, are 20,000 standard issue, finest British made, common or garden stuffed teddy bear toys doing their bit for our international balance of trade, together with their impeccable, and I have to say, absolutely correct export paperwork.'

'I just don't get it!' muttered the senior detective to himself angrily.

Yes, well I can see that, thought the Customs Officer, adopting what he hoped was a suitably blank expression.

'I mean what the hell are they doing exporting soft toys to South Africa?' he continued, to no one in particular.

'So can we close it up now, sir?' asked the Customs Officer politely, twisting the knife ever so slightly.

That was it, the detectives knew they were beaten, for now.

'Yes, yes, alright,' the senior man said, as he handed back the manifest emblazoned with the company's strap line and logo, rendered as B$_{ulk}$ T$_{ransport}$ L$_{ogistics}$ – F$_{co}$TW, and turned to leave. 'Thanks. You can send it on its way.'

*

The sawn-off was properly prepared in advance, they made sure of that. They both knew it wasn't just a matter of taking an angle grinder or a pipe-cutter to it and chopping off both barrels to make a functional lupara. That was the sort of thing an amateur would do.

The barrels were hardened steel so needed to be cut right and cleanly. So they carefully wrapped the metal to protect them as they were clamped in the vice, before the cuts were precisely marked and double checked for accuracy. And when it was done, they took the time to properly file down and dress the cut edges, making sure there weren't any projecting ridges, loose shards or swarf that might come off when they were fired. They knew they needed to be careful with things like that, if not, you ran the risk of splinters that could go anywhere and be dangerous.

The stock came down as well, turning it into just a pistol grip so the whole thing could be both concealed and manoeuvred more easily, important in a confined space. The way it was planned to go down there was no way the target was going to get a chance to see it until it was time, but still, you could never be too careful.

What they ended up with was something that looked like an old fashioned flintlock firearm, the sort of thing a self-respecting high-wayman might have aspired to for having stagecoaches stand and deliver. Clyde Barrow, as in Bonny and Clyde, used to have a favourite sawn-off he nicknamed his Whippit. He'd fitted it with a foot long leather strap attached to the butt at both ends so he could carry it concealed, shoulder holster style, hanging between his arm and his chest and could 'whip it' out quickly and easily to fire.

They loaded both barrels with a common buckshot shell, 12 gauge, 00 buck, holding 9 pellets. The only unusual feature was they had opted for reduced-recoil shells. From practice they'd found this made the gun easier to manage when firing in the absence of a stock to brace against a shoulder, without having any noticeable effect on the impact at the sort of close range situations they would be working in.

In theory it also tended to make fast follow-up shots easier but again, given the ranges involved, generally that wasn't ever going to be an issue, even though having lost the choke at the end of the normal barrel, the effective spread would be wider than normal.

They were professionals, and being a professional in their book meant being careful.

Prior Planning Prevents Piss Poor Performance.

They lived by that.

It meant proper preparation right from the outset, careful reconnaissance and researching of the target, or in this case targets, for as long as it took. They were interested in learning everything possible about them, and certainly everything they needed to know from a practical perspective. Where they went, who they saw, what they did. Their haunts, their routines, their foibles. How they acted, what they watched for, how aware they were. The places, the times, the security. All of this and more they were looking for and it all went into the mix.

And only when they thought they had enough, and only then, could the planning start.

What was going to be done. The where. The when. The how.

What was needed and where was it going to be sourced. The tools. The transport. The cover. Did they need anyone else? Did they need papers, or uniforms? All those practicalities that needed sorting out, and arranging properly in advance.

But that only took them so far. Then there was what was going to happen afterwards. The clean up. The exit. The getaway. The collection. Staying active as a professional meant realizing that the job didn't end the moment you pressed the trigger. It meant planning on how you got away, without leaving a trail for forensics to follow. As well as making sure you collected the balance of your payment of course.

And for real professionals, that wasn't the end of it.

Because for real professionals there was also the scenario planning, the truth as preached by their chosen patron saint, Helmuth von Moltke the Elder, that no plan survives contact with the enemy.

So they took risk management seriously the way they'd been taught.

They thought through the what ifs, the alternatives, the fall backs. It was just the normal thing for them to do. They were professionals and to them, this was just another job. There was nothing personal about it. It was a piece of work, something that they'd specialized in ever since they'd come out of the forces expert in every black art their government had spent serious money training them in, honing their skills over the years until muscle memory and constant exercise had made them, they knew, among the best in the world at what they did.

And then once they were out, they found the private sector, or certain elements of it at least, were willing to pay well for these skills. Those that appreciated professionalism and discretion at least.

So now all there was to do was wait in the warm Mediterranean sunshine, sitting on the balcony of their rented apartment drinking sweet freshly squeezed orange juice and enjoy an early morning shared *ensaïmada* and coffee, before heading out to the car.

*

It was to be what the client called Aussie rules. The client had specified they wanted it done that way, and as professionals they didn't ask, know, or care why. Perhaps they thought it might be to throw the investigation off the scent. Whatever the reason it didn't matter to them. It was something they could handle without a problem.

They had arrived first, as agreed, and sat waiting in the car at the rendezvous point, earphones in, wraparound shades on.

They'd chosen a spot up in the mountains. The twisting winding road climbed steeply from the orange groves and picture perfect tourist attractions of the valley floor with its little wooden train and old fashioned tram down to the port, and the promenade of seafront restaurants at which they'd eaten the last few nights while they scouted out the area.

As they gained height in the early morning sunshine, long falls were visible between the trees, and occasional glimpses out towards the brilliantly shining sea at the apex of some of the hairpins, before the road turned back on itself to plunge between the grey rocks and even greyer ancient olive trees hunched over in gnarled groves, the tracks off to isolated stone built houses growing fewer and fewer as the land became harsher and less hospitable with each kilometre marker they passed. Until at last the road flattened out and began to snake its way through and around the mountain tops where it had been carved, blasted and tunnelled, to head along the west of the island.

They took the road carefully. The island was a magnet for cyclists riding in clubs, all matching sponsor splashed lycra outfits and already this morning they'd passed two pelotons of mamils, arses in the air as they pumped their way up the mountain, one emblazoned with a *Sky* logo, and the other with *Connecticut-E* which they hazarded a guess at being an energy company, while whistling down the other way had come a group in black, red and gold with *Dieter-moto* scrawled across their chests.

They reached their destination only a few moments later. It was a small island after all, so nowhere was really very far from anywhere else, and they turned off the tarmac and down the rough track towards the parking area, rattling over a cattle grid as they did so.

At the weekends it was a busy park, part of a larger nature reserve, with a play and picnic area just beside the car park and the usual facilities, a toilet block, tables, and a range of barbeque pits for families to cook at, all tucked away just a few hundred metres from the road but screened from view by the trees.

Driving sedately so as not to kick up any unnecessary dust, the car wheeled slowly around over the rough earth of the car park, turning so that it stopped facing out towards the entrance.

This early on a working day late in the week, the place was as deserted as they'd anticipated. No cars, and no signs of people. It was too soon for any of the cyclists to be taking a break. They were too busy making the most of the relative cool of the morning air before the sun rose over the high cliffs either side of the road and turned the tarmac into a furnace.

Other than a pair of mountain bikes chained to a rack in the far corner, it looked as though no one had been near the place for days, but ever the professionals, as the driver waited at the wheel the passenger got out and carefully checked all around to make sure.

'Clear?' asked the driver, his elbow hanging out of the wound down window, as the passenger returned to the car.

'All clear,' he confirmed, sliding back into his seat.

Here in the mountains this early in the year the air was chill, and despite the brilliant blue of the sky, the sun had yet to climb high enough to shine down into the valley from above the surrounding peaks. By the afternoon this place would be roasting, but just now they could enjoy the cool, still, clear air.

They didn't have long to wait, as about ten minutes later they saw the car they were expecting cautiously nose its way down the track.

'Here he comes,' the driver said quietly, as the cattle grid rumbled and clattered under the advancing car's wheels.

'Hello though, who's he got with him?' asked the passenger, as they saw the silhouette of a second figure in the vehicle, but by that time it was too late for talking or scenario planning, as this was going to be it.

The approaching car stopped just past the entrance as though the occupants were surveying the scene and then there was a flash of its headlights in enquiry.

The driver responded with a languid wave of his hand where it was resting out of the car window in confirmation, beckoning the new arrival to approach, and it began to edge forward.

The driver pointed down at the ground next to his door and the new-comer got the message, the car crawling across to them and coming to a halt just next to where they were parked, driver's door to driver's door, so close that neither could actually have got out.

The driver and passenger stared blankly at the old and flabby face they were expecting to see as the new car's window whirred down. If they felt any surprise at the second, equally old, but more deeply lined and haggard face on view sitting in the passenger seat across from them, they didn't show it.

*

There was a flash of annoyance across the new arrival's florid expression at the sight of the two of them sitting there in silence behind their shades.

'You going to take those things out so we can talk?' he said, gesturing to the driver's earphones, 'Or what?'

The driver motioned wordlessly to his ear in mute query which if anything seemed to piss of their podgy guest even more.

'Yes, those, for Christ's sake. You asked us to meet to talk, so let's talk.'

'I thought you were coming alone?' the driver said, as he shucked the earphone facing the open window out of his ear.

'So I brought a friend,' came the reply. 'I see you did too, so I guess that makes us quits, doesn't it?'

'Does it?' asked the driver, glancing sideways towards where his companion was sitting patiently in the passenger seat, the new arrival's eyes following him to look at the passenger's cold expression.

Which was just what the driver wanted, as, with his left elbow still casually resting on the window sill, he reached down out of sight with his right hand to where the sawn off was lodged, resting by his leg against the transmission, both hammers already cocked in readiness.

With one swift motion he swung the weapon up and fired straight into the astonished fat face across from him, before leaning slightly forwards and sideways to edge the barrel round the first man as he slumped against the steering wheel, he emptied the second chamber into the body of the other man in the car.

As he did so, his passenger calmly picked up his own weapon, a Smith and Wesson revolver, from where it had been resting down the side of his seat and reached for the door handle. They always preferred revolvers if it wasn't a silencer job; they were more reliable and less likely to jam than an automatic, while they also retained the shell casings, leaving less potential evidence at a scene.

Stepping out of the car, the passenger pulled his earphones off and dropped them on his seat. He didn't need them any more as they hadn't been to listen to tunes. They'd simply been for ear protection against the noise of the blast as the driver shot from inside the car, in the same way that the wraparound shades weren't just there for comfort against the bright Mediterranean sunshine, but to protect their eyes against powder burns or blast from the shotgun's discharge at such close quarters.

He walked round to the passenger side of the other vehicle and peered inside.

It was difficult to tell if the fat driver was alive or not. His passenger, who'd taken the second barrel's blast full in the chest, was still breathing but obviously in a bad way.

No matter, the shotgun salvo hadn't been intended to kill. That was the Aussie rules bit. If it had, well fine, but that wasn't the purpose.

The passenger raised his revolver to the shattered car window and calmly shot each man once in the head just behind the ear with a .357 Magnum shell, delivering the classic *coup de grâce*.

Job done, the two men moved swiftly but without any element of panic or concern. The driver pulled forward a few feet so that he was clear of the dead men's car and he could open his door. Stepping out he reached into the vehicle for a cloth that he ran over the sawn-off's touchable surfaces before it went back onto the seat.

The passenger meanwhile already had the boot open and was lifting a petrol can out to begin soaking their car's interior. They were professionals. It had been rented with false papers and dropped off to them the previous evening already equipped by an anonymous third party, so there was no incriminating CCTV. They didn't need to have watched CSI to be crime scene aware about the need to avoid leaving any DNA or other tell-tale trails from their time in the car. The two men peeled off their jackets which would have the worst of the gunshot residue on their sleeves and threw them into the car as well. They had brought hand degreaser, a bottle of water and paper towels so it was a matter of moments for the driver to do a quick first clean of his hands. His passenger had had the luxury of gloves that he was also disposing of in the same way.

A few minutes later, and as their burning car roared in the clearing behind them, the two men were charging downhill along the cycling trails leading back to the town below on the mountain bikes they had carefully deposited there the night before, locking them securely in the stands.

As they descended from the mountain's slopes and came closer to town, the revolver which the passenger had retained until now, wrapped in a plastic carrier bag, in case they had to deal with any incidents or problems on their escape, went into a small but deep ravine they had spotted on their field trips while the bag itself could wait for a proper litter bin closer to the town. They were already five or six miles away from the scene of the shooting and so the police were unlikely to look for it there.

Another half hour or so and they were sitting in front of a café, freshly showered on return from their ride, bikes hosed down and stowed away at the back of the rented villa, having another coffee. Up in the mountains they could hear the wail of sirens as the fire service screamed up the mountain to where a column of black smoke hung ominously.

There were notices all along the road warning about the danger of forest fires as the vegetation dried out. It was something the local authorities took very seriously indeed.

*

The telephone call came the next day and was answered after only a few rings.

'You know those cleaning jobs you were after?'

'Yeah?'

'Well it's all done. Turned out on the day there was a bit of an offer on.'

'Oh yes?'

'BOGOF, mate.'

'Bog off?'

'Two birds with one stone, mate. Bump one, get one free.'

'OK, so it's sorted?'

'All taken care of.'

'That's great, owe you one.'

'No problem. Anytime. You know that.'

'Yes, yes I do.'

*

The face appeared on the screen, glowering out at the team assembled in the darkened room as they sat around a rough horse-shoe of office tables in an ordinary looking meeting room while the projector buzzed quietly to itself from where it hung from the ceiling.

It could have been any ordinary business presentation, a real death by PowerPoint job. Slide after slide after slide of bullet points that the speaker insisted on reading out more of less verbatim in the mistaken belief that this added some kind of value, never mind that if he stopped to think about it, he could reasonably assume that everybody in the room had learnt to read for themselves quite a few years ago, long words included.

Except that the business the speaker had been describing was, by most people's standards, anything but ordinary.

And when it came to bullet points, well, some of them were bullet points.

But then the men in the room weren't most people. As the national committee for co-ordinating information and action on organized crime by outlaw biker gangs, they never dignified their activities with the word clubs, across each of the major UK constabularies' serious crime units, they were seen it all before, done it all before, professionals. They knew why they were there and they knew what they were expecting to hear as the speaker droned on, and what he was saying came as no real surprise to anyone in the room.

Until the end of course.

Until he put up the photograph of the face.

Because the face, was, well, a Face. A player. A kingpin. An untouchable.

Everybody in the room knew all about the untouchables. Those fifty or so men, and they were all men, who broadly controlled most organized crime across the country.

These were the men who headed up gangs, ran families, had firms. The men who had climbed the tree and learnt by and large to have others do the dirty work for them. The men who now didn't get their hands directly messy, but who ran things through others. The men who had cut-outs that insulated them from direct implication in any action.

The men in short who were untouchable, because there was nothing that touched both them and a crime.

'And this,' said the Chairman, as the room absorbed the picture he'd presented them with, 'this chap is, we are apparently reliably informed by one of our sources, our recently retired target.'

'Retired?' one of the silhouettes beyond the projector objected. 'Mr Swazi Gold? Bollocks, he's retired. Who fed us that load of crap?'

'Yeah, blokes like him don't retire!' agreed another voice.

The speaker nodded at the views expressed, not disagreeing with them one iota.

'So that raises an interesting question doesn't it, gentlemen?'

'If he hasn't retired, what the fuck is he doing?' came the first voice again from out of the darkness.

'Precisely, gentlemen,' said the Chairman, nodding at the audience member closest to the door to hit the lights on again and gathering his papers in front of him so as to be able to cover the next section on his list, 'and that is the really interesting question isn't it?'

And as the room surreptitiously glanced down at their agendas for the meeting and collectively worked out how long it was going to be until the next coffee and fag break, the faded grey and white picture on the screen continued to lurk like a ghost at the feast.

The hungry wolfish look of the sharp features, neat clipped goatee beard and long greying hair pulled back into a ponytail of Stu, as of the start of the year recently and allegedly retired Scottish P of the Rebel Brethren MC, and reputed main importer to the UK of some of the rainbow nation's finest hash and weed, glared out across the room from a police mug shot.

*

'The rumour mill has it that he's writing,' came the surprising news from one of the Met detectives at the front of the group.

'Writing? Writing what? His memoirs?' Came scoffing laughter from some of the others.

'Yes,' was the simple answer, which generated some debate around the room.

'What the hell?'

'They're all starting to do it now, the old guard.'

'Whatever happened to them all keeping quiet?'

'Well, they don't spill the real beans do they? It'll just be the story he wants to tell, won't it?'

'All about how he's a just a poor old misunderstood and persecuted businessman who likes to ride bikes with his friends...' came a voice, in mock sympathy for his predicament.

Up to now the representative from Strathclyde Police had stayed silent, thinking through the possible, hideous implications of what a real tell all by Stu might involve, and in fact, why a real tell all was probably the last thing that Stu would ever want to write. Although for obvious reasons, he didn't share these thoughts with his colleagues around the room.

Given his current position and status, what Strathclyde Police knew about Stu and his background was something Strathclyde Police were keeping very close to their chests, a secret known only to a handful of very, very, very, senior officers on the excuse, if anyone ever did find out the truth, of operational security; but in reality, it was in the knowledge that this was a scandal that had the power to sink careers and even whisper it in horror, put pensions in jeopardy at the absolutely highest levels, and nobody wanted that, did they?

Particularly not just right now, at a time when plans were being negotiated to merge all eight Scottish police forces into a new single entity, Police Scotland.

Stu and the whole potential toxic shit storm that could erupt if the truth about him ever emerged, had the power to torpedo the entire enterprise, as the senior ranks at Strathclyde Police knew all too well.

So, needless to say, the man from Strathclyde Police was here to listen, to steer gently as and when it seemed appropriate in the interests of Strathclyde Police, but not to over-share.

'Well he is a businessman these days, isn't he? Lots of them are, you two ought to know that if anyone does,' he asserted in his hard Glasgow accent, only to be met with a snort of derision, in particular from the two detectives who'd spent a fruitless night on Felixstowe docks not a month before.

'What Stu and Bomber's toy stuff? Import and export? Come on, pull the other one. There's only one thing they and the rest of them're interested in importing and it's not furry friends for tiny tots! Take it from us. We had a look see.'

'Aye, and you didn't find anything, did you, for all your hanging around the docks, eh lads?' he challenged them, to the amusement of some of the other regional representatives around the room. The junior of the two Met officers sunk back into an angry silence as he knew they hadn't an answer to that. 'So, all the same, like it or not, it is part of what he and the rest of them do so we need to deal with it.'

The more senior officer wasn't cowed though. He'd seen enough of his share of turf wars and infighting to be able to handle himself in a room like this. He wasn't here to win any popularity contests, every-one knew how much most of the rest of the regional forces hated and despised the Met. But he was buggered if he was going to let the Jock roll over them like that.

'Oh bollocks. They want to have it both ways all the time. They're always complaining that they're stigmatized as criminals because of the patch they wear, but at the same time they want, revel in even, their reputation for living outside the law, not being bound by it.'

He glared around the table as if daring anyone there to challenge him on it. 'Well I'm sorry, but as far as I'm concerned I'm afraid we've got a word for people who break the law, stop me if I'm getting too technical for you, but in my force we call them criminals.'

'But what about the others?' asked another voice in the room, meaning other club members and in particular, other Freebooters. 'Will it be a story they want told?'

The man from Strathclyde Police just shrugged.

'Not our problem is it?' he suggested.

'No, I suppose not...'

'Not until it turns nasty anyway...' someone else intervened.

'And then it will be our problem won't it?' snarled the senior Met detective.

'Not if he's still in Spain...' offered a voice.

'Or Cyprus,' suggested another.

'And you're not worried about blow back?' demanded Mr Strathclyde Police sharply, for once feeling some sympathy with the Met's point of view.

'Not really...' was the reply. *Which is just fine for you I guess*, thought Mr Strathclyde Police, you just don't think it'll hit your patch, 'we'll worry about it when it happens.'

'Ah but, now there's a problem straight away,' chipped in the more junior Met officer.

'What is?' asked the relaxed Devon & Cornwall representative.

'Well he's not in Spain any more is he?' the Met officer announced flatly to a collective intake of breath.

'Isn't he?' Thames Valley wanted to know.

'No, he's back,' the Met man replied, with a flat gesture of his hand that said there was no doubt.

'You're sure?' Surrey pressed, with sudden interest.

'Sure we're sure,' the senior Met office chimed in, taking over from his colleague. 'He's back. Arrived at Gatwick last week on an Easy Jet flight just like any other pensioner back from Spain.'

'So where is he now then?' asked Surrey, looking back up at the scowling face on the screen.

The Met officer just shrugged his shoulders as he contemplated the consternation and disquiet this news had introduced into the group. 'We've no remit or budget to have him tailed as yet, so we're buggered if we know. He was picked up, we're assuming by an associate, and driven off and that's all we know at this stage.'

'Oh shit!' muttered somebody from around the table, Thames Valley possibly.

Quite, thought Mr Strathclyde Police to himself, although of course he didn't say anything.

'Now, talking about Spain,' the Chairman intervened, 'if I can be forgiven for jumping around in our agenda on this point, it's probably a good moment to have a look at item 7 in your briefing packs.'

There was a general shuffling of papers as he waited for the people around the table to get organised and have the section with its reports and photographs to hand. There was a low whistle from somewhere down the table and some murmurings as he gave them a moment to scan the pages and put their thoughts in order.

'Now, as I see it,' he began, once he felt they'd all had enough time to be on the same page as it were, 'this may or may not be something to do with our priority targets, but I think we need to review the horrific murder last week of these two retired detectives...'

'Execution, you mean,' interjected the DI from Surrey. 'That was a professional hit plain and simple if I've ever seen one.'

'That's never going to be nothing, not in a million years,' agreed the senior Met man.

'Yes, well,' the Chairman said, regaining the floor as he put his own copy of the file down on the table and looked around the room.

'As you will all have read by now the victims were retired DI ███████ ████████ and retired DS ████ ██████, both previously of Strathclyde Police, who led the force's investigations into the Rebels until their retirement at the start of this year.'

There was a snort from somewhere down the table and eyes flickered to the Strathclyde Police representative to see what reaction he might give, but he was playing his poker face.

We all knew the rumours. Between cops things run round the grapevine like wildfire. The word had it the pair of them had claimed to have been running a source in The Rebels, for years some said, but despite all the time, effort and money spent on it, with little or nothing to show for it by the time they both handed in their papers and headed off to the Med. The only disagreements I ever heard about it were whether they'd just been milking the force and snaffling the operations funds to feather their nests, or whether they'd actively been on the take from the club. Either way, there didn't seem to be that much doubt amongst those in the know that they'd been dirty.

'So we have to keep an eye on the possibility that there's a link there to these deaths...'

'Possibility? My arse! What else was it going to be about?' demanded Surrey, and then the discussion ran freely around the room and opinions divided.

'They were dirty cops. It could be anything...'

'You don't know that, nobody knows that for sure.'

'We all know what the signs are though, don't we?'

'They ran operations against the club for years, got sources inside, built their careers and God knows what else on it, because at the end of it they weren't telling, were they?'

'And then they both retired.'

'Jumped before they were pushed, you mean.'

'Whatever, but it was a cosy way to go, wasn't it, for them both? Off to villas in Spain the pair of them and you do start to wonder where the dosh for that all came from, don't you? Nice houses, pools, smart cars. Very comfortable. That lot didn't all come out of just a copper's pension did it?'

'So the question has to be asked about where it came from and why?'

'Which makes you wonder by the end, who was actually running who?'

And all the while Mr Strathclyde Police kept his own counsel, quietly watching and listening.

'...until they ceased to be useful.'

'Once they were out of the force you mean? So you're thinking loose ends? This was somebody tidying up?'

'Maybe. If there's anything to this they'd be people who knew a lot, too much perhaps for comfort for somebody?'

'But why wait? They've both been retired for a few years now without singing? Why do something like this that you'd have to figure was going to stir a major shit storm. A public hit on two ex-cops? You'd have to expect that's always going to bring serious heat down, whatever the circumstances. So why take the risk?'

'Who knows? It depends what the risk is you're dealing with, doesn't it? You'd balance the likely fall out against whatever the alternative is and decide which is going to be the least worst option.'

'But why kill them? Why not just warn them off?'

'Perhaps they were warned. Perhaps they just didn't listen.'

'Still, it would have to have been something pretty major, you'd have thought?' the junior Met man was chipping in again now. 'Somebody must have really had something serious riding on this...'

'Well that goes without saying, doesn't it, given what they've done?' the Chairman observed tartly. He had no love for the Met either. 'To me the more interesting question is, why now? What's provoked it, has something happened or is something going to happen that meant they had to go?'

He looked straight at Mr Strathclyde Police and asked him directly, 'So now, you're very quiet on this. These were your blokes after all, so I'd expect you to have a view. Any thoughts you'd like to share with the group?'

There was a moment's silence as the two of them locked eyes, before Mr Strathclyde Police gave a slight shrug of the shoulders.

'As far as I know, as a force we have no official view,' he said carefully, 'about the death of these two ex-officers.'

The rest of the room took a moment to parse that statement very carefully. They noted the stress on the 'ex' in ex-officers, and they noted also that it wasn't 'the sad deaths' of 'valued colleagues', and that gave them what they needed to know.

'Who knows?' the Surrey rep came in to break the silence eventually. 'Perhaps circumstances changed? Perhaps they started to seem more of a threat than before? Perhaps they got greedy and started asking for dosh? Perhaps they got involved in some business either with their old contacts or on their own.'

'Or perhaps whoever it was just wanted to wait until they thought they were safe and their guard was down,' added Thames Valley.

'Perhaps. It could be anything. That's the trouble, this is all just speculation, since we don't know buttons really, do we?'

'Well that's not quite true, is it? We know something about the hit, don't we?'

'True. They were both blasted point blank with a shotgun and then finished off with a revolver. That's quite a mess isn't it? It seems a bit over the top to me, don't you think?

'It suggests Australians, or at least an Aussie connection...' the junior Met guy offered.

'Why?' asked the Chairman, curious at this titbit.

'You've never seen *Underbelly*?' the junior detective looked around the room in increasing incredulity at the sea of blank faces looking back at him. *Couldn't any of these duffers stream a video*, he wondered to himself?

'Oh come on now, you all need to catch it. Absolutely worth a watch, it's a dramadoc about a Melbourne gang war...'

'The relevance being?'

'The point being, their standard approach to a hit was firstly a blast with a shotgun to incapacitate the victim, it made sure he was down and couldn't get away or retaliate, and then they'd finish them off at point blank range with a handgun.'

'There's lots of bikers in Oz, could that be the connection?' suggested Devon and Cornwall.

'They're called bikies down there,' interjected Mr Strathclyde Police, with a hint of irritation in his voice, that didn't have to add an unspoken *get it right*, before actually conceding, 'But maybe.'

'So do we need to be looking for a link to Australia, then?' asked the Chairman, in his role as facilitator. 'Does anyone have anything going on in that direction that we know of? Anything on any of the call logs we're watching?'

There was a general shaking of heads around the room as nobody had anything much they were aware of.

'Does anyone else have anything on this they want to share before we move on?'

Again a few eyes in the room turned towards Mr Strathclyde Police, but he just sat there silent again.

'No? Well then, in that case I think it's time for a coffee break,' the Chairman announced, glancing at his watch and adding above the din of chairs squeaking on the floor and a suddenly rising level of chat. 'So if we can keep it to fifteen minutes, then please gents I'd be grateful. We've still got a lot to get through this afternoon and we'll kick straight back off with our friend here,' he said, gesturing towards where Stu's features had continued to stare out from the screen all the while they had been talking, as if he'd been listening in.

After everyone had settled back down from coffee, other than a couple of stragglers who were still catching up on returning their voicemails in the corridor outside, the Chairman brought the subject back to ███ ███ ████████, also known as Stu, one time president of first the UK end of The Rebels MC, and latterly joint president of The Rebel Brethren and his undoubted, so far untouchable status.

'This is a man, I would remind you, gentlemen, who has been the target of an ongoing investigation by Strathclyde Police for many, many years, but has however, a criminal record amounting to a grand total of two speeding tickets...'

'And a speed awareness course,' Mr Strathclyde Police added, 'don't forget that.'

'Well, thank God all those police resources aren't being wasted then,' came the needle from the senior Met office, as he slipped back into the room, raising a laugh around the table.

'So gents,' the Chairman continued smoothly, 'the matter for discussion here today is really very simple. We all know he's dirty, we've just never been able to prove it. So, if we don't want him to continue to get away with it, what are we going to need to do to catch him?'

And with that he threw discussion open to the table, although in reality, there was only ever going to be one answer to that question, and the room quickly settled on it as the consensus.

By going after his known associates and working up the chain. People like Bomber.

'We know he'd been talking to a journalist for a while before he retired last year and we have reasons to believe he's looking for a real way out,' Greater Manchester briefed.

'A Plan B?' came a quiet voice from down the table where the Met and Surrey were sitting, raising a snort of amusement from somewhere around the room, until the Chairman's silent glare quelled whatever private joke was being shared.

'So we give him one?' asked the Chairman, breaking the renewed silence after a moment's pause, 'A deal to co-operate, is that the idea?'

'The sort he can't refuse...' agreed the Met, to general amusement in the room.

And that was how we came to target John Harris, otherwise known to his associates and club brothers as 'Bomber'.

*

We had an editorial meeting around the managing director's desk the moment the phone went down.

We knew who the caller was, of course, straight away from the files, as soon as he'd given us his name. Iain had interviewed him a number of times and he'd come up in other pieces Iain had researched, from discussions with bikers, to both on and off the record sessions with various people in the police.

In the Spring of 2008, Iain was invited into Long Lartin jail to talk to Martin 'Damage' Robertson. The interviews he conducted over the next few months then became his book, *Heavy Duty People*. By this point Iain had been covering the outlaw biker scene in his capacity as crime correspondent of *The Guardian* for almost a decade, during which time he'd also come to interview a number of The Rebels MC in Scotland, traditionally and internationally The Brethren MC's most bitter enemies.

However, behind the scenes as it were, across the UK this was obviously a period of significant change and politics for both the clubs and the key individuals in it. Since the mid-nineties, despite the continuing differences and conflicts elsewhere around the world, the two clubs had established a strong working and trading relationship which only a year or so later would lead to their eventual merger to form an independent UK-wide club, The Rebel Brethren MC.

As one of the senior Rebels MC members he had come into contact with, Iain had interviewed Bomber directly on a number of occasions. As one of those patch-holders whom Iain had found willing to talk at length, their conversations ranged widely across Bomber's time in the club from his first introduction to it, right through to, at the time, his thoughts on potentially retiring and leaving the lifestyle.

The combined editorial view was a unanimous consensus best expressed by the managing director's comment.

'Oh shit! What the fuck have we got ourselves into now?'

*

There was no choice really, we had to arrange to see him, but he made it clear that however this went, we had to play by his rules.

He would set the time. He would set the place, and ominously he told us, he would ensure security, whatever that meant.

He wanted a meeting, a meeting at which he would show us the files, tell us the story, off the back of which he was convinced we would at once sign up to publish what he wanted printing.

*

And there was something else Bomber had made clear to us on his call. He'd arranged a go between. Someone he trusted who would be in touch in advance of our meeting to tell us part of his story and get us up to speed for what he wanted us to know.

Someone very surprising.

A detective inspector by the name of Paul Chambers, and from the West Mercia Police of all places.

Now what the hell did that mean, we wondered and where did he fit into the picture?

Why would someone like Bomber trust a copper to talk for him? How would he know him, Bomber having been based in Scotland as far back as we could trace him, and with no known links to anywhere south of the M62 as far as we could see.

And why would a copper want to act as spokesman or go between for a hard core biker like Bomber?

Whatever our questions, we decided, there was only one way to find some answers, and so we agreed to meet. That was it. That was all we signed up for. A meeting and that's it.

Needless to say, it wasn't what we got.

*

But before we did anything else, there was one other thing we knew we'd have to do. And that was read Iain's files, go through every word he'd had with Bomber and Stu, every interview, every note, every scrap we could find, searching for background, clues and anything that could help us. Anything at all.

And so, for what it's worth, and to what extent you or anybody else believes a word of it, what follows is the stories we got, those Iain was told, those we were told, and those we found out since.

CHAPTER 2   CHARACTER WITNESS

Blood makes you related. Loyalty makes you family.

Various formulations and attributions including Chris Diaz

As we might have expected from a policeman of his seniority, Detective Inspector Chambers arrived bang on time and we showed him into our little meeting room. It's not much, we're not a posh outfit, just room for a table with half a dozen chairs around it and a unit in the corner where we'd sorted out a thermos of coffee, a jug of milk, and some more or less matching mugs.

We shook hands very formally and made introductions as our managing director played mother. DI Chambers didn't take sugar.

He was on his own, so there were just the three of us. We wanted to keep this tight until we knew what we were dealing with.

And then there we were, all sat down facing each other across the Formica, mugs on the table, pads of paper flicked open and a pot of biros in easy reach in case we wanted to take notes. We were ready for the off, and wondering where best to start.

Luckily DI Chambers, 'Paul, please, otherwise we'll never get anywhere,' solved that problem for us with an 'I guess I'd better introduce myself then, hadn't I?' which seemed to sort it nicely.

'So as you know, I'm a detective inspector with the West Mercia force so you're probably wondering how I've got involved in all this, which is as it happens, the best place to start.

'Well, as Long Lartin prison is on our patch, for my sins I'm the senior officer with responsibility for the ongoing investigation into the murder on 17 July 2008 of one Martin Robertson, aka, as you obviously know from your chap Iain Parke's interviews, Damage. Since at the time of his death he was also, again as you know, the serving president of the Brethren MC in this country I have therefore also taken on the lead in our force for all intelligence gathering on OMG activity...'

'OMG?' we asked, interrupting.

'Outlaw Motorcycle Gangs,' he clarified, 'and all ongoing police investigations into OMG related incidents within our area.'

'You're the go-to guy about bikers for your force?' we clarified,

'That's about the size of it,' he agreed.

'OK, so we get that I suppose, but the Midlands are a hell of a long way from Bomber's turf in Glasgow and points north, so can we ask what your connection with him is?'

DI Chambers sat back in his chair as he started to tell his story. 'Well to start with, when I first picked up these roles, not much really. But to answer that we need to look at a bit of history. Less than three years after Damage's death The Brethren in the UK under his successor Wibble, and The Rebels led by Stu, did what up to then had been unthinkable and merged together in this country to form a single independent club.

'I can't tell you the shockwaves that sent out, both right across the club scene here and overseas, and throughout UK law enforcement.

'Don't forget, we'd just had a short, sharp, and quite nasty little biker war with some very public and serious casualties as the newly combining club saw off an attempt by the Mohawks to set up shop. And then we had fighting at an airport of all places, when the local firm ambushed Americans arriving from the mother club to take back the patches, so at the time no one in law enforcement really knew what we were looking at here.

'Would the mother clubs internationally, on either side, just sit back and take it? Would they try and come in heavy to sort out the local clubs? Would they patch-over new local franchisees and tell them to sort out the renegades? Would we have a repeat of the Mohawk thing, but on a larger scale?

'And what about the new club itself? Would there be house cleaning of anyone not fully with the new programme? The clubs aren't big on diversity and dissent. Would people be jockeying for position in the new entity. Merge two organisations and there's bound to be some duplication of roles that needs resolving, one way or another.

'And what were the clubs' plans once they'd merged? Would they be looking to use their new found unity and size to muscle in on, or take out, the remaining smaller independent clubs?

'The truth was, no one on our side of the house knew what the hell was going to happen but the safest thing was to assume the worst, that whatever was going to happen, it was going to be trouble.

'And so what was the police's reaction to this situation?' we wanted to know.

'In short, it was the setting up in September 2010 of Operation Derby. The powers that be decided that to deal with a potentially national issue like the newly merged club, a national response was needed.'

'And that was Operation Derby?'

'Yes. To give you some idea of how seriously this was taken, it was headed by an assistant chief constable from the Northumberland force no less. He was chosen given the powerbase of the senior ex Brethren membership who were heading up the English side of the merger at the time, and the whole thing had a twofold brief.

'Firstly, it was to be about information and co-ordination, the idea was to have a clearing house across all the UK forces. The bikers were getting organised nationally, so the thought was we had to too. Each force right across the country from Devon and Cornwall right up to Strathclyde Police, together with national agencies such as SOCA, had to designate a senior OMG officer if they didn't already have one, and each of these representatives was then their delegate to Operation Derby, which meant attending the monthly co-ordinating meeting which rotated between Bramshill Police Staff College down in Hook and Harperley Hall College of Policing up in County Durham.

'The idea was that each force and agency would share its information on all OMG activity and intelligence on all patches, as well as brief on the progress and results of any operations they had aimed at OMG linked activity...'

'So get all these agencies into a single room and ask them to co-operate for the common good, was that it?'

'Yes.'

'Sounds like a recipe for disaster to me,' we joked.

'Well, I wouldn't put it quite as strongly as that but unsurprisingly there were, let's just say, some differing agendas on show right from the outset...'

'I bet there were, but you said there were two objectives,' our managing director asked, checking back on the notes he was taking. 'So if sharing information was one of them, what was the other?'

'Well, this was the very interesting part in some ways. Co-ordinating, intelligence sharing; that's been tried before across forces with varying levels of success as I'm sure you'll appreciate, so in many ways other than the particular target there was nothing really novel in this. But the second part of the brief, well that was something new. In fact, as far as I know, it wasn't something that had ever been tried in this country before.

'We don't have a national police force. Partly that's historic, while there have been mergers over the years of local forces to form more regional ones, politically there's always been a view that policing needs to be under some form of local control so as to be held accountable to the local policed population, although in reality that's always been a bit of an academic fiction when it comes to day to day operations.

'The idea of forming a national police force comes up every so often, and there's talk about amalgamating all the Scottish forces into one at the moment, and you can see why it might make sense. It's argued you could save money by cutting out a lot of duplicated back office functions, as well as being able to establish national standards and approaches. Small forces wouldn't have to worry about being over-whelmed by a big event, there are all sorts of practical advantages been touted, but so far no dice.

'Partly that's down to internal resistance. You push together what-ever it is, thirty or forty forces into one, and that's a lot of top coppers fighting for the jobs on offer. But politically it's never been an attractive fight to pick either as there's a bit of instinctive hostility to the idea of some overwhelmingly powerful national police force. Whatever the reality of local control as a fig leaf, there is something about local legitimacy that still seems important to confidence in the force and a commitment to civil liberties, whatever anyone outside says. What Home Secretary wants to go down in history as having set up some copper as the most powerful bloke in the country?

'Yes, we have some national outfits, SOCA's a good example, but if you look at what they do it's just an intelligence sharing agency, they aren't operational. I guess what I'm saying is we don't have a British equivalent of the FBI.

'Or we didn't until Operation Derby came along. Because the second part of our brief was to go beyond the simple sharing of information. It was to co-operate in the planning and executing of co-ordinated multi-agency operations targeting the senior officers of the club.'

'So you weren't just a talking shop any longer?'

'No, that was the point. Like I said, the real mission of Operation Derby was to be something we've never really had in this country before, at least to my knowledge. We were to be a national police taskforce, targeting a specific group of alleged criminals...'

'I notice you say alleged.'

'Well it has to be alleged, doesn't it? Even if you do ride a Harley with a patch on your back, innocent until proven guilty still applies, doesn't it?'

'You'd have thought so,' we agreed.

'Well it does in my book anyway,' he said emphatically.

'Fancy a refill?' our MD asked, picking up his empty cup and gesturing to the flask.

'Don't mind if I do,' DI Chambers said smiling, 'because I think this is going to take a while.'

'Alright then,' we resumed, sitting back down, 'so we understand what you were involved with, but where does Bomber fit into all this?'

'How much do you know about Bomber?' he countered, by way of reply.

'Just what we're reading in Iain's files. We've been trying to get up to speed ever since he called.'

'And how much is that?' he followed up, with a raised eyebrow.

'A fair bit, we suppose,' we shrugged, 'Iain conducted some lengthy interviews with him, but we've no idea how reliable what he says is, or what else there might be...'

'Not sure you're getting the truth, the whole truth and nothing but the truth?' he suggested, with a note of irony in his voice.

'I suppose. How would we know?'

'You wouldn't,' he announced flatly, putting down his coffee, 'OK then, I guess I'd better fill you in on Bomber and what's been happening, hadn't I?'

'Sounds good to us,' we told him.

*

It's important to remember at this stage that whatever he had to say, DI Chambers wasn't our only source when it came to understanding Bomber's story. In fact, as well as Iain's interviews with Bomber himself and other bikers, we now had two main police sources. Whatever DI Chambers was telling us, and the records of Iain's discussions with his police contacts going back many, many years.

The problem was, reconciling all these versions of events wasn't the most straightforward thing in the world.

As part of his research into the clubs, as well as speaking to the bikers themselves, Iain had also been talking regularly to a number of police officers, ranging from officers in the Serious and Organized Crime Agency, through regional detectives, and even some who'd worked undercover in the biker scene, although for obvious reasons the identities of this last group were heavily protected in his files.

These people had talked not only about the clubs and the police view and information on their activities, but also in some cases about individual members, including in some cases Malcolm, Dobbo, Stu, Sandy, Bomber, and others, as high profile officers within the club.

One of the policemen Iain interviewed had, for example, spent a number of years undercover on the fringes of the club in the late 1980s and early 1990s, at the time Bomber had first become involved, and had then continued to focus on the club scene in his later career, including acting for a while as part of his force's liaison with SOCA on biker club crime.

And it was noticeable that from these interviews it was plain to see that in days when some, fed by a diet of press stories and law enforcement autobiographies and budget-promoting press releases, see outlaw bikers and their clubs as branches of organized crime, Bomber was regarded even by cops who had gone up against him, as whatever else he might or might not be, a biker first, last and always.

'Even guys in rival clubs, ones you would think as an outsider would be hostile, given some of the bad blood that exists, talked about him with respect, even with grudging admiration in some cases,' the ex-undercover cop had told Iain.

'He was hard, and hard core, fiercely loyal to the old school biker code, and he was old school in other ways as well.'

*

'The thing that was obvious from everything I'd read on our files about Bomber,' DI Chambers told us, 'was he was seen as a one percenter's one percenter.

'Looking at him through the interview room's CCTV he didn't look anything out of the ordinary. He was a reasonable sized bloke, about six one, he'd obviously done weights at some point as a younger man to build himself up but now at fiftyish you could see it was starting to go. Neat shortish haircut, matching neat close-cut beard, and dressed in fairly smart casual but working style clothes, shirt, jacket, that sort of thing. In fact he looked just the way you'd expect him to look if you met him on business. A trucker who'd made good, self-employed, built up his own firm. Calm, confident, no nonsense. Someone straight to deal with.

'Look, as a policeman, I'd have to be the first to say that they're not all hardened criminals. Lots of them will have criminal records, but many won't. Some of them undoubtedly make their living from selling drugs and involvement in other sorts of crime, from car and bike theft to protectionism and prostitution, but plenty of others just have straight day jobs in a range of things from skilled tradesmen through to professionals. Bomber's a good example of this himself as he started out as a mechanic before becoming a long distance lorry driver, and then eventually setting up his own logistics business which now trades internationally.

'They do describe themselves as outlaws but that in itself isn't a crime. Just because they don't want to feel constrained by the laws that others have set, doesn't mean that they all immediately want to go out and break them either. It's more a question of deciding to live by their own rules, their own assessment of what's right and wrong, and taking responsibility for their actions.

'So like I say, despite what some of my colleagues may think that they're all just criminals, as I've always seen it there are real reasons why guys get involved in the club and they're not all about money and crime.

'It seems a bit odd to even have to say it, but it is a bike club after all, and a love of bikes is one thing. Then there's the camaraderie. But above all, if you ask me, it's a family.

'It's not a coincidence that they call each other brother. That's really how they feel and if you look into their backgrounds, back to when they were kids, I'd say a hell of a lot of them had dysfunctional childhoods – broken homes, abandoned, whatever. These are guys who've grown up looking for a family and they've found it in the club.

'In a funny way as a copper I can even understand it. In our way we're a bit cut off from society in the police as well. We all work together and then socialize with each other so we tend to make our own little world that's a bit suspicious of outsiders, people who aren't in the job don't understand us or what we do and we have to rely on each other when the crap hits the fan. So the job's a bit like a family as well, a demanding one, requiring a commitment and a loyalty that can come first. And I think it's much the same on their side of the fence although I doubt either of us would ever really want to admit it openly.'

*

Which certainly seemed to resonate with the way Bomber saw things from the transcripts of his conversations with Iain when he talked about the club, his ideas about its philosophy and what it meant to him.

'So what are mates to you?' Bomber had asked Iain in one of their first conversations.

'What does your friendship actually mean to anyone? How valuable is it really? And anyway, your mates, who are they?

'Some blokes you share some time with at work? The crowd you hang around with as and when you're out at the pub? The guys you go to a match with whenever you can grab a free Saturday? The team you have a kick about with one night a week?

'It's all pretty small scale though isn't it? All part time stuff.

'They're outside of your real life, your day to day, when you all go back home to the wife and the kids or whatever you've got. They're an exception, people you see occasionally. People you like, sure, people you get on with, share a history with perhaps, share some interests with, probably. But how deep does it really go?

'You know for thousands of years we all lived as tribes of hunters. That's what we're adapted to do, to be. Each tribe was a small extended group of families, of people bound to each other, not just by the ties of blood, but by the way they lived together, seeing each other day in day out for the whole of their lives. The blokes would head out, day after day, working together year in, year out, to hunt, to kill, to provide. For that they had to rely on each other absolutely and without question. They had to share their resources, to co-operate, to look out for each other as brothers. They had to know without question that they would always be there for each other when it counted, whatever came, whatever it took, whether it was to kill the big game, or to defend themselves if they got attacked out there amongst the wild animals.

'And when the day's hunting was over, they didn't all just down tools, sod off back to their homes and the wife and kids and shut the door on each other. No, they all sat around the fire and ate and talked together, chewed over the day, told stories, enjoyed each other's company until, sure it was time to kip, and then the next day they went back out and did it all over again. And the next day and the next.

'Do you see what I mean? To be mates then was to live, to work, and to live or die together; to be part of a band of brothers who depended on a total commitment to each other, on trusting each other with their lives, not just about being a couple of guys to share an odd fucking pint with a couple of nights a week.

'That's what most people don't get, that's what they don't realise

40

they've lost, I suppose. Because there's nothing that ever comes close to that for most people, there really isn't.

'In fact there's only two places you'll find that level of absolute commitment these days, that way of life, those real levels of brotherhood.

'Bits of the forces, and us.'

'Nowhere else?' Iain had asked.

'Nope,' Bomber had grunted, 'And people wonder why we attract so many ex-squaddies.'

*

From the interview notes Iain had on file, by the time he'd come to speak to Bomber at any length, Bomber was however already well down the path of deciding he wanted to leave the club.

But as the piece above clearly demonstrates, even while he wanted out, Bomber was still keen to talk to Iain about the upsides of being in the club, from the obvious: the parties, the runs, the feeling of being part of something bigger than yourself and the security of knowing that your mates had always got your back, no questions asked; through to the things that were less obvious to outsiders, the way brothers would look out for each other, the network of people, not just in the club in the UK that you would know, but all around the world in charters that you didn't, that you could call on, who would put you up, feed you, lend you a bike and look after you like you were one of their own, secure in the knowledge that if they landed on your doorstep at any time they could rely on you doing the same.

*

'To start with, being in a club, any of the real clubs, the one percenter ones, local, regional, national, whichever, we all have the same sort of ethos. Holding a patch, being a member, it's a righteous thing.

'The club's your new family, a real family where everybody looks after everybody else.

'Most, not all of them I grant you, but most of the guys worked, you have to so as to afford the bikes and the parties, so they had full time jobs. It's an expensive lifestyle in some ways.

41

'Sure there's always some who're on the dodgy side. A fair few dabbled in any sort of shit that came along to turn a quid or two, but this wasn't a criminal gang by any manner or means, you know?

'Most of the guys had steady girls. Sooner or later they had kids and everybody mucked in and helped each other. You needed tools or parts to fix your bike? If anyone else had them, they were yours and you'd pay them back as soon as you could. My house was your house. Food, booze, dope, money, whatever you had you would share when a brother needed it. And you knew, if the tables were turned, he'd do exactly the same for you.'

What Iain couldn't work out was how far Bomber really meant it and still believed it, and how far he was trying to justify the last twenty odd years of his life to himself.

*

But with DI Chambers sitting in front of us, there was one thing we wanted to know to help us make sense of what we were being told.

'So,' we asked, 'if he's such a died in the wool one percenter, how come a police officer like you is here talking to us on his behalf?'

'Simple,' he told us, without actually answering the question directly, 'we arrested him, and it all went from there.'

'The first thing we did was as soon as we'd found out where Stu was staying, which given the surveillance we had organised didn't take that long, was to pull him in.

'And as we'd arranged, we lifted Bomber at the same time. Having them both in for questioning was the start of the plan.

'They'd both been processed as usual by the woodentops: finger-prints, mug shots, DNA swabs, the works, and then stuck into separate interview rooms to wait.'

'And you went at Bomber first?'

'Yes, that was the plan. In theory, the idea was to see if we could get anything from him to put to Stu.

'No one expected it to generate much. We all reckoned they were both too experienced players for that. They'd been round the block before and besides, the bikers generally all just refuse to engage, no comments all the way there and back again. But it was a marker and a question of laying the groundwork. Particularly for what was planned to come later.

'Of course at the time I hadn't known anything about the so-called Plan B. I just thought this was a straightforward investigation, and as it happens I was lead in the initial interview with Bomber, along with Detective Sergeant Richard Timms, the junior Met officer on the taskforce who was acting liaison, for some reason the Met always wanted two guys there.'

'So how did that conversation go?' we asked.

DI Chambers just laughed, 'Not too good to start with.'

And not only was he going to tell us about it, DI Chambers had the transcript, and the tape for us to listen to. Clicking the cassette into the player he'd placed on the table, through the inevitable static and tinny distortion of the microphone, we heard that voice we were already becoming familiar with from Iain's tapes, with its strange English accent for someone who'd been such a player in the Scottish based charters of The Rebels.

'Look Bomber, we're not after you,' said DI Chambers as Bomber sat across the table from him, arms folded and looking bored.

Bomber grunted in contempt, 'I should think not, I've done nothing wrong.'

'It's your boss we're after, we've arrested him as well, you know?'

'My boss?' Bomber shook his head in mock bewilderment. 'Well shit, mate you've got me there. I'm self-employed so I don't really know which one it is you're after. The wife? Or do you mean the tax man, 'cos I'll help you take him down any day, the thieving bastard.'

'But there must have been more than that sort of stuff coming out of it for you to be here,' we observed, and DI Chambers nodded.

'Yes, yes there was.'

'So what happened?' we pressed.

There was a pause as though he was working out how best to describe the events.

'He talked to me,' he eventually told us simply.

'How did you get him to do that?'

Hearing that a one percent biker like Bomber had talked in a police interview was a surprise in itself, never mind what he said. As DI Chambers had just alluded to, the bikers were famed for their code of silence whenever it came to the law, often just informing police that they were banned from speaking without the club's approval.

'I just asked him to start at the beginning,' he continued, 'We were after background initially, anything we could get, so even though it was all those years ago, I was still interested in how come he'd got involved in joining the club.

'The way I'd read it from his file and the intelligence we'd gathered over the years, it was something to do with Maggie, his first old lady, or that's how we'd heard it anyway.'

'You'd been listening to gossip?'

'If you like,' he said, 'if that's all we've got to go on by way of intelligence at times, it's all we've got to go on.

'The thing you need to appreciate is that at the time he first got mixed up with them, as I understand it, he was quite an odd bod, an outsider.'

And again, that rang true. As Bomber had told Iain once, *I'd always been different, I'd always been an outsider, I'd never known why but I'd just never fitted in. I'm not complaining mind you, just saying that's the way it was, until I found the club and acceptance.*

'Word was he'd been seen as shy, awkward even, when he first turned up. He was young, early twenties and as I read the file, quite fucked up in his own way without the first clue about what to do about it. And Stu, well, Stu saw that and took advantage. But I'm getting ahead of myself.

'The first thing was just to get him talking.'

'About what?' we asked.

'About anything really. I just wanted to hear him talk so I'd listen to anything he had to say. I even asked him about why he didn't talk.'

'And he told you?'

'Eventually, yes. He was never going to say anything incriminating, so I guess he thought, what harm could it do?'

'So, Bomber, why don't you talk to the police as a rule? You must know that to most people it doesn't look good? That you've got something to hide?'

'What the fuck do we care about what ordinary people think about us?'

'Well that's not quite true is it, Bomber? Why the toy runs and stuff? If you really didn't give a shit why do you bother? So why the rule? I mean, there's going to be loads of times when just saying something could save a whole load of grief?'

'Simple, it's self-preservation isn't it? Every time one of our guys talks to a cop about anything that's been alleged against us, then you take what he says, or even more than that, you make shit up, and you turn it around to paint the picture that you want to, against him, against the club. And that doesn't just hurt the guy who's said something, it hurts the rest of us too, it hurts the club.

'And no matter what the guy tells you he said, you can never really know can you? So it can sow doubt, suspicion even, inside the club. What if he really talked? What if he ratted someone out to buy himself out?'

'Well we all know it's the way your lot work isn't it? I'll give you a bye on this son, it's not you we want, it's your boss, just like you've tried it on me already, so give us what we want on him and you can walk.'

'No, so as to protect everybody else, it's had to be a simple rule. No one says nothing, full stop. That way, we always know that whatever you cops say, it's all just shit.'

'And journalists? You're not too keen on talking to them either are you?'

'Same deal really. Ever since Thompson did his number on the HA back in the sixties, the guys have learnt we can't trust what that lot'll say or not say once anyone's opened their mouths to 'em. You cops just want shit you can use to look good, give you a job to do, an excuse to give us crap and stitch us up. Journalists just want shit that'll make good copy and sell papers, the worse the better. And because we're so visible, because we don't fit in, we fit both of you lot perfectly as targets.'

'So, you're still sure you don't care what people think about you?'

'Is it all here?' we asked, leafing through the file of transcripts.

'Everything we talked about in his interviews at the station, yes,' DI Chambers confirmed, as he fast forwarded the tape to get to the next section he wanted to play us, just so we could hear for ourselves what it had been like at the start.

'You know who I hate? Smug bastards, people with a sick sense of entitlement, belonging.

'I've always been an outsider. Never fitted in, never belonged, could never buckle down, knuckle under and make it work. And if I couldn't be part of it, then I was having none of it.

'You want me to be an outsider, I'll be a fucking outsider. I'll live by my rules and screw yours and everything they stand for.

'There's us and them, one percenters and the rest, citizens, whatever you want to call them, sheep who just follow the rules, fit in, play along, do what's expected, what they're told and live life safe and secure just so long as they don't rock the boat.

'Most people are sheep. They get up, go to work, get on a bus with everybody who got on the same bus the day before and moan about their shitty work, crap boss or last night's game and then they go to some poxy job they hate, day in day out, year after year, and for what?

'To be trapped into working like some drone for some faceless corporation or bureaucracy, sitting in the same seat, seeing the same people, so you can come home and pay the mortgage on your rabbit hutch each month for the next twenty-five years, so you've somewhere to house your kids and put food on the table, and have a fortnight off each August to go and sit on a beach in some crowded sunny shithole surrounded by other people's screaming kids before it's time to go back to the grind and save up for next year's trip?

'Well not me, sunshine. No fucking way. Screw that, I was always going to get what I wanted, I was going to go my own way, come hell or high water. Fuck it.

'I don't just want to rock the boat. I'd gladly smash it in, sink the fucking thing and let everyone just sink or swim, it's up to them.'

'So he was angry?'

DI Chambers nodded, 'Yes, he was angry. I just let him vent. I wanted to find out why...'

'So you could use it?' we asked.

'Yes.'

'So what did you think he was angry about?'

The policeman's answer was surprisingly pragmatic.

'To be honest, to start with I thought it was promotion. Or rather, lack of it.'

'His career?'

DI Chambers sat back in his chair from where we'd been sharing a look at the transcripts as we'd been following along while we listened, and gathered his thoughts.

'The thing about being made in a club like this,' he explained, 'is it's like any organisation. It's not so much about what you do, it's about who you know and how much they'll sponsor you, fight your corner. It's about office politics.

'There's guys who've been working for years, in puppet clubs, as tag-alongs, doing dirty work, shovelling shit for the club, but who have never made it, are never going to make it because despite the fact they're doing a good job, they haven't hitched their ride to a wagon that's going to take them places, support them, push them forwards into membership. While other guys, guys who might be younger and have given less service, if they become someone's protégé, someone they trust implicitly, someone who's seen as having real earning potential, then you'll see them overtaking these older guys and leaving them way behind.

'It's just the way it is, that's life. But as far as the club's high ups are concerned, it's also potentially quite dangerous. Because eventually, and it's usually when he's sitting in some cop shop with bars on the view, sooner or later there's a chance the older bloke is going to start asking himself what the hell he's been doing with his life? Wonder who's been fooling who, and why the hell he's putting up with all this rubbish, all this grief, when he's not been seeing the rewards in terms of a bottom rocker, let alone a sniff of a patch or whatever the next rung up the tree is from where he is now. And that's when they could be tempted to grass, particularly if they're facing some serious weight.'

'But that doesn't fit Bomber does it?' we objected. 'He wasn't some tagalong wannabe was he? He'd been a patch for years, he'd been made president of some charters even. What would his complaint be?'

'No, that's true enough,' admitted DI Chambers. 'But I still think in his eyes he was in the doldrums. I think he felt himself being passed by.

'Whatever else he was, as far as I could see he was straight. He had a legitimate business, a successful one at that, an honest job that made him a decent living and had supported him in looking after his wife and bringing up his kid which had obviously been very important to him. He wasn't into dealing and as I see it, that was his problem.'

'Because Stu was?'

DI Chambers nodded. 'If he wasn't into the business side, Bomber was never going to be sitting at the Top Table because that's where the wheelers and dealers were. He'd reached a glass ceiling if you like.

'I guess it doesn't matter what you're doing, what sort of organisation you're involved with or where you actually end up in it, whether it's near the top, in the middle or down the bottom; there's always going to be someone above you on the rungs, or some level up you realise you're just never going to make.'

'And you think that's what got him angry enough to start him talking?' we asked.

'It's got something to do with it I think, because after a while, and after getting some stuff off his chest he gradually began to open up. And slowly, nothing incriminating mind you, he began to give me his background.'

'If you don't mind me saying so, you sound as though you had a decent education.'

'Me? I suppose so, my folks split up when I was still just a kid. Dad went off to the States and mum ended up shacking up with a bloke over in Germany. They had dosh OK, so I got stuck in a boarding school.'

'Sounds a bit rough. How about holidays? What did you do then?'

'They made arrangements to start with. Relatives, that sort of thing. You know, I was never a kid who ran away from home. My home ran away from me.'

'They abandoned you?'

'Too fucking right they did. Just dropped me 'cos I was a nuisance, so I had a fairly shit childhood, and now you know why I don't feel like talking about it. You satisfied?'

'Yes, I get that now.'

'But there is one thing you ought to know that I did get out of what happened to me, how they treated me.'

'Which was?'

'I swore to myself that I'd never let that happen to a kid of mine. I had a fucked up childhood and I if I ever had a family I'd look after it, I'd never, ever, abandon a kid of mine. I'd be there for them whatever happened, whatever they needed, whatever it took.'

And then there didn't seem to have been anything more to say on the subject at that point in the interview.

*

Iain had also found with Bomber that there were some no go areas that he simply didn't want to talk about and his childhood was one of them. Iain had tried asking about his background a number of times in his interviews and had never got very far.

49

'Do you have a criminal record?' Iain had asked him.

'Me? Yes I've been inside once…' Bomber hesitated, as if uncertain about dredging up a long buried memory.

'But it was a long time ago, before all this,' he added, glancing around.

'Before you were in the club you mean?' Iain clarified.

'Yeah, I was just a kid.'

And as it was obvious that he didn't want to talk about it and the subject was closed, Iain left it at that.

The main thing, as far as Iain was concerned for the purpose of the piece he was writing about how far the reality of the biker's life was adrift from the popular image, was that ever since first becoming associated with the club as tagalong and then through his career as a tryout, patch-holder and then officer in the club, Bomber had never been charged, much less convicted, of anything more serious than some parking tickets and speeding fines.

*

'So what did you do next? Where did you go with the interview?'

'Well he would never tell you this himself,' DI Chambers said, 'but one of the key things you had to realise about Bomber if you wanted to understand him at all, was the way he took care of his kid Jenny after her mum disappeared.

'Whatever else you might think about him, what he is, the things he's done, the one thing he did do, was he did the right thing by Jenny. He took her on when plenty of other blokes would have walked away, and I'm not saying other bikers mind you, I'm talking about all sorts of men in any walk of life. He stepped up and brought her up.'

'So you decided to use that as an angle?' we asked.

DI Chambers nodded. 'I said I'd like him to tell me about his kid and how he'd met her mum…'

'And he talked about that?' we asked in some surprise.

'Oh yes, and it turned out the gossip was right, because he'd met her through the club.'

But Iain had been way ahead of the police on that one as we knew from having read his files and the story of his life Bomber had shared with him.

Iain had asked Bomber where he met Maggie.

'At a party.'

'Was it a club party?'

'Yes.'

'So how did you get involved with the club in the first place?'

'I was at a party, I ran into them there.'

'The same party?'

'Yes.'

'You met them both at the same time?'

'Yeah.'

While there were times when Bomber could be loquacious and willing to talk at length without prompting, at other times Iain recorded that getting answers out of him could be a bit like pulling teeth.

'So how come you were invited to a club party?' Iain continued, 'Sounds a bit odd if you didn't know any of them.'

Bomber just shrugged. 'I didn't know it was them to be honest. It was an open house sort of thing. I just tagged along with a mate from work.'

'Was this when you were lorry driving?'

'No, before that. I'd just moved to Edinburgh and got a job as a mechanic. It didn't pay much but I liked working with bikes, I always had.'

'So why Edinburgh? You don't sound Scottish, Iain observed.

'I'm not, I was brought up in Manchester, there and...' Bomber stopped for a swig at his beer before continuing... 'other places.'

'And that's where you got into bikes and mechanics?'

'Yeah.'

'So how did you end up in Edinburgh?'

'Oh, well, a bit of a fresh start I suppose, but what's it matter?' Bomber growled with a hint of annoyance in his voice at the question. 'That was then, this is now, so did you want to ask about the club or what?'

'I was just curious...' said Iain.

'Curious? About what?'

'About you, your background, your story, what makes you "you" if you like...'

But Bomber made it abundantly clear he wasn't interested in any of that.

'Oh fuck that bullshit! I'm not interested in that ancient history and I don't want to talk about it. You want to ask about the club and what it means to me, that's fine we can talk. You want to get into that old shit before I got involved with the club, then I ain't got anything to say, right?'

'OK, OK, no offense,' Iain held his hands up in mock surrender. 'I didn't mean to pry, I was just interested that's all. So then, tell me, how did you first get involved?'

Mollified a bit by having established some boundaries, not to mention the arrival of another pint, Bomber settled down to telling his story.

'I got a job spannering, at a local bike dealer, servicing commuter bikes and that sort of thing. It was a little old family owned shop, had the town Honda and Suzuki franchise. You don't see many like it any more, with a showroom full of 125s and 250s in the front with helmets for sale along a wall and shelves behind the counter for your spark plugs, two stroke, and bits and pieces, and a work-shop and yard out back where we did the PDIs and services. Old Mr Crouch was the owner and he ran it wearing one of those long brown coats, and other than Saturday when his wife helped out, there was just him, me, and another lad, Jack. Jack and I'd take turns covering for Mr Crouch at the counter if he got busy or was off having a cup of tea, and we became mates.

'I liked it there, it was the first place I'd ever really worked and they just let me get on with stuff that I was good at, which I enjoyed. I never expected it but I was even happy to deal with the punters coming in. You'd got older guys, factory workers who needed a C90 or whatnot, cheap wheels to get them to work. You had old dears who wanted something to pop to the shops and back on, and then you had the biker kids in their leathers, grubby jeans and cut off denim covered in heavy metal band patches, coming in from the local sixth form at lunchtime to get a new chain for their Superdream, or a set of ace bars to help them get their zits closer to the tank.

'Jack knew some of them, he was a local lad and they'd all been at school together and so when he went out for a ride with them I found myself being invited along too. There wasn't much money around in those days and amongst the half dozen or so of us we had a variety of fairly clapped out machines. Other than Jack and me, most of the others didn't have a clue about how to properly maintain and fettle their bikes so there was always someone breaking down with something or other, so eventually we nick-named ourselves the EDBSA.'

'The what?' Iain asked, as he made notes.

'EDBSA, it stood for the Edinburgh and District Bump Starters Association.' Bomber was staring off into the middle distance while he spoke, seemingly lain thought, transported back to a younger time.

'It was just a bit of fun you know? We were kids, don't forget. So we hung around, drank at the same pub and took rides out at weekends for a blast or the occasional party as and when any of us got an invite. And that was how I first met the club.

'One of Jack's mates turned up one evening and said that there was a bash on over Motherwell way. I wasn't quite sure exactly where that was, not being a local lad I was still getting my bearings, but the blokes seemed to know where they were going. Some big house, loads of bikers were being invited and it was going to be a sort of unofficial rally thing over a weekend. Head over, stick up a tent, there'd be a barbecue, a bit of a disco but playing good stuff, not pop crap. All we had to do was pitch up on a bike with our tent and bring some beer and we were in. It sounded great.

'I didn't know whose party it was, didn't have a scoobie-doo.

'As far as we knew it was a friend of a friend of a friend who'd just put out the invites. But we didn't give it a thought. I suppose we just reckoned let's go and check it out. If it is what he says it is, well fantastic, if not, well we can always hang onto our booze and whatever gear we'd scored for the weekend, or if we can't get in we can always fuck of somewhere else to pitch our stuff and get wrecked.

'But when we got there it was cool and we were in no problem without any hassle.

'As we were arriving there was just a column of bikes ahead of us, so we tagged along at the back. I don't know if someone was supposed to be checking against a guest list but if they were they'd given up on it by the time we turned up.

'It was great, I'd never seen anything like it before. There was a big old Victorian villa type place, great stone block built, detached, standing in the middle of an acre or so of grounds on the edge of the village which was obviously the centre of the action. There was a lit area round to one side where there was a sort of part marquee job set up to house the disco and a bar, and as we pulled in I could smell a big barbie going somewhere. We looked around for a place to set up and eventually found one towards the back by the hedge as the rest of the grounds were already filled with scattered tents and parked up bikes as more bikers than I'd ever seen got ready to seriously party.

'It was a fantastic evening, really wild. We'd brought plenty of beers and one of the lads had some decent leb so pretty soon we were well into it. There was music playing through the sound system, these multi-coloured fairy lights strung up along the bushes beside the house and a load of people sitting round the edge of a swimming pool which had lights on underwater as well.

Shit I think it's the first time I'd ever been anywhere that someone had had a pool.

'And we still didn't know whose place it was, who was giving the party.

'Sure, we saw there were club guys around, a bunch of them, but they had set up their own bar round the side of the house the other side of where the barbie was, and them being what they were, it wasn't like me and my mates were going to go barging in and start bothering them was it?

'But even then I still hadn't twigged whose party it was, who owned the gaff and pretty soon I was too stoned to care.

'No, we were just going to enjoy it, drink our beers, headbang to the tunes we liked, check out the bikes and the birds.

'And that's when I first saw Her. Maggie. Fuck it, it was Her that started all this shit for me really.

'And it was only because of Her, well sort of, that I eventually made the connection.

'When I fucked up big time.

'We'd got there early evening. I forget exactly when, but say seven or so. By the time we'd got the tents up and sorted it was beginning to get dark and the party was starting, so we cracked into the beers, and the spliffs started doing the rounds.

'It was one of those things you could wander round at, do what you fancied, so we moseyed on back towards the house. That was where I first met Dobbo. You could drink the stuff you'd brought yourself so we'd stashed that in the tents for later as just to one side of where the rock DJ was playing there was a sort of bar running. You bought a strip of paper off a bloke at one end for a tenner with ten boxes printed on it and then every time you wanted a drink the bloke who served you at the bar crossed them off for the drinks you'd had, and Dobbo was one of the guys on bar duty.

'I'd gone to get a few cans in for the lads to take the edge off the buzz when it happened.

'I was standing there at the bar waiting for a moment while Dobbo was ripping open a new slab of tinnies when I looked round.

'The DJ had just put *Stairway to Heaven* on and to be honest no one much was dancing, everybody was just too chilled out, until suddenly She just appeared.

'There were a couple of lights set up to shine on the ground in front of the DJ's deck making a sort of outdoor dance floor, in the middle of which, silhouetted by the lights against the darkness had materialised this swaying ethereal vision.

'She had been slim, lithe, her long hair tumbling like a wave as in a dream she spun on her toes,' as Bomber painted a picture in words for Iain.

'I felt a tap on my shoulder and swinging round I saw it was the bloke from behind the bar. He was grinning at my obvious, slack jawed stupefied fascination. I tried refocusing on him, my mind reluctantly emerging from some kind of trance as back here on earth he proffered me the six pack I had come to collect and my neatly ticked off tokens.

'I mumbled "sorry" as I took them off him and turned my head again fearful that the magic would have faded.

'The bloke said something like "She's quite something isn't she?" nodding at where the sinuous vision was ushering down folds of heaven as she smoothly wrapped the music around her.

'And I could only agree and stumble away into the darkness to hide my confusion, while behind me beauty twirled, sank and floated in time to the music.

'Like I say, it was a real hard core biker party, heavy duty people if you know what I mean, and our little mob were well gone by eleven or so as we sat around the bonfire we'd built down the end of the garden on the far fringes of the bash, crackling sparks floating high up into the warm night sky.

'By this stage we all had a bad case of the munchies, no surprises there, so a few of us heaved ourselves up and headed over to the pool in an unsteady giggling gaggle to grab some food from the barbie; which was where I got into an argument with a bloke called Eddie, about whether you could jump a bike over the pool or not. You know what it's like, it was just one of those stupid things you get into, with him saying, Nah you'd never do it and me insisting, Yeah reckon I could. I mean, if fucking Evil Knievel could jump this, that or the other canyon, then I sure as hell could jump a bloody pool.

'And then the inevitable happened, because someone said, "Well if you're so fucking sure, why don't you do it?" And mate, that was it. Once those words were out there, there was no way I could back down and leave them hanging in the air, no frigging way.

'Because I saw She was there again, watching and laughing on the edge of the crowd, the lights sparkling in Her eyes and taunting me to show Her what I was made of.

'So off I stomped, back out into the darkness down the long garden towards where I vaguely thought our tents were and where we'd left the bikes. Of course by this stage there was a bit of a kerfuffle as some of my more sensible, or at least, less pissed or stoned mates, tried to persuade me that this wasn't a good idea, but I wasn't having any of that.

'I nearly lost it trying to get back to the tent, stumbling drunk and tripping over guy ropes and stuff, but eventually more by luck than judgement I found my way back to my bike.

'For a moment I seem to remember I stood staring at it, slack jawed and half wondering what it was I was supposed to be doing before my reptilian brain kicked back in with my brilliant idea. Sticking the key in the lock I kicked it into life. I'd picked up an old XT500, Yamaha's big thumper Enduro single and with its off road set up and low down grunt, after my years of scrambling about as a kid, I reckoned I had a real chance.

'The familiar bark of the engine and thrum of vibration through the handlebars felt as though it brought my brain back into focus as I shook my head a bit to clear the fuzziness from my mind and snicked it into first. Slipping the clutch I headed out, threading my way through the narrow gaps between the randomly scattered tents and kicking down with my feet as I did so, until I reached a path and could get properly moving.

'Heading towards the house I caned it, absentmindedly flicking on my headlights, and over the noise of my engine accelerating hard I heard someone scream that I was coming. I could see a gap opening up in front of me amongst the people around the pool as figures pushed and scrambled to either side to get out of my way as I raced towards them.

'Approaching the house and pool, the ground sloped upwards slightly and I stood up on the pegs as I reached the end of the path and gunned the engine for my approach, cresting the rise and bursting into the light and then –

'Bang!

'I remember it all in slow motion, just like you would with an accident.

'I jumped down on the pegs to compress the suspension as I hit the tiled area surrounding the pool, and as the bike rebounded, all at a single moment I pulled back on the handlebars for a classic bunny hop to get me airborne, blasting the throttle and dumping the clutch to get that zap of extra acceleration from the energy stored in the flywheel. There was a lip at the edge of the pool, nothing much, just a little rise of an inch or so, but it was enough to act as a kicker, bumping the front wheel up and enabling me to keep the power full on as the rear wheel hit it and lifted me into the air.

'I was flying.

'A sensation of free falling.

'In a world of my own.

'And silence.

'There must have been noise. I know there must, people shouting or whatever, but I didn't hear any of it. Just then, just there, for that moment there was only me, the air and the bike. And Her, watching somewhere in the darkness. And you know what? I almost fucking made it. I almost fucking made it. Almost, but not quite.

'My front wheel hit the edge of the pool on the far side but by that

58

time I was going down. The next thing I knew was the shock of the water as I crashed straight into the pool. You know what it's like when it gets forced up your snout when you get a dive wrong? Well think that, in spades.

'By the time I surfaced and was shaking my head to get the water out of my eyes and ears you should have heard the commotion. People shouting, screaming, laughing, all sorts. I looked down and there was my bike, lying at the bottom of the pool. As I swam to the side I remember thinking to myself, Oh shit, now how am I going to get that out?

'I remember there were people up on the side of the pool reaching down, so grabbing proffered hands, I was hauled out of the water to slump down sitting on the edge, sopping wet, my feet and boots still in the water as I became aware of the cold clinging sensation of my sodden clothes hanging from me, and the streaming rivulets of water pouring down as I reached up and brushed the wet hair from across my face.

'And all around me the noise went on until with a sudden hush it faded away, and over and above my immediate consciousness of chill I sensed a change in the atmosphere, people drawing back, a sudden tension and fear as I heard a voice shouting, "What the fuck's going on here?"

'It was a serious sounding voice and I could hear someone answering him with, "Some twat's put a bike in your pool."

'Some twat.

'That would be me then. I decided as, squelchily, I staggered to my feet and turned towards the approaching figures. Once again, a path was magically opening up amongst the surrounding crowd for an approaching danger, only this time it wasn't me, it was Mal, the club's P, with a couple of his crew following on in his wake as backup while he came to find out just what the fuck was going on.

'He walked straight up to where I stood dripping waiting for him, and now the whole place really was completely silent.

'He had a beer bottle in his hand as he stopped to face me by the side of the pool. He looked down and took in the sight of my bike against the blue tiles of the pool casting weird shadows as it rested against one of the underwater lights at the side.

'Having satisfied himself he wasn't seeing things, he looked back up at me.

'"Your bike?" he asked.

'"Yep," I told him.

'"What's it doing in my fucking pool?"'

'I shrugged. There didn't seem to be much to say other than the truth, "I didn't manage to jump far enough."

'He looked down at it again and it was his turn to shrug.

'"Well I guess you'd better get it out again tomorrow then, hadn't you?"

'I just nodded. Again there didn't seem to be much to say other than the obvious. "Yeah, I guess so."

'He took a sup of his beer as he seemed to consider this for a moment and fixed me with one of his I'm-going-to-remember-your-face-son looks that I later found he did so well. Then after an age he said, "OK then."

'And that was it. He turned around, and he and his guys just headed back off to their own bit of the bash, leaving me surrounded by a circle of other party goers who I guess were just wondering how come I was still alive, having pulled off a stunt like that.

'But really, I didn't care about any of them. There was only one person in the crowd that I was looking for and that was Her.

'But I couldn't see Her.

'Eventually some of my mates got me back to our tents and I got sorted out with some bits and pieces of dry clothing, but the steam had gone out of the party for me by that stage, so I crashed an hour or so later, but not without having necked most of a bottle of Southern Comfort that someone had presented to me when I'd got back to the bonfire.

'And all the time, all I was doing, was looking out for Her.

'But She was nowhere to be seen.

'Next morning was special. Really special, a slice of my own private hell. It was bright, sunny and hot and I felt just like death warmed over. My head was throbbing and yet when I got to the side of the pool and looked down, squinting against the sickening glare of the glinting waters with its rainbow slick of oil and fuel, there was my bike, just as I hoped I'd only imagined it.

'Now how the fuck was I going to get it out?

'As the makeshift campsite slowly emptied out of revellers and stragglers heading out and home, Stu and the rest of his crew settled onto loungers around the poolside to watch the entertainment I had laid on and make helpful suggestions.

'Me and my mates found there was no easy way to lift it out and eventually there was nothing for it but to drain the pool, which given the crap that had come off the bike was something that needed to happen anyway. Then we could roll it to the shallow end and manhandle it up some steps.

'It took a couple of hours drying out, the heat of the morning sun beating down on my throbbing skull, kicking it over with the sparkplug out to make sure the cylinder was clear of water, and draining the carb's float bowl, during which time we started on the job of scrubbing the pool tiles clean so the bloke could set it to refilling again when he was ready.

'But then, after a bit of fettling, a can's worth of good old WD40, and what seemed an age of me jumping up and down on the kick starter, fuck me if she didn't have a cough and a blow or two and then start again, bless her.

'By which time I was completely beat and just wanted to get the hell out of there. Eddie had hung around to help me and get it going, but he was already packed up and so he headed off, while I lay back for a moment with my eyes closed, feeling that dry metallic taste of shit in my mouth and desperately willing the pain in my head to go away. I was just trying to summon the strength to heave myself upright again and start to think about breaking down my tent so I could sod off home and crawl into my own bed, while beside me the bike chuntered and clattered away to itself as if complaining and grumbling about its treatment.

'"Beer?" came a voice and I opened my eyes, blinking against the sun, to see the twin figures of Dobbo and Stu looming over me, silhouetted against the clear blue of the sky in all their rotten splendour, typical of the day.

'What everybody forgets now is just how filthy dirty and scruffy bikers were back then, as a deliberately chosen screw-you look. The rockers had had their leather jackets and studs but as the outlaw biker scene coalesced in the seventies and early eighties they seemed old hat, conventional even.

'Besides which, we'd all read Hunter S Thompson and just thought that was how it all worked. We didn't get how much he'd been wound up by the Angels.

'No, we all just swallowed it whole, hook line and sinker.

'We'd all read how chickenshit it was to wear leather jackets, studs, anything practical like that. What, were you scared of a spill or something? Looking for protection against road rash like some modern ATG-ATT pussy in a one piece with fake sponsors logos to match his crotch rocket? And don't get me started on Barbour jackets, that was real granddad stuff.

'Nah, black leathers were for heavy metal kids into the fashion and wannabe bad boy bikers. The real thing in those days was riding out in knocked off donkey jackets, army surplus store greatcoats, great places to shop for your combats and German para boots if you weren't a DMs man, or occasionally the skinhead style bomber jacket in olive green or black.

'There weren't any of the fancy black leather biker vests in those days either. Your all-important colours were always worn over the top of whatever your cobbled together collection of rags were, on a denim cut off.

'Meanwhile, for any self-respecting outlaw, your originals naturally would have been left under your bike to collect the requisite degree of oil staining, and if you didn't have a bit of leaky Brit-shit to do the necessary for you, you could always help them on their way with a deliberate soaking, before you then wore 'em until they simply rotted away, stinking grey shredding strips of fabric clinging to your legs and patched with stolen beer towels across your arse.

'And personal grooming was very much to match. Shaving was for straights, so beards were the order of the day, from spade to the full Santa. Hair was long and straggly as a rule, although looks ranged from the full on thicket, through the mullet for the sophisticated and stylish, to the so called angel cut, a close cropped stubble on top combined with long lank locks at the back beyond the helmet line.

'Squinting against the light the two of them looked every inch the young dangerous outlaw bikers that of course as tagalongs, they actually weren't yet.

'Grinning behind a pair of silvered aviator sunglasses with the slogan *All I Ever Think About Is **SEX*** printed in red across each lens which made his eyes invisible, Dobbo squatted down so he was closer to my level, while I levered myself up on my elbows. As he became easier to see I took in his lumberjack style shirt with rolled up sleeves open over a faded Sabbath tour T-shirt.

'But mostly I took in that his outstretched arm was proffering a can.

'"Have a beer mate. Good to see you got it going again," he said approvingly, nodding at the bike as propping myself on one side I reached out with my free hand to take it. "I thought it might take a bit more than that."

'"Nah," I said, "they're bullet proof these things. Take more than a bit of water to knock it out for very long."

'"Well, even so," he said with a bit of a grin, "you know, I have to say, that was a bit of a show." He was talking about my display last night I guessed, rather than my efforts with a scrubbing brush and a can of WD40 this morning. "Gave me a right laugh."

'"Well... cheers," I said somewhat warily, as I took the can from him and popped it open with that satisfying hiss, mixed with sense of relief that I seemed to be going to get away with this.

'"No problem," he said, as he stood back up again and glanced back over to where the rest of the club were camped out where somebody was gesturing.

'"It's Mal," Stu said, nodding back towards the pool, "He wants to see you kid."

'"It's going to cost me money that," Mal nodded, sat back on his recliner by the empty pool, a fag smouldering away in the ashtray beside him and looking up at where I was standing uncomfortably in front of him, "sorting the pool out, filling it up, chemicals and shit."

'I wasn't sure what to say to that so I opted for keeping my trap firmly shut.

'He let me stew for a moment until with a wave of the beer bottle in his hand he asked, "So, d'you really think you can do it?"

'I glanced over again at the distance. It really wasn't that far across, I thought as my rusty brain reckoned up the calculations, I'd jumped as much, if not more, as a kid on my little scrambler, but I'd been lighter then and had arranged a better launch as out of mouth came, "Yeah, but I'd need a bit of a ramp…"

'"A big one?"

'"No, a couple of feet should do it, just enough to give me a bit of a lift, get me properly airborne."

'He sat up, swinging himself forwards and around to plant both his feet on the warm tiles and lean towards me with a grin on his face, while he plonked his empty bottle down on the table beside him which seemed to be a sign for Stu to start to head across bearing a new one.

'"OK then, sounds to me like we can have a bit of fun with this then, so I'll do you a deal, how about that son?"

'I just shrugged and wondered what was coming next.

'"I'll get the lads to knock up a ramp and you have another go. You make it and we're quits, screw it up and you owe me for the pool, how's that? Can't say fairer, eh?"

'"Well…" I started, but it was obvious this wasn't really one of those offers that you could sensibly refuse.

'"OK then," he said, sticking out his hand.

'I took it, "You're on."'

'He stuck up a hand and waved to a couple of the guys who were sorting out the barbie to join us.

'"You sort your bike," he was saying as they stepped over, "and we'll sort a ramp and let's see how we get on..."

'It only took them an hour or so. It wasn't anything fancy, just some timber out of his shed screwed together into a pair of triangles and then braced across with more stout timber, and a long sheet of ply cut down into a couple of strips and layered across the top to give me my ramp.

'It was crude but it would do. We slid it into place on the tiles at the edge of the pool and to try and stop it slipping forward when I hit it I had them drill some holes on either side at the foot of the ramp where it ran off over the grass and we banged in some tent pegs to secure it in place. It wasn't much, but I thought it was better than nothing.

'Eventually, shoving it with my foot, it seemed sturdy and stable enough.

'Mal came over to inspect the project as the smell of cooking was wafting over from the barbie.

'"Good to go?" he asked.

'"Reckon," I told him.

'"Good lad," he said, clapping me on the shoulder in a surprisingly friendly way, "right, we'll grab some lunch and I'll get the boys organised afterwards."

'And off we went in our different directions.

'About five minutes later Stu wandered across and plonked a paper plate with a burger, semi-cremated chicken leg and a dollop of shop bought coleslaw on the seat of my bike, together with a cold one.

'"Lunch," he said simply, before turning around and heading back over to where the blokes were gathered around the pool.

'I was sat on the bike at the end of the path, the engine responding rortily as I blipped the throttle, checking and rechecking that it was running right and amazingly none the worse for wear for its little bath last night. The last thing I was going to need just now was a misfire if I was going to do this. But no, she was running fine.

'It was a lid on job now, if only because if I didn't make it this time, I was heading for a meeting with the concrete and tiles of an empty pool.

'Ahead of me at the other end of the path the way was cleared straight up to where the makeshift ramp was sitting and either side of this was the crowd, all gathered round for the show like rowdy spectators at the coliseum encouraging lions versus Christians, only for me there was a stomping rhythmic handclap that matched the rising chant of...

'Jump! Jump! Jump!

'Mal was holding up his hand as he counted me down...

'"Three! Two! One!"

'And his arm dropped.

'I swallowed hard and gunned the engine, wringing the throttle grip to the max before I dumped the clutch and launched the bike up the path.

'This was it.

'Why the hell I just didn't do the obvious, I'll never know. I was on my bike, moving, I could have just scooted across the grass, hit the drive and been out and away, escaped. It would have been easy. I'd have had to keep my head down. Disappear maybe, make a start somewhere else, but so what? I'd done it before, I could do it again.

'But I didn't. Instead I was blasting up the path, the engine screaming as I redlined it in first and booted it up mercilessly into second.

'All I could hear was the roar of the engine in my ears while somewhere in the back of my brain I registered the image of the stomping of the feet, the clapping of the hands and the mouthed shouts as the time track to my memory, counting down the moments until, with a wooden sounding clunk and a sudden slight sagging as the ply gave slightly under the weight, my front wheel hit the ramp and with a Zen like calm, I repeated my jump.

'I was up out of my seat now, sailing through the air. Good height, I was thinking at the apex, as the bike's nose started to come down and then – Bang, I was down again, the front and then rear shocks telescoping as the bike and I thumped onto the other side, my arms and legs bent as I absorbed the shock and kept it together as we ran off the tiles and onto the grass beyond.

'Daring to breathe again, I scrubbed off the speed and pulling it round in a lazy U, puttered back up towards the edge of the pool to kill it, kick out the side stand and slip off my lid with a shake of my head to clear my hair from my eyes.

'Across the other side of the pool the crowd was laughing and cheering as money changed hands. Of course, they'd had a sweepstake.

'Stu fetched me round again to where Mal was standing in obvious good humour, a fag dangling from his mouth as he accepted some cash one of his blokes was handing over.

'"Nice one son," he said, as hand on my shoulder, Stu plonked me in front of him, "You've got a bit of class, you know that?"

'"Cheers," I nodded, with a sheepish smile.

'"So we're cool?" I asked.

'"Yeah, we're cool, son," he nodded, sticking out his hand, and then to my amazement pulling me into a biker hug as I took it. "Saved me a job son, it was about time the pool had a good clean."

'"You ought to tagalong, son," Mal was saying, as he let me go and someone pressed another cold one into my unresisting hand. It wasn't so much an invitation as an instruction. "See what you think."

'And then someone else was calling him away, something they wanted him to see or do or rule on, and I was alone again with Stu as my guide amongst the milling chatting crowd of club guys.

'"You cost me a fiver there," Dobbo muttered in my ear later as he walked me away back round the edge of the pool to where my bike was standing, "I had it on you bottling it."

'But even that was said with a smile.

'Just at that moment however I wasn't really listening to him, as across at the far side of the group I'd caught sight of Her again. Dobbo's eyes followed my gaze.

'"So what's it with Maggie then?" he asked later that evening.

'I'd somehow gathered that given my new tagalong status I wasn't going to be heading home anytime soon. Mal had called me over for a chat during the afternoon. We'd talked for a while over a beer. He'd wanted to know who I was, how I'd heard about his party, it was all very casual, relaxed, and then I'd sort of ended up just hanging around and chatting to Dobbo and some of the others. By early evening I somehow seemed to have been detailed to stick with Dobbo and Stu who were both still tagalongs as well back then, and give them a hand about the place, which seemed to involve a hell of a lot of fetching cold beers for patches who couldn't be arsed to stand up and get one themselves.

'"So, you fancy her or what?"

'I was confused, I really didn't have a clue what he was on about as at that stage I didn't even know Her name. It had never even occurred to me to ask anyone.

'"Who?"

'"Maggie, the bird over there," he said, nodding to where She was standing again over by Stu as he was tending the barbie. 'You were staring at her all last night, you twat. I saw you, you couldn't keep your eyes off her could you?'

'"Oh her, is that her name? Do you know her?"

'He looked at me appraisingly for a moment and eventually said, "Maggie? Yeah I know her. You want me to fix you up with her?"

'I think I must have just stared at him open mouthed. Did I fuck?

'Tongue tied, I was just shaking my head in confusion as raising his arm he gave a wave and a shout to call Her over.'

The story we had in Iain's files fitted in with what DI Chambers had told us as well.

As DI Chambers had already mentioned, Bomber was by his own admission a bit gawky when he first came onto the scene. He had always been, and still was as far as we could gather from the observations in Iain's files, a very private person, introverted, shy even, so he was naturally someone who didn't tend to give much away. Given his background and seeming issues as a kid with his family, it seemed as though he always found it took a while to get to know and trust people.

But as Iain observed, once you'd won his trust, you were a friend for life, he had an intense loyalty that way.

'...and as a youngster,' the Inspector was saying, 'I really don't think he'd have been comfortable at small talk and as for chatting up a girl, well, I'm not sure he'd have known where to start.'

Of course as it happened, Dobbo knew Maggie, she was one of Stu's current squeezes. So setting Bomber up with her could be simple. But given she was Stu's bird, it could also be extremely dangerous for him.

So the question DI Chambers had in his mind was why did he do it?

What was in it for Dobbo, and what was in it for Stu to agree?

But the truth of the matter was really quite prosaic. As Dobbo also knew, Stu got through squeezes at a fair rate and while it seemed she didn't appreciate it at the time, even if Dobbo did, Maggie was on her way out as far as Stu was concerned. Truth be told, he'd simply got bored both with her, and her prodigious appetite for whatever gear Stu had on him whenever they were together.

So Dobbo knew that as far as Stu was concerned, shucking Maggie off to Bomber was going to be no skin of his nose, far from it. In fact, if it got her off his back and out of his stash without a fuss it would be a bit of a win as far as he was concerned.

So telling Bomber later that evening *Let me see what I can do*, and having a word in Stu's ear to get him to set Maggie up with Bomber was an easy win for Dobbo as well.

And doing so was either a very lucky move on Dobbo and Stu's part, or very astute as a way of enticing Bomber into the fold. As it happened, a simple offer of friendship, combined with helping him get involved with the girl he'd fallen for heavily from the moment he'd seen her, was an overwhelmingly powerful combination for Bomber in his fragile state at that moment in time.

Dobbo and Stu, whether knowingly or not, had laid out a prospect in front of him. Of a route to happiness, fulfilment, a sense of belonging; of an opportunity to become part of a new family, and for someone like Bomber, it seemed there was just no escaping its magnetic pull.

CHAPTER 3   RESPONSE AND RESPONSIBILITY

Stu: I bumped Bomber up to being an officer because I thought he had what it takes.

The thing is you can have a good guy one day, a really great club member. Then you make him up and find the next day that you got a really shit officer because they can't handle it, don't know what to do.

Sometimes they just want to stay everybody's mate, be one of the boys, not throw their weight around, which is fine in terms of getting on with the blokes, but it doesn't mean they'll respect you or do what you tell 'em to do.

Other blokes go the other way. Give them a tiny bit of power and it goes to their heads. They come back in the next day like a mini Hitler with a stripe on their sleeve and a huge attitude that the blokes should just do what they say because they've told 'em so, which just causes a whole load of agro and resentment.

Worse still you get some who yo-yo between the two. Most of the time they just want to stay being one of the lads, but then when they can't get what they want, eventually they snap, they turn into Godzilla ranting and raving around the place, until they calm down and want to go back to being mates again. Trouble is, no one knows where the fuck they stand with them and it just causes all sorts of grief.

What you want is someone who can be consistent. Someone who's clear about what they want, what standards they expect from everyone they meet repping the club, from patch-holders downwards.

And you can be challenging like that, pushing everyone to do the best for the club, so long as you lead by example, so don't ask others to do what you won't do yourself, and you show your total commitment to the club and everything it stands for. But you've got to show you're dedicated to your guys at the same time. You're there to help them be the best they can, you're committed to the club because of what it stands for and what you can do for all of us.

If you're going to want to lead then you have to lead by example, by the standards you maintain, expect and demand, and by your commitment you show to your principals and your guys. There's no other way and that's what I'm looking for in anyone I want to bring through the ranks.

And that's what Bomber had as I saw it. Potential, potential to lead.

So I gave him his chance, and he took it.

Iain: *So how did that work out?*

Iain Parke's files – Interview with Stu 2009

'I'm telling you mate, it's a dying way of life.'

Iain and Bomber had been speaking, quietly, in the corner of a clubhouse.

'Look around you,' Bomber had said, 'We're all getting on. There's blokes here in their fifties, sixties even, I wouldn't be surprised if Gramps isn't pushing seventy if he's a day. But forties? Very few. Thirties? Hardly any.

'And you've got to ask yourself, with all the heat and shit that comes down on you once you're wearing a patch; with it starting to be made illegal altogether in some places like Germany and Australia, what's in it for a younger guy to want to join?

'You used to get into this game young, well, relatively young at least. Back in the day when the club was forming; the sixties, the seventies, the guys joining it were a bunch of lads, real tearaways, blokes in their twenties, early thirties at the most. But as it's gone on, the age at which you get in has started to creep up. The club wants more mature guys, blokes they know have seen a bit and have made a decision that this is something they really want to commit to for life, rather than something they've drifted into as a youthful indiscretion that they might think twice about later on when wife and kids come along. So most guys striking these days are probably in their thirties, they've been a squaddie, done time, whatever.

'But even so, the thing that no one thinks about when they get in is what happens later. This ain't the sort of deal where there's a pension is there? So sure, you can live it large, have a real good time, do whatever the fuck you want while you're in, but sooner or later you're going to wake up and think, How does this end? How do I get out? Can I retire? Will "they" let me? What will it mean if I do?

'And will they let me is a big one. While you're in the club you're useful and to a degree, there's confidence that you're going to be keeping your mouth shut. But once you're out, well you're out. So are you of as much use? And how far can you be trusted? You can see the sorts of questions that someone at the Top Table is going to be asking themselves about you and what the obvious risk avoidance strategy might be.

'Fuck it, I'm proud of my time in the club, even after all the shit. We were the best, you know? We were really something, we didn't take any crap from anyone outside.

'There's nothing like it you know? Being part of something, something great. Nothing like it at all.'

'So were you a wild kid?' Iain asked him, checking back on what he was saying, 'I just wanted to get clear on where you came from, what you were like as a lad, how you fitted in with the other guys...'

'Me?' he snorted in disgust, and shook his head, 'You know you read all the books coming out these days guys from the clubs are writing and they all talk about how tough they were as kids. They're all the same more or less aren't they? Being fourteen or fifteen, bunking off school, stealing bikes, TWOCing motors, not taking any shit, getting into fights and shagging the local birds, so it's only joining the army or something that gets them out of it and shows them there's something more?

'Well I wasn't like that. I wasn't like that at all,' he said, with what could have been a tone of regret in his voice.

'Anything but, really. I was always the quiet kid, all I ever wanted was to be left alone to get on and read my books. The wimpy kid, a bit of a weed to be honest, a specky lanky streak of piss. So yeah, fuck it, I hated being a kid and my time at school. Best days of my life? Bollocks. Good riddance is all I have to say and I don't want to talk about it or think about it.

'That clear enough for you?' He glared at Iain as though daring him to say another word.

Iain always said he felt he knew when he'd pushed his luck and almost gone too far, and this was absolutely one of those moments, a time to turn away and chart a safer course.

'So why do you want out then, Bomber?' Iain asked, his voice low, as neither of them wanted the details of this conversation to be over-heard. 'What's got you thinking like that after all these years?'

'I've just got a bit tired of going to bed every night not knowing whether the plod were going to be kicking my door in at five o'clock the next morning,' came the weary voiced reply. 'I mean, who needs that eh? It gets a bit wearing, you know?'

'Well yes, I can see it might.'

'Particularly if it's all because some other sod's making money.'

'And are they?'

Apparently Bomber just nodded at that point, reluctant to commit his words to Iain's ever present Dictaphone, although Iain added his own succinct assessment to the end of his tape once he was off the premises and heading home for the evening.

'Disaffected is not the word.'

*

Bomber was one of the bikers Iain had interviewed at length during his association with the clubs.

At the time they first met, Bomber was in the process of retiring from the club and unlike many other members, in sessions then and after-wards, he was prepared to talk.

Iain had written about his experiences interviewing bikers, and although it doesn't name names, we believe he had Bomber in mind in particular when he spoke in a piece published in a UK biker magazine in June 2009 about what it was like to talk to outlaw bikers.

So whether Iain had been being disingenuous in also asking Stu about Bomber, or whether he was just looking to get a different viewpoint, he already knew how it had worked out. He'd had it straight from the horse's mouth.

'So you're thinking about getting out, retiring, leaving it all behind?' Iain had asked Bomber, returning to the subject again the following evening.

'Oh yeah, sure I do. I've been thinking about it a lot, particularly recently.'

Bomber looked down at his beer as if deep in thought.

'Just focus on my business,' he added after a moment, 'Getting that straight, you know?'

'And that is a straight business, isn't it?' Iain checked.

'Yeah, sure it is,' said Bomber, with a flush of pride in his voice, 'Built it up over the years and always kept it right. No choice really, with the club thing, especially once I got into logistics and then imports and exports. I knew I'd always have the man sniffing round it so I've always run it straight as a die. Taxes on time, no funny business, all that. There's no other way really, not if I wanted to make a proper go of it.'

'You've built it to quite a size?

'Yeah, I've done alright. Not bad for an ex-trucker eh?'

'Not bad at all,' agreed Iain before probing, 'So what is it with you?'

'Me?'

'Yes, you. Why would you want out? I'm curious. What's eating you?'

'I've just got tired, I guess, and I feel like I've paid the price, paid my dues anyway.'

'The price?'

'Yeah well, it's cost me you know? The club, the job. It's cost me plenty, anyone could see that if they wanted to look, even if they didn't want to admit it. Friends, family, you name it. And eventually I guess, it's all started to catch up with me.'

'And...?'

'And I guess I just started to wonder if it's all been worth it.'

'So what happened?'

Bomber gave Iain an unsettling stare as he mulled that question over, and then eventually, hesitantly and circuitously at first, he began to talk.

'People think that when you've made P, you've got it made, but really, they've got no frigging clue. I mean Christ, you've no idea the hassle involved, the responsibility you're taking on.

'It's like you end up being dad to the whole of the charter. You're the one in charge, you're the one who's always got to be looking out, keeping an eye on what's happening, how things are going to affect the club.

'Sure you get respect, sure people look up to you, but it comes at a price and it ain't that simple you know? It's like you can never, ever, relax, chill out, just enjoy it anymore, because somehow you've become the one who's responsible for everyone else and for the club.

'Sometimes it's like being in charge of a big bunch of kids and the worst are the heat magnets.

'It's like, I look at what some of 'em do sometimes and all I can do is think to myself, what the hell did you go and do that for? It's like they just run off wild and they just don't think for themselves. It never occurs to 'em. They'll do something without considering what it means for the club or what sort of shit it's going to cause that someone's going to have to clear up.

'The thing about heat magnets is they never take responsibility for what they're doing and how it impacts on everyone else. They just carry on doing what the fuck they like whatever the grief that follows and you know what I realised eventually? At the end of the day it's our own fault, officers like me I mean, that we get this grief, because we let 'em get away with it.

'They're the sort of guys who if you give them an inch, they'll take a mile. Try and be reasonable and trust their judgement and sure as hell you'll quickly find out that they've not got any.

'Turn your back for just a moment, and they'll have dropped the whole of the charter in deep shit because they've blown up over nothing and attacked a civilian, or they've been so pissed or wired that they've thought they'd show some class and freak out the citizens with some very public stunt or other.

'And of course they don't ever think to stop or pull it in because at the end of the day we, the officers, we have always ended up clearing it up for them, setting things straight, tidying up loose ends.

'And even then when you do that for 'em, are they grateful? Are they fuck.

'When they think you're getting at 'em then they're just like stroppy teenagers, being arsey, arguing back about what you want 'em to do, just interested in partying and lazing around and doing whatever they like, rather than pulling their weight. So then you're the dad that's getting in the way, stopping them having their fun, chasing them to do shit. The dad they're always bitching, moaning and whining about whenever they're alone with their mates and they don't think you're listening.

'I tell you, as a new P for the first time when Stu first made me up down south, I tried being Mr Nice Guy to start with.'

'No good?' asked Iain.

'Shit no. Herding fucking cats would have been easier than managing the mob I had at times, and pretty soon I was sick to death of it. I thought to myself, why the hell should I play it that way and end up with all this shit? So I learnt, I learnt fast, that there was only one way to do it.

'It's tough love mate. You want 'em to do what they need to do for their own good, then you need to be fucking hard right from day one. When you're P, you're the boss and people had just better do what they're fucking told. Eventually you'll start to know who you can trust, who'll act the way they need to without being ridden all the time and then you can cut those guys some slack. But that's very much on an earned basis. Until then you've got to keep your distance from them, keep your rep as the guy who says how it is and what happens, and be the one who can make it happen.

'Because with the sort of guys we have in a club like ours, they're no shrinking violets. These are guys who've made it to getting a patch, they know who they are, what they want and how to get it. And if you ain't got a firm grip on all the guys in your charter, they'll be off doing their own thing and pretty soon it'll be complete fucking chaos and putting that genie back in the bottle becomes a way bigger problem than if you'd just bloody well kept the lid firmly on it in the first place.

'And I guess that was the lesson Stu wanted me to learn, and I guess he thought I'd learnt it because when all the shit blew up with Munster in Granite City, I was the one he tapped to sort it out.'

And settling back into his seat, Bomber told his story.

'Aberdeen was an ex-Clansmen's charter.

'After we took out their acid in 2001 they lasted a while as an independent club but the writing was on the wall from the moment the raid went down. Once we'd bundled their chemist into our van and got him out of there, it was all over for them bar the shouting, and they knew it.

'They had a bit of fat to live off that could buy them some time, supplies to sell at a premium, that sort of thing, but without their guy that was a dwindling resource, particularly as they knew it was only a matter of time before we had him back up and running, producing for us. And in our game at the end of the day, money is power.

'So eventually, whatever the emotions, they knew they were going to have to make a deal with us and what the only deal in town was going to be.

'Give Merlin his due, he kept his club together and afloat for a year while he explored the options.

'On the face of it, the Menaces were an obvious potential avenue for them as he knew the players. Fuck it, he'd hosted a sit down between them and Stu back in the mid-nineties at a time when we were just getting things on to a less confrontational footing, so seeing if there was a deal to be done on supplies with them that could let the Clansmen continue as independents was just the sensible thing to do.

'Hell, in the old days the Menaces would probably have gone for it for all sorts of reasons, from the straightforward business to the satisfaction of supporting an irritant in our own back yard, and if it came to a war between us and the Clansmen, then so what as far as they were concerned? Something that sucked up our time and guys in grief against a mob who were acting as the Menaces' proxies? It would just be a sweet no lose situation as far as they were concerned. They could just sit back and watch us slug it out at no cost to them at all.

'But the reality was, this wasn't the old days any longer, and ironically enough, that was partly down to the role Merlin had played in hosting those early talks.

'Because by the time we had taken out their acid operation, whatever the international politics between us and the Menaces, here in the UK when it came to business, things were nicely settled to both sides' satisfaction. Turf was sorted, trade was good, things were peaceful and we could all get on with riding our bikes, having a good time and for those that wanted to, making money, without having to watch our backs just because of the patch we were wearing.

'So by the time Merlin went calling on the Menaces for help and support, there was no way he was going to get it. Why would they risk what they had going with us and the *modus vivendi* we'd worked years to set up, for the sake of picking what was always going to be the underdog in any fight up here?

'No, while he had to try it, the truth was Merlin didn't have a prayer of getting any meaningful support there, and so it was eventually just a matter of facing up to the reality, which was fight and lose, or join and share, and Merlin was always a realist.

'So eventually the Clansmen did what was always going to happen, and patched over to become Rebels, and their Granite City charter came as part of the deal.

'It was Stu who started it off. It was Stu who sent me up there to take over after the trouble.

'I mean I'm not blaming him or anything. Fuck it, I was up for it, you know? This was my big chance, a real step up the greasy pole, a chance to be P of a sizable charter, show what I could do. So I went for it big time. In for a penny in for a pound sort of thing. I decided if I was going to go for it, it had to be all the way. So I just upped sticks and moved us up there lock stock and barrel, me, my wife Kath, and Jenny.

'Your daughter?'

'Yes. It made sense, you know? After all, I was expecting to be there a while. That was what the job was going to be after all. Knock heads together, do a bit of housecleaning if needed; whatever it took to get things back on track. This was just after all the trouble with Munster, don't forget, so getting his charter sorted out was an important job no doubt about that. But then once it was sorted? Well then, that would be it for me for a while and my chance to establish myself as a player...'

By which Iain read as organising a local powerbase, sorting out a sweet little operation, where Bomber could build up his rep and bide his time while he watched out for the next opportunity to take a step up the rungs.

'All I had to do was not screw it up.'

'So what happened?' Iain asked.

'In two words? Poison and chalice.'

'You've got to remember that the patch-over was all ancient history as far as I was concerned when I got there. It had been back in 2003 and here we were, what eight years later?

'So by the time I got there the charter was a mix. There was still a quota of old ex-Clansmen patches who'd made the change and survived the sort of shakeout that always happens. There's always a fallout after any patch-over. The club takes a good look at the guys who've come in to see who's really going to make the grade, while the guys who've come in take a good look at their new club and decide if it's really for them.

'And then there were the new recruits who'd come on board in the years since the patch-over.

'So I wasn't expecting too much trouble.

'Sure there'd been the problem with Munster, the previous P. He'd gone a bit, let's just say off piste, in a way that I'm really not going to get into, and so Stu just had to step in to sort him out which meant get him out of the club, after which, Stud had decided to send me in to make sure the rot stopped there.

'I couldn't have been more wrong.

'Most charters tend to be made up of similar types of people; after all, like attracts like. So let's be honest, some charters are full of crims, where you'll find most members make most of their dosh from dodgy stuff of some sort or other, other charters are just full of straight working guys where everyone's got a job and relies mainly on earning an honest wage to keep a roof over their heads.

'The trouble with this charter was that it was a dangerous mix.

'Aberdeen was the wild north east at the time don't forget. Oil money was everywhere, and the lads coming in from the rigs had worked two week shifts of twelve hours on, twelve hours off. They all had money to burn and were looking for serious fun on their two week breaks, so the drug trade around the club scene was booming and some of Munster's boys had been filling their boots.

'Munster had been very much that way inclined and once he'd made P, discipline slipped as he'd focused more and more on using the patch and the club to further his "business" interests. He'd brought guys in who really shouldn't have been there. Some were serious crims who wanted to do quiet business, some were just wannabe gangsters who were yet more heat magnets, and neither of these mixed particularly well with the old school bar room brawler bikers, each section wanting to pull the charter in their own direction.

'You interested in history at all? I am. Fascinating stuff. You can learn a lot from it.

'Take medieval times. All the stuff that Shakespeare covered. Henry V, Macbeth, Richard III, all those. It's all there, mate, if you just look for it.

'You had a king, right, and he was in charge, he was the guy that all the barons had to swear allegiance to, and then it all rolled downhill as the barons each had their knights and men who served them.

'But the king always knew that the barons would only be loyal so long as he delivered what was in each of their interests, or when they were afraid of what would happen if they didn't support him, because he always knew that deep down, whatever any of them would ever say to his face, each of the barons would be watching out for their own interests, wondering to himself if he had a shot at making king, and keeping an eye on the other barons who might be rivals in case they made a move first that could put them at risk.

'One of those situations where everybody knows that whatever the rhetoric, however close you were, however much trust you had day to day, when it came down to brass tacks, everything was in the end a matter of expediency and *in extremis*, everyone would be looking out for themselves and that's just the way the world was. No point in crying about it. Everyone knows it, no one says it, and you all just pretend it doesn't exist.

'At the same time, the more certain you could be that someone would get your back, the stronger you were as a team.

'So the king had to be a leader, he had to be someone they would want to follow because it was in their interests.

'So if a strong king wanted to go and kick the shit out of the French he'd need troops and he'd have to rely on his barons to provide them. And so long as the barons thought they had a decent chance of winning and there'd be plenty of opportunities for loot, then they'd be up for it and back him as it would give them what they wanted, while if he was seen as a strong king with lots of loyal troops, you wouldn't want to cross him either.

'But at the same time he couldn't push it too far. Start to use his position as king to pick off powerful barons too obviously and he could panic the rest into an alliance against him to protect their position. John didn't pitch up to sign Magna Carta because he felt like it, he was dragged down to Runnymede kicking and screaming because his barons had a united front and forced him to the table to confirm their rights.

'But the moment a king started to be seen as weak, then everything began to be up for grabs, didn't it? Why pay tax to a king who couldn't make you? And what risk were you running as a baron, of someone else pushing past you and seizing the throne? So you'd start jockeying for position, setting yourself up for a shot at the top slot if it looked like a possibility, while not showing your hand if you didn't have to and keeping tabs on your rivals.

'In the worst case, you end up with factions. Red rosed Lancastrians and white rosed Yorkists supporting rival claimants for the throne, and then you were into a struggle that could rage for years, decades even, as the two sides slugged it out in a slow motion stop-start civil war that devastates everything in its path, where nobody can trust anyone else.

'From what I could see the moment I walked in, the charter was on the edge of chaos, civil war even. Instead of a united brotherhood, I saw factions, and little groups and cliques were eyeing each other across the clubhouse with increasing suspicion, hostility even. It had to stop and it was going to stop right now. I wasn't having any of that on my watch.

'We'd seen what could happen when clubs disintegrated, here and elsewhere around the world. Scenes of brother murdering brother.

'The crap had to be canned before it turned really nasty. So I was there to pull it together and to clean house. And I wasn't going to do that by being everybody's friend. I was going to do that by reimposing some good old fashioned basic club discipline, and if you didn't like it and what it was going to take from now on to wear the colours, well you knew what you could do.

'Obviously that didn't go down well in some quarters, particularly coming from a guy who the local patches saw as having been pushed on them from down in the central belt.

'Local charters are always touchy about their prerogatives. No one likes anyone else interfering in their business, national officer or not, and the local charter always wants to pick its own guys as officers and deal with its own dirty laundry in house. I can understand that, it's a pride thing apart from anything else. So when the club at a national level steps in to take somebody out, let alone a P, and then impose an outsider on them to sort things, that's a big deal and it breeds resentment.

'Having come in hard and read the riot act, pretty soon I thought it all seemed to be going OK. At the time, what with everything that had gone down with Munster, people were keeping their heads down and looking to see which way the land lay, and I guess I thought I had it all quite quickly sorted. There weren't any obvious hostilities as such, a bit of tension sometimes but hell you'd expect that, what with everything the guys had all gone through, with Malcolm and the like, and with me having been forced on them by Stu down in Glasgow.

'All in all I thought it was, what's the phrase, mission accomplished? I mean within a few months we were having family events and all sorts, and Jenny who was just 19 by then had even become a bit of an item with one of the younger guys, Stretch.

'I wasn't overly impressed with that to start with, I'll admit, but politically it was potentially good news for me as Stretch and his brothers – he had a real life brother Pete and a half-brother Tazz who were both patches as well – were respected local members. But I came round to it actually quite quickly. Truth was, he was a good stand up guy who I could respect, and being practical about it I knew if I could win his little mob round that would make my life a whole hell of a lot easier, and her going out with him wasn't going to do me any harm in that department.'

'So you let it go?' asked Iain.

'Yeah, I let it go, which even surprised me a bit I have to say.'

'Why?'

'Oh you know, just the usual reasons,' and then he added with a grin, 'you know what they say, guns don't kill people...'

'Don't they?' Iain asked guardedly.

'No, dads with pretty daughters. They kill people...' he said.

'So there we were, everything seemed to be going well. You know I've looked back afterwards and wondered if there was anything else I should have done?

'Did I start to relax? Let things slide?

'Should I have played it differently?

'I don't know, it's all second guessing in hindsight, besides which, what's the point? You do what you do and things happen. That's just the way it is and you live with it, deal with the consequences. No point in crying over spilt milk.

'We'd had a lot of heat over the years. Given the history you could understand why, what with everything that had occurred, so the message came down the line, loud and clear, Stu wanted things quietening down.

'It was a major change in tone for the club. We were to take things coolly, drop off the cops' radar.

'Cut down the number of parties, avoid trouble, whatever it took. Back in the old days freaking out the straights was part of the act you know? Now all that sort of shit was off the agenda. They even started suggesting guys needed to clean up their look; get haircuts, smarten up their appearance, all that sort of stuff.

'Well you can imagine how that went down with some of the blokes, but you could tell how serious the Top Table was about sorting out our image. And at the end of the day, like always, it was the club's way, and if you didn't like it, well, you knew what your options were.

'It was my own fault. Something blew up between some of the guys. It was some bullshit rubbish, no biggie, but I had to get involved didn't I? I was P, I was still intent on letting everybody know this was my show and I controlled everything that went on, so I just had to decide to chuck my weight about, instead of letting them sort it out themselves.

'And once you're in, you're in, you've put your rep on the line and there's no backing down from it.

'The thing was, given the history of the guys in the charter, their friendships, family ties even, it quickly became one of those things that had people lining up on either side behind the guys who had the beef.

'The charter was splitting apart in front of me, and my getting involved hadn't quashed it. If anything, it had brought the punch-up and divisions into sharper focus, exacerbated them, made them more of a thing.

'A stupid personal beef rapidly turned into a hook some of the patches could hang their resentments on, of the fact I'd been para-chuted in from outside by Stu to take over the charter and clean house. I'd trodden on some toes while I'd been doing it, fuck I knew that, but what did they expect? It needed doing and I did the job I'd been sent to do. Still, it didn't stop a hard core resenting the fact I'd been forced on them, not elected from within the charter.

'Worse still, by doing anything at all about this ruck I'd put my authority on the line, and inevitably rather than being above the fray, I ended up getting dragged right into it. So by the time I did eventually squash it, I got exactly the situation I'd wanted to avoid, being accused of taking sides, favouring one lot over the other.

'And equally inevitably, by the time I'd sorted it and imposed a settlement on all concerned, some of the losers weren't just going to shut up and quiet down, quite the opposite.

'I'd stamped on the fire and put it out, but there was still a fuck of a lot of smoke, hot air and red hot smouldering resentment glowing away underfoot that I knew could, would even, burst back into flame again just as soon as another piece of kindling happened along. Particularly when some guys just couldn't help running off at the mouth and fanning the flames.

'If there was a problem, I knew I needed to sort it out for myself. Stu had put me in charge but it wasn't just a matter of wanting to prove myself, that I could handle shit. It was more than that.

'You don't go running for help when things get tough. That's not the way it's done. If you're big enough and ugly enough to be an officer in the club, then you're expected to take care of club business, and that's it.

'So I decided I needed to set an example, to really piss on this problem once and for all.

'Now Pete was a heat magnet, and like I've said, that just wasn't what we were looking for by that time. The whole club's policy, the policy it was up to me to enforce, was to quiet things down, slip under the radar.

'But that just didn't fit with Pete's old school ways. As far as he was concerned, baiting citizens and the cops by showing a bit of class was what being an outlaw was all about. If you were going to go all respectable so you could pass unnoticed, what was the point, he wanted to know?

'And of all the problem elements, Pete was the mouthiest of the lot. He'd been warned, a number of times; if anything I'd let him have a whole length of rope, but he didn't take the hint. He wouldn't let it go and worse, by being mouthy about it, everybody could see he wasn't letting it go.'

'Which was a problem?' asked Iain.

'Which was a problem, because it was such an obvious challenge.

'I guess he thought he was fireproof. After all, he had two brothers in the club, including Stretch who was going out with my Jenny, was a long standing local patch and had quite a chunk of the club guys behind him. So I guess he thought he could get away with shit.

'What he didn't get, was that was exactly why I simply couldn't let him get away with diddly squat.

'Either I was P or he was, and there was no way I was going to let crap stand.

'So eventually he ran his mouth off once too often and I booted him out. I used some half arsed minor thing as an excuse to pull his patch. And it wasn't just about him, it was a warning, *pour encourage les autres*, a way of showing once and for all who was in charge.

'Now it was my way or the highway.'

'And did it work?' asked Iain.

Bomber just snorted in wry amusement.

'Did it work? Did it bunnies!

'Outside the club, Pete continued to just mouth off against me to anyone who'd listen, I mean, I should have seen that coming shouldn't I? After all, once I'd booted him out, what did he have to lose? In fact, I quickly started to find if anything it was worse having him outside the tent pissing in, and that was when I really fucked up.

'I was a bit rat-arsed to be honest, I'll admit that.

'We were at a club party down our local boozer when I got filled in on Pete's latest broadside. Worse, there was a rumour going around that Pete had been talking to the Kelpies. They'd taken in some of the Sheep Shaggers who hadn't made the cut, and to top it all, the bloke was telling me he'd heard Pete planning on sounding out some of the remaining disaffected members about defecting across.'

'Was he? Talking to the Kelpies?'

Bomber just shrugged.

'Who knows? The point was, at the time, that evening when I heard about it, it sounded as though it made sense to me, and that's why I said what I said.

'Look I'm not making excuses for myself. It was a dumb thing to do, and if I had my time again I'd hope I'd keep my fucking mouth shut, but in my defence I didn't mean it, it was just the sort of stuff you say when you're hacked off.

'It was just something that came out of weeks of frustration with the bastard, you know how it is? You can see how that sort of thing can happen.'

'So what did happen?' Iain asked.

There was a long moment of silence before he continued in a weary voice.

'Well, I did my whole *who will rid me of this turbulent biker* rant didn't I?

'I can't remember exactly what I said, but that was the gist of it right enough.

'Like I said, I didn't mean anything by it of course. I was just letting off steam really, and if I'd said it in my office, in private, then that would have been it, wouldn't it? Nothing worse than a well kicked filing cabinet or something, and so what? I'd have got it out of my system and then been able to sit down with a clear head and work out what my, what the club's, next move needed to be.

'But that wasn't the way it happened, was it? Because I wasn't in my office and I was somewhere far from private, wasn't I?

'Loads of people heard me swearing and going off on one. And the problem with that was the wannabes.

'There's always wannabes at any club party. I mean, hey it was a party, you invite people right? That's the point of parties isn't it? Having people there. Friendly clubs, friends of the club, the great British public, Uncle Tom Cobbly and all sometimes, depending on the sort of party it is…'

'You knew that…?'

'Of course I knew that, and if I hadn't had a few lines and most of a bottle by the time the tryout came up to talk to me, then I'd have kept my mouth well shut. But by that stage of the evening, I was just too well oiled, so I just let rip. I was calling Pete all the names under the sun and mouthing off with how somebody needed to do something serious about him, and soon.'

'And people heard you?'

'Shit yeah, I mean it wasn't like I was yelling it at the top of my voice to anyone who wanted to hear, I wasn't that out of it, you know. I was the P, this was a club party, I was there to enjoy myself, but as a P there's a certain sort of dignity, distance you've got to keep, you know? You need to manage your rep and you can't be letting people see you getting completely shit faced or out of control, certainly not civilians.

'No I was just talking, in a normal voice like to the guys around me, but anyone could see I was really pissed off, not just from what I was saying, but the way I was saying it…'

'And you were overheard?'

'Yeah, of course. Well there was the tryout who'd brought me the tip off, and his mate he had with him who was the one who said he'd seen Pete cosying up to one of the Kelpies in a bar the other end of town, and had done some ear wigging. He said they'd been talking quietly, and being careful about what they were actually saying, but that he'd been able to hear enough of what they were on about to get the drift of what Pete was proposing. And then when they got on to talking about me a few beers later, Pete hadn't been able to help himself, his voice rising in his anger as he mouthed off.'

'So you were unlucky?'

'I wouldn't go that far. Well a bit, I suppose, but even so, if I'd thought about it I'd have kept schtum until the little shits were out of earshot. But even then I guess, I didn't really think anything very much about it.

'And by the time I did think about it the next day, it was too late. Yeah, way too late.'

*

We knew the story, both from Iain's files and from the extensive press coverage at the time.

The tryout Mark 'Weasel' Nugent and his mate Charles 'Muttley' Booker allegedly left the party soon after Bomber's inciting remarks. Pausing only to pick up a selection of kitchen knives and two pairs of rubber gloves from under the sink at Booker's mum's flat, headed across town in Nugent's car to the pub where Booker had seen Pete drinking earlier that evening.

They were convinced that what they were setting out to do would demonstrate their commitment, their willingness to take on whatever the club, as they thought, wanted done, regardless of the risk to them- selves, or the consequences, and so earn them immediate status within the club.

Inside the pub it was dim and approaching closing time. As the two men passed straight through the boozer's public bar, their feet making little sucking sounds on the beer tacky floor, they ignored or were seemingly oblivious to the knots of drinkers clustered around some of the tables and even the CCTV camera mounted in its protective cage up in the corner of the room, before pushing through the swing doors and into the lounge bar beyond.

Here the lighting was, if anything, dimmer still and the room quieter, with the noise of the few scattered punters absorbed a bit by the softer furnishings of the banquettes and booths, beer-smelling densely patterned carpets, swagged curtains that were never there to be drawn, not quite matching fabric to the floor, and even the dark green flocked wallpaper above the fake half panelling.

They two men didn't need to talk, as just as soon as they turned the corner of the bar they saw the figure of Pete sat alone in the booth at the furthest end of the room. By this stage he was on his own, his Kelpie visitors, if that's who they were, if they even ever existed, were nowhere to be seen. Whatever he'd been like earlier, by all accounts Pete was relaxed, an empty pint and shot glass to one side of him and a fresh pair in front of him, while his eyes were fixed on the big screen on the wall of the pub to his left which was showing the darts.

It's believed he only looked up as Nugent and Booker, drawing the knives out from under their jackets as they approached his table, suddenly rushed him, Booker allegedly yelling, 'That's the cunt there, let's stick him.'

Peter 'Pete' Branson was unarmed and stabbed twice in the chest, collapsed across the table almost immediately as one of the wounds severed his aorta, a fatal blow in its own right. Nugent and Booker weren't to know this of course, and with the dying biker face down and helpless in front of them they proceeded to stab him another dozen times in the back, side and neck, before turning and running from the pub.

Needless to say, by the time the cops turned up, no one had seen anything, and wouldn't you know it, the camera seemed to have suffered a glitch that night as well and accidentally wiped the tape.

*

'So then what happened?' asked Iain.

Bomber just shrugged resignedly.

'Look, it was a tragedy, right? A complete fucking waste, I'm the first to admit it. If I could have my time again, if there was one thing I could change, it'd be that.

'But you can't, you know? What was done was done, wasn't it?

'I just had to deal with the fallout as best I could and given the circumstances, one of the things I decided was that as he had been mouthing off against me and the club, and he'd been kicked out in bad standing, I said no one was to have anything to do with the funeral arrangements or show up for the burial.

'You've got to appreciate, I was having to make a shed load of decisions, all at a time when the shit had truly hit the fan and it just seemed to make sense then and there. I wanted to distance this thing from the club. So making sure everybody kept their heads down, ensuring there were no patches there, no chance of any incidents that might create more crap for the cops and press to chuck at us, it all just seemed to make sense.

'It was a spur of the moment call, but when you're P, when you've made a decision, you've made a decision and you've got to make sure everybody sticks to it, particularly when this sort of very public shit storm is going down. Make a rule, keep a rule. As P you've got responsibilities, you're there to rep the club and you've got to do whatever needs doing to make sure the club's interests are looked after, whatever anybody else thinks.

'You can't afford dissention, second guessing, guys arguing back. The club needs to act as a unit, solid, loyal. It's about leadership and keeping the guys together. It's the sort of time that tests you as a P, that's when you see whether you've got what it takes, whatever the flash on your chest says.'

'But then there was Stretch...' Iain observed.

'And then there was Stretch,' agreed Bomber.

'Like we found out later, the cops were bugging us. We weren't so tech savvy back in those days, not nearly so surveillance aware as we are now, well not that sort anyway.

'They had recordings of pretty much everything. They even caught Stretch's call to Tazz and the pair of them talking it over. They played the tape of the phone call to me when I was in custody and they had to give a copy of the transcript to my lawyers so I could prepare my defence.'

'Have you heard what's happened now? You've heard what he's said?'

'No, I've not heard anything. That's all I know. What is it now? Christ, Pete's dead. What else could there be?'

'That's what I thought, it's why I wanted to call you.'

'Why, what is it? What's the matter?'

'He's spread the word, no one's to go. Says he'll pull the colours of anyone who shows up.'

'Oh Jeez... that's not right.'

'He says he was out in bad standing and that's it. So there's to be no colours, no turnout, no club presence at all.'

'Nothing, not after all these years? They're going to stick him in the ground like that?'

'Nothing. He's said he'll pull the colours of anyone who shows up. Maz came straight over to see me. The bastard sent him to make sure I knew and I guess he'll be out looking for you as well.'

'So what are you going to do?'

'I don't give a fuck about what he says. He's my brother, he's your brother and he was a club brother until this last bit of bullshit, and he deserves our respect.'

'So what are you going to do?'

'Do? I'm going to bury him of course, what the fuck else do you think I'm going to do? I'm on my way over to the undertakers now. That's not the question.'

'That's not the question? So what is the question then?'

'Are you coming?'

'Me?'

'Yes, you, what do you say? Don't you want to be there and see him off properly?'

'Of course I want to be there but...'

'But what?'

'But it'd be worth my colours. And yours as well.'

'So?'

'So, think about it. Think about what you're risking, what you'd be giving up? He'll do it, you know, he'll pull your patch and you'll be out in bad standing. You want that? And for what?'

'To do the right thing.'

'And what fucking good is that going to do? Is it going to bring him back? No. Look, I don't like it any better than you do but I can sort of see where Bomber's coming from.'

'I don't give a fuck what you sort of see.'

'We're on the edge, you know that. Pete going off at him running his mouth off when he shouldn't have, don't deny it, you know what he was like when he'd had a skinfull, the crap he used to say and he didn't give a toss who heard him. It was dangerous shit and Bomber's the P. He's got to set an example and if you carry on with this, you're going to be it.'

'I don't care what example he wants to set.'

'He'll say you're going against the club...'

'And I'll say it's none of his fucking business!'

'Stretch, this is a line, don't cross it. Pete's dead, there's only us two left. You're just like him, you're always pushing the limits, and look what happened to him. Don't let it happen to you as well. Listen to me, I'm right.'

'I don't care about being right, not your sort of right anyway. I'm going to do the right thing by Pete and that's it. Now are you with me or not?'

'For fuck's sake, what do I have to do to get you to understand? If it's you, or us, or the club, Bomber's going to have no choice.'

'I'm not interested in understanding. I'm just interested in seeing what you're made of.'

'He's welding the whole club together. That's what he's here for, that's why he's appointed a complete bastard like Maz as Enforcer. There's no way he'll tolerate any shit out of anyone over this, he can't afford to, so if you go up against this, you're going up directly against him and the whole of the club, not just here, but right across the country. Do you really want to do that?'

'He's our brother.'

'Yes, I know he is. But you have other brothers as well. Living brothers who love you. This is a shitty situation. You know it, I know it. It should never have got to this. There'll be a time to mourn Pete. When all this crap's died down things will be different, you'll see. Then you and I and the rest of our brothers can do what needs doing. But just not right now. Not when it's too dangerous.'

'Too dangerous? For who? For you?'

94

'For you, for me, for the club, for everything we've all worked for here for all these years in setting it up, growing the club, making it our patch. There's club rules you know? They're there for a reason.'

'You've got it all figured out haven't you?'

'Yes, yes I have. It's an issue for him now because things are hot. But just give it time to cool and then it'll all be very different...'

'Give it time?'

'You know what he's like. You more than any of us.'

'Don't bring Jenny into this.'

'Hey, I'm not bringing Jenny into anything. If anyone's doing that, it's you isn't it?'

'Oh fuck off, Tazz. You know I wouldn't take your help now if you offered it, if that's the way you feel.'

'Oh bollocks to the way I feel. Just think about it will you? Think about her.'

'I'll think about her alright.'

'Look, just don't do something stupid, right? Come and talk to me before you do anything you might regret, OK? I'm worried about you.'

'Don't bother about that.'

'Hey look, I'd better go, I've got a call coming in.'

'It'll be Bomber or one of his guys.'

'Yeah, probably. Look I mean it. At least keep this quiet and call me before you do anything. Love you mate.'

'Yeah...'

'To me it was simple. We're all members of the club, we're all supposed to be loyal to the club, and it's only that loyalty that keeps it all together, keeps us strong, keeps the club what it is.

'Without that, it's over.

'So I don't care whoever the fuck else it is, brother, sister, wife, kids, parents, whoever. The club comes first and anyone who doesn't get that, doesn't live it, isn't my brother. They're nothing to me, they're out and that's it. You join this club, you agree to live by its rules. You can't just chop and change when it suits you, or because you don't like how they've worked out for you. Either you are in, and you stick with it through thick and thin, or you are out.

'I'd been brought in to sort out the mess up here. And it was a mess because people had put their own agendas and fun and interests in front of the club. And that was what I was determined to put a stop to, whatever it took.

'It's like Stu always said. You never know what someone's really like, their character, their principles, their judgement, until you see them in action, until they've taken on a job like being a P. People can talk the talk but what really counts is can they walk it when it counts? Stepping up to a job like this, that's the test.

'If you take on the job of P, and it's a real job, something that you really need to think long and hard about before saying yes to, then you're taking on responsibility for where your charter or club goes. You're the skipper, it's your hand on the tiller steering the ship and if you want the job then you've got to take everything that comes with it.

'You have to decide what's right, what's wrong, what's going to be done and what isn't, and you've got to do it without fear or favour.

'You can't be scared of doing anything because of anyone and if you are, then you've not got what it take to be P. And you can't let friend-ship get in the way of your decisions either. Mate or not, when it comes down to it, the club and all the interests of all your brothers has to come in front of what you feel for any individual, in or out of the club. Our strength is our brotherhood, our loyalty to all of our brothers, and if you ain't got that, then you ain't got what it takes to be a patch and I've got no use for you in the club.

'You need your guys to be able to talk to you sure. To do the best for the club as P, you can't do it all yourself. You need top notch advisors who aren't afraid to say what they think and let you know how the rest of the guys are feeling. That's what I've always said, but it's about giving advice, feeding into the decisions that you as P need to make, because once a decision's made, that's it, and there's no arguing the point, particularly not given the history I had to deal with up there.

'If you set yourself up against the club in any way, anything at all, you're making yourself an enemy of the club. It's that simple.

'Absolute loyalty and absolute trust. Those are the strengths that make our club the greatest club in the world, and make our brotherhood stronger than blood. And they're the only standards I'm prepared to work to.

'So as I saw it, I'd no choice. Pete was out and to me there's only two types of people in the world. Those who are brothers, and those who aren't.

'This is a club for guys who are loyal and stick together through thick and thin, guys who'd ride to hell and back for each other. If you're loyal to the club and you died then you're going to go with every bit of honour and respect the club can show.

'But if you're out and bad mouthing the club, like Pete, then you're out and as far as I was concerned, there was no way anyone from the club should be dignifying his send off at all. I didn't want to hear his name, I didn't want to see anyone mourning him and I didn't want anyone going near his funeral.

'He had already been dead to us from the moment he was out and as far as I was concerned he could rot in hell.

'He'd been a traitor to the club and that meant in my charter, he was nothing to us. Nothing.

'And so I'd given my instructions to my crew and I knew they'd carry them out.

'But I knew there might still be guys around who didn't see it the way I did. He'd been a member for years of course, long before I came on the scene as far as these guys were concerned, so I knew that club or no club, there would still be people with a misplaced personal sense of loyalty to him. It wasn't just Stretch and Tazz I was worried about, although of course, as his actual brothers I'd made particularly sure that they both knew which way was up, and what was expected.

'In fact in a weird way it was actually something of an opportunity, as it gave a bit of a test of the older guy's commitment. So quietly I had Maz set some of the tagalongs up to keep watch on the undertakers. As Enforcer he was my head of security.

'If anyone was going to break the rules I wanted to make sure I caught them at it.

'It would be a chance to sort out any waverers once and for all. And anyway, apart from anything else, I wanted to know what was up.

'The cops obviously had us in the frame for Pete even though truth be told it wasn't really anything to do with us. It was more of an accident like, but anyway, they were taking a big interest, seeing how they could fit us for it. The post mortem was quick, well there wasn't much of a debate about how he'd died really, was there? So it wasn't long until they released the body to his folks to sort out arrangements for his funeral.

'I knew the cops would be keeping an eye on things, looking to see what was happening, so I did the same, had some of the boys keep a watch on the undertakers, keep a record of who was coming and going.

'And that's when I said that everyone was to stay away. Given all the crap that had gone down I didn't want anyone from the club being seen around. I didn't want the cops to have anything that they could use to link it back to us. I was thinking about the club, see?

'We'd already got those little shits Weasel and Muttley out of the way. They'd come back round straight after, acting it large about what they'd done, and shit, we couldn't have that could we? As a couple of the local low lifes, the cops knew full well who they were and even without anyone at the pub talking it wasn't going to take them too long to work out who was responsible, so we had to get them out of the way sharpish.

'Maz and his boys bundled them into a van. We told them they were going to a safe house somewhere they could lie low for a while until the heat had died down, and they jumped straight in the back like good little kiddos.'

*

The thing was, we'd heard on Iain's tapes the police's view of what they thought had happened to Mark 'Weasel' Nugent and Charles 'Muttley' Booker who have never been seen since.

His SOCA contact's view had been brutally simple.

'Bomber's mob took care of the muppets that killed Peter 'Pete' Branson. It's just basic security as far as they're concerned, always kill the killers so that way there's no tracing back up to the top through someone further down the tree who might be persuaded to talk.

'We can't prove it at this stage, but our sources say they were both shot and buried somewhere up in the forests.

'You just have to drive into the hills in just about any direction from Aberdeen and there's miles and miles of Forestry Commission land out there. There's The Bin, Bennachie, Kirkhill, and half a dozen more you can take your pick from, and that's just if you don't want to drive too far. Helicopters are useless because of the density of the tree cover, while it's impossible to search it all on foot. So there's plenty of room for a few holes that'll never be found, which is just what they'll have wanted in terms of covering their tracks.

'Trust me, no one is ever going to see or hear of either of them again.'

*

Which, when we thought about it, was just one more set of reasons to ask what the hell DI Chambers was doing here repping for Bomber?

CHAPTER 4   RUN TO THE SUN

'Maggie? I never thought she was much of a looker myself. All skin and bone. You'd just be worried about cutting yourself.'

Some of Bomber's club brothers had had a different view of Maggie as Sandy had told Iain.

'Oh she had something alright, but it was all about her up front attitude and ballsiness I guess, not anything conventional. I mean she'd been up for anything once, a real wild kid in her day. If it was me I'd have dipped it in Domestos afterwards you know? Just to be safe, but Bomber, well he fell for her hook line and sinker first time he saw her. Bam! Just like that. He couldn't keep his eyes off her.

'And she was something to watch in action, I'll give her that, she was a real piece of work.

'It's just given what she'd get up to, I wouldn't have fucked her for practice.

'The thing is, she wasn't just a complete and utter nutter, but manipulative, and a complete mess with it. You know you get some blokes who're real party animals, just always looking to get as wrecked as possible and who don't care what agro they kick off? Well she was the female equivalent.

'She'd do anything, with anyone... and you couldn't turn your back on her or she'd have your gear and be off with it. She was forever nicking stuff from up the high street and flogging it on to turn a bit of cash for her next score. A one woman crime wave she was. You'd see her in Woolies and just know the pick'n'mix was going to go walkies, you know what I mean? Too much hassle for me, mate. The guys put up with her because she was a bit of fun and always available but no one took her seriously or would have been prepared to put up with her crap longer term.

'Not until Bomber.

'None of that mattered to Bomber. He just put up with all her shit.'

'Why?' Iain had asked.

'Why?' Sandy looked perplexed as though it was possibly the

dumbest question he'd ever been asked. 'Because he was in love with her, the poor sap. It didn't matter what she did, Bomber didn't care, he was always there for her and that was the sad part.'

'Sad?'

Sandy nodded, 'Because she really didn't give a shit about anything or anyone else apart from number one. All she cared about was getting wasted, even after they'd had the kid. When I heard she was up the duff I thought well at least she'll slow down a bit with a sprog to look after, but nothing doing. The next time I saw her she was chasing around a party after Stu and hoping to score while Bomber was left holding the baby.

'And that's the way it went on until she upped and left him.'

'And where is she now?'

Sandy shook his head. 'Don't know and to be honest, I really don't give a fuck. He's, no they're, him and Jenny, they were much better off without her, had been ever since she cleared off.'

'And of course then Bomber married Kath, and she was great for him, the both of them really, him and Jenny. She had the right attitude. Saw that he was a deal, a package; him, the club, Jenny, and she took the whole thing.'

'How well did you know Jenny?'

Sandy gave a broad smile of semi paternal pride. It probably wasn't misplaced if half of what Iain had heard about how Jenny had been brought up, not just around the club but with Bomber's club brothers' active support and help, was true.

'Jenny? Oh she was a great kid. She'd been in and out of the club-house ever since she was a nipper, grown up around the place.

'Everybody knew her and loved her. We'd all looked after her while she was growing up, the guys spoiled her a bit, I guess. We always had dogs around and she loved looking after them and at Christmas we'd have a party and Gramps always dressed up as Santa Claus so we'd have our own grotto for all the kids, and even grandkids these days.

'It's a real family atmosphere sometimes you know and she'd

'You want to know why I'm here speaking for Bomber don't you?'

'Yes we do.'

'Have you ever heard about an Osman Warning?'

From the expression on DI Chambers' face we must have looked suitably blank as we shook our heads and confessed, 'No.'

'Well neither did Bomber,' he said with hint of bitterness in his voice, 'officially at least.'

'Is it something to do with what he told you?' we wanted to know.

'Sort of. It came out of that anyway. As far as I was concerned. Like I said, to start with all I wanted to do was get him talking to us at all, I didn't really care what it was about.'

'It was a bit of a fishing trip?'

'If you like, but it was more about breaking a habit and establishing that he could say something. And of course although I didn't realise it at the time, that was just what others were waiting for as we listened to him tell his story.'

*

'I was in my twenties when I first got involved. You know how it is at that age, you think you're all grown up and a bloke, but looking back at it now, I reckon really I was still just a kid, even then.

'You change as you get older, and I grew up in the club. This is where I stopped being a kid and learnt what it meant to be a man.

'All any of us ever wanted was to ride our bikes and have fun with our mates. That was what it was all about, to start with at least.

'After the party, there wasn't a lot said out loud but then the guys didn't really need to say anything as such to make their views clear. I'd made it to tagalong status and I was sort of hooked up to Dobbo and Stu amongst the tagalongs who were around at the time. Sort of the dogsbodies' dogsbody deal, running here there and everywhere for whatever any of the guys wanted. It was a lot of work but hell, I didn't mind, because it was a lot of fun as well. I got to hang out at the coolest parties and tagalong at the back of the pack on the coolest rides. Sure I might have just been on the edge of it all, but at least I was in it, if you get what I mean.

'And best of all, I was with Her.

'Dobbo and Stu had sorted me out between them. Maggie had been Stu's bird but he told me it was over, so he was cool about me and her getting together.

'Eighty-eight might have been a shitty time, it seemed like we had more than the usual share of disasters that year, from Lockerbie to Piper Alpha, but as far as I was concerned, it was a great summer as the club seemed to cruise easily from party to party, with our little crew swarming along behind.

'Of course it wasn't all easy. It's not meant to be when you're a tag-along, because all the while the guys'll be keeping an eye on you, testing you out, seeing if you've got the potential, the spark that'll make you worthy of being offered the chance to strike, which is where the real hard work begins.

'So inevitably there was a bit of mud testing, to see what you were made of.

'When you're a tagalong or a tryout the general rule is, when a patch tells you to jump the only question is how high?

'But alongside that there'll be trick bags, test runs, things you're asked to do, or go along with, just to check you out.

'And some of them'll be deliberately out of order stuff. A patch'll tell you to do something completely unreasonable, like taking off some flash you've been awarded, or maybe doing something completely suicidal like jumping off a cliff. And they're not doing it to see if you're committed enough to do it, they're doing it to see if you'll stand up for yourself.

'Sure, as a tagalong or a tryout you're expected to put up with a lot of crap to show your commitment. But no one wants a doormat who'll let themselves be walked over in the club either, so you've also got to show you'll stand up for yourself whenever it matters to earn respect, whoever it is who's giving you shit. And you have to do it where the guys can see you, 'cos otherwise how are they going to know you're going to be a stand-up guy and rep the club right when they can't?

'A key part of surviving before you get a patch is having the instinct to walk that narrow line and know which sort of situation is which, as well as being tough enough to take what comes when you screw up, as you're inevitably going to do every so often.

'After all, if sometimes standing up as a tryout and telling a patch *I'm not going to do that so if we have to have a dance about it, well let's get on with it now*, is exactly the right thing to do; then equally, some-times it's going to be the very last thing you ought to be doing, and you won't have to wait long to find out which is which.

'It's all part of the start of the long slow process of learning to be a club guy.

'In some ways I think it gets to be like playing a role you know? I guess a lot of life's like that isn't it? You figure out what people expect to see and how they'll react, and if that gives you what you want, then you give them what they're expecting.

'And I guess that whatever I was doing, I must have been doing alright because when it came to the club's big run that year there was no question, I was going.

'The Run to the Sun they called it. A two week blast, over on the ferry and then down through France – Marseilles and the Med – to hook up with a friendly French club. That was the plan. I was going to need a passport and everything.

'The trip down through England was uneventful. We were wary, the club had some charters that side of Hadrian's Wall that we hooked up with as we headed out, but we knew it wasn't our turf for much of it, certainly the further south we went the more we were heading into enemy territory, so there could have been trouble from the Menaces. Whether there'd been some quiet diplomacy or not about negotiation of the fact we'd be passing through I didn't know, but the fact was we didn't run into any ambush. As it happened, we had no hassle of any kind and everything went off peacefully. There was obviously some degree of practical contact at top levels between the clubs, communication channels, but what went on in them back then, well that was way above my pay grade. Still is.

'So, soon we were rolling into the echoing steel belly of the beast at Portsmouth, the guys sliding the bikes laden with their panniers and bedrolls onto their stands to be strapped down by the deckhands for the crossing to Caen. While behind them as tagalongs, Dobbo, Stu, Maggie and I brought up the rear in the club's old white transit crew bus freighting the rest of the gear for the trip.

'Sure I'd have loved to be riding as over the next couple of days we worked our way south, heading out down long plane tree shaded roads, occasionally streaming along wide straight empty French motorways, or sliding along fast sweeping bends down from the Massif Central as we headed inexorably towards the shimmering Mediterranean.

'I could close my eyes and imagine the feel of the warm wind on my face with Maggie squeezed against my back as pillion. But that time would come, I thought, soon enough. All I had to do was work my passage and one day it would be me out there in the pack up front and it would be the next generation of tagalong and tryouts driving along behind me.

'We took most of the week to work our way down. The gig wasn't starting until the Friday so we had plenty of time for some long hard days of riding. France is a big place I discovered, not having really thought about it before. We'd pitch camp for the night, and by we that means tagalongs and tryouts dong most of the pitching, and fetching of wood for the bonfires, and carrying of booze and food as usual. But did I care? Bollocks, no!

'I was too busy learning about wine *en vrac* for pennies a litre, the taste of fresh croissants and bread like we never seemed to have at home, the feeling of warmth at night and the shade of plane trees in the morning, the aromatic smells of the areas we passed though, of lavender, sage, rosemary, the sight of teeny weeny tractors pulling trailers piled high with grapes, crashing out on campsites under huge skies filled with millions more stars than ever shone on Glasgow or Edinburgh. And there were psycho runs screaming through sunflowers waving over our completely stoned heads, and all the time rolling, rolling, rolling down the wide sun drenched highways bathed in the comforting nurturing roar of bike engines ahead of us and bearing us along down to the promise of sea sand and sun.

'The party was out at an old airfield, just by a little town somewhere in the sandy hills inland from Marseilles.

'I didn't know if it was just the anticipation that was getting to every-one as we got close that evening; whether it was the sheer pleasure the guys were feeling at riding through the warmth of the gathering darkness as we passed the signs counting down the kilometres to the town, thirty, twenty, ten; or whether it was just this was the club arriving at a party, but even from back in the truck bringing up the rear of the column we could feel the increasing excitement, the revs inching up, the tension building.

'The thing was, we were, well the club was, arriving at a party, and if the club was going to arrive, it was going to fucking arrive in style you know? Show some class.

'There were speed limits at the edge of town. We flashed past, ignoring them, the pack's engine noise roaring now as we thundered into the built up areas.

'Out on the highway a club run had a certain formality, a discipline to it, with riders in pairs and a strict pecking order of Prez and Road Captain up front, then the officer and patches with the Enforcer and his oppo bringing up the rear, followed by the tryouts, other hangers on and then us in the crew bus to pick up any stragglers.

'But now it felt as though that discipline was breaking down as the pack began to surge forwards, egging each other on, it hurtled through the streets, with us in the crew bus straining to keep up. Now tryouts and tagalongs were being hustled forwards, sent screaming ahead of the pack like outriders to block off side roads as the river of bikes plunged forwards like an unstoppable flood along the road, sweeping through red lights without a blink of brake lights trusting to the invincibility of adrenaline to clear the way.

'When the pack was in this frenzy there was no stopping for anyone. It was an elemental force, a thing bigger than anyone in it, brushing all before it out of its way with no mercy for anyone failing to keep up. You fell, you were left behind, the pack wasn't stopping for anything. Give way signs, stop signs, cops, traffic, all would be taken in a rush.

'"The club doesn't stop for shit!"' shouted Dobbo in my ear, as he hauled on the steering wheel and we heeled over on the corner out of town to make the final run in. We could see where we were headed a mile or so up ahead.

'That would be the place with all the blue flashing lights round it then.

'The *gendarmerie* had the approach roads locked down as the club roared up, seven, eight abreast across the road, finally halting only at a barbed wire barrier that had been strung across the road at a point where it was flanked on either side by a culvert that made dipping off the tarmac to get round the roadblock a non-starter.

'From where we were at the back we couldn't hear what was going on as some more senior frog plod engaged with the head of the pack. I doubt Mal's French was much good but then, W*e've got an invite coppe*r seemed to cover most of what needed saying and it wasn't as though the frog plod fancied having some pissed off bikers on this side of the picket line when they could just let us inside to have all the undesirables in one place. So a moment later and with a cheer from our guys and an aggressive revving of engines and dropping of clutches we leapt forwards again as the barrier swung out of the way, and then our headlights were bouncing over the rougher ground as we rattled over a small wooden bridge across a ditch and through the gate in the security fencing.

'We'd made it. We were in.

'Kicking off on that Friday night it was a wild weekend bender with everything you could think of.

'It wasn't just us there, the host club *Les Carcajous* had invited a host of different independents, so there were bikers from all over – Spain, Italy, Germany, Holland, Scandinavia – you name it. There were even some of the English independents there, luckily ones we got on with, the Janners from the West Country, The Hangmen. So once Mal and the officers had hooked up with our hosts and the formal introductions were done and dusted, we tryouts and tagalongs got dumped with the usual sticking up the tents and scoring firewood while the club guys headed off to check out the party. We didn't mind. That's how it was.

'All the entertainment and events were organised around the airstrip and each club pitched up its own set of tents somewhere in the surrounding scrubland so that by the time everyone had arrived the place looked like a Bedouin city.

'During the day it was like a fair for big boys and their toys. There was a bike show, competitions, slow riding, tyre pulls, a makeshift drag track with a quarter mile marked off down the runway and a proper Christmas tree, guys doing stunt riding demos, beer tents, food stands, a mobile ink man was doing souvenir tats in a tent with his gear plugged into an extension running out of the control tower.

'Normally tryouts at a party would pull a lot of security stuff, looking after the bikes, standing guard and shit to see off busy bodies, the nosy, and the terminally stupid who wanted to have a look see or have a go. But not here.

'Here we had the frog plod handling all that for us. Sure each of the clubs supplied a token tryout or two as security on the gate, but to be honest, they had it easier than the tryouts who were on hand to fetch and carry booze or whatever for the guys around the circuit. The tryouts on security could sprag out, lounging around on a mixture of deckchairs scrounged from somewhere under a sun shade, stolen from God knows where, drinking beer and smoking spliffs, while across the ditch the cops were sat sweltering in their cars or stood around in the heat manning the barbed wire barricade we'd come through.

'But it was as night fell that the bacchanalia began. In the centre of the airfield there were the band tents, hosting whatever your heart desired, so long as that was mainly loud rock music and a range of strippers, through to some way out sex acts, just the sort of good wholesome entertainment you'd want at this sort of a bash, while sprawling out into the dark from the central crowds were the circles of club tents, lit up by crackling bonfires and humming with the noise of petrol gennys to drive lights, beat boxes and for the very well organised like us, a proper big fridge to keep the beer cold.

'Which was where the problem started on the Saturday night, because with the heat of the day, the supplies of cold beer we'd arrived with weren't lasting very long. As a quick stock check and hurried estimate of the rate of consumption showed at about nine o'clock, we realised if we didn't do something we were heading for a dry patch. Which, as the tagalongs whose fault it would inevitably be, we also realised meant that, let's just say, we wouldn't be the most popular blokes around.

'Sizing up the situation Dobbo knew that if we didn't want to set ourselves up for a good kicking, there was nothing for it but we'd need to make a beer run. We remembered passing *supermarchés* in some of the local towns so if we got our arses in gear and grabbed some cash from the kitty, we reckoned we could get out, get stocked up and back in time for the main night-time session.

'"OK," Dobbo said, coming back from scoring the cash off Mal, "let's grab Stu and go."

'So we had to find Stu, which took a bit but eventually Dobbo stopped him skinning up with Maggie who was pissed as usual.

'"We've gotta go get some beer," Dobbo explained, as Stu shrugged at the interruption and scrambled to his feet, "we're running out."

'"Wait fer me!' giggled Maggie, hauling herself up after him, 'I'll come too…"

'"What the fuck for?" asked Stu, shaking his head.

'"Wanna get some fags," she slurred, staggering off under her own steam in the general direction of the van.

'Stu and Dobbo exchanged looks and I chimed in saying, "What the hell, why not let her come if she wants to?"

'Stu didn't look pleased at the prospect but shrugged and let it go.

'"Your bird, your problem," he observed darkly.

'When we got to the store, it was a small one bathed in the blue white glow of fluorescent lighting off the side of the main drag, occupying a shuttered windowed gap between the outskirts of town with its graffiti painted walls and low rise flats and a deserted industrial estate.

'As we pulled off the road and into the small dusty car park at the side, the yellow tinged interior light spilled out through the doorway plastered with its notices of offers of the week. We didn't really pay much attention to what was around as we slammed the van doors shut and strolled across to the entrance.

'Inside, after wrestling to find the right coin, Dobbo disentangled a trolley from the chained corral at the start of the aisle and we sauntered across to where the beers were stacked.

'Well I say we, as, ignoring us, Maggie headed straight off to the tills to get some smokes and then disappeared outside again, presumably to skin up.

'Not that we paid any attention to her, or the looks we were getting from the few other late night shoppers, or slightly nervous looking shop staff. We were used to that by now and it was water off a duck's back as far as we were concerned. Instead we were concentrating on the business in hand as we worked our way through the selection of cans and bottles on offer to make sure we got the best bang for our buck.

'To be fair, one of the reasons we were attracting attention was probably Stu, who had decided that walking around the store wasn't really for him so he'd clambered into Dobbo's trolley as soon as it had been procured and had refused to get out again, insisting on being pushed down the aisles as he directed operations. He didn't even want to get out once we'd chosen the beer so in the end we'd just had to pack it round and on top of him so that by the time we approached the slightly startled girl manning the checkout, our trolley was groaning under the weight of both a biker whose head was up by the handles and legs were dangling over the front of the basket, and what we hoped was enough beer to keep our crew going until the morning.

110

'"He's not got a barcode, love," Dobbo told her, nodding to Stu with his usual infectious grin as she started to ring up our purchases. I'm not sure how much English she had but she seemed to get the gist as she smiled back at him. Or it might just have been the effect Dobbo always seemed to have on birds. They all just seemed to melt at the sight of him. A bit sickening really.

'Anyway Dobbo was soon counting out the roll of folded notes we'd brought, peeling off the necessary and taking the proffered change with an exchange of warm pleasantries with our mademoiselle, before with a heave to get the Stumobile moving again and around the corner from the till, we were back heading out into the warm night.

'"So where's that bint of yours gone?" Stu asked from his rolling perch, scanning what we could see of the car park in the light of the shop front.

'"Beats me," I said, looking around.

'Maggie was nowhere to be seen.

'Once we'd rolled the trolley up to the van, Stu deigned to start to clamber out, demanding a hand from both of us to extricate himself, while we also had to hang onto the trolley to stop the whole bloody thing going tits up and sending the bottles of beer crashing to the ground which would have been decidedly bad news.

'Eventually he was out and I had the doors at the back of the van open.

'Dobbo had some dosh left, so he and Stu decided they'd nip back inside and see about sorting out some spirits as well, leaving me to hump the beer into the van. I didn't mind, I was still just happy to be involved in those days.

'As I picked up one of the slabs of tins and slid it in to join the others, I heard a familiar laugh, so stepping round the far side of the van from the store, I peered into the gloom across the car park. Now my eyes were adjusting a bit to the darkness again I could see a small knot of figures perched on and around the low wall at the furthest end of the car park, including a familiar small one, and straining my ears in their direction I could hear a murmur of voices.

111

'"Hey, Maggie," I called, with a wave to get her attention. "We're getting loaded up here so we'll be off in a moment."

'I just wanted her to know, as I knew Stu wouldn't bother about waiting for her. If it was up to him he'd quite happily drive off without her. If she wasn't at the van when he wanted to go, it'd be her look out he'd reckon.

'The figure waved back in acknowledgement but made no sign of starting to head my way, so I turned back to the job in hand of loading the beer. It was typical Maggie, I thought at the time. She'd be just having a good time doing whatever the hell it was she was doing over there and not give a shit about us, me, and what I was doing, or wanted. She could be a right selfish cow at times.

'Then the scream came.

'Now the thing you need to understand is, I like a ruck, me. Just thinking about it now is getting me going. The energy, the adrenaline as your heart starts pumping, everything becomes super real as for that moment the world is just about you, you and the other guy. Win or lose, it's all up in the air and down to you. It's a test. Who's harder, faster, more committed. Jesus, you really feel you're alive, it's what we're about isn't it? Survival of the fittest? It's the absolute best.

'That's what people don't get. This is what blokes have done for thousands of years, ever since the stone age. Testing themselves. You create your rep, you live it and then you fight to defend it, and every time you win, you come out that little bit harder that little bit closer to Superman. What does not destroy me makes me stronger and all that bollocks.

'A tightness in the pit of your gut as things start to kick off. There's just nothing like it.

'It was Maggie of course. I knew she'd have pulled some stupid stunt or other. She was always trying it on, as she reckoned nine times out of ten she'd get away with it. Being a fit bird, she just had to smile at most blokes to wrap 'em round her little finger, so whether it was nicking your last beer, fag or spliff, she just had to bat her eyelashes and wriggle out of it as a joke or something you wanted to let go so as to have the pleasure and promise of her company – most times.

'But every so often she just pulled this shit on someone who wasn't going to play ball, someone who didn't give a fuck about her, who took, not gave; and this was one of those times.

'Some lanky *beur* in a hoodie had caught her with her hand in his pocket filching his gear and from the eruption of shouting in non-schoolboy French was seriously upset by this. His evident displeasure showing by the fearsome grip he had on both her wrists as he forced her down onto the ground while his crew suddenly circled round her.

'"Oh fuck," I thought, as dumping the slab of tins I had in my hands onto the floor of the van I launched myself across the car park towards the commotion, arriving with a flying kick from my steel toe-capped boots to the back of the guy's knee that folded him to the ground in an instant.

'As he and she fell to the ground, it all kicked off. I had taken them by surprise but that only lasted a second or so and as their hands went for their pockets I knew they'd all have knives and this was going to get very nasty, very quickly, but there was no backing down now.

'There were four of them, ignoring Monsieur Screamer on the ground who was rolling around, both hands clutching his knee and out of it for the moment. But that worked against them a bit. When there's lots of you against one bloke your problem is you get in each other's way, which is what these guys were doing, whereas me, I just had to pick one to try and fuck over.

'So I grabbed the nearest one by the loose cloth of his hoodie and kneed him hard in the balls, swinging my back against the wall and yanking him towards me to act as a human shield against his mates as I did so.

'It helped a bit but they were coming at me from either side and I was in real trouble until the cavalry arrived as Dobbo and Stu steamed in full force to save my neck.

'Between the three of us with our blood up and the evidence of two of their crew already out of action, the others decided this wasn't their fight and turned and ran, leaving each of the lads on the ground to get a bit of a stomping for form's sake before we bundled ourselves, Maggie and the *kif* from out of the lads on the ground's pockets into the loaded van and got the hell out of there before the natives returned with a proper sized war party.

'Meanwhile, unbeknownst to any of us, Mal had decided the event was an appropriately public one to use to award some flash. So almost as soon as we arrived back at the site and unloaded the van, we found ourselves at the centre of a circle just beyond the ring of our tents for what was a club tradition.

'As we stood and wondered for a moment what the fuck was going on, Mal stepped forward from the surrounding ring of grinning bikers and announced that Stu and Dobbo were being offered tryout bottom rockers and I was getting an official tagalong flash. With a flourish Mal dropped the patches which he'd suddenly produced on the ground in front of us.

'And then there was a ruck. As we dived to grab our flash, everyone else dived in on us, because if we wanted it enough the club's tradition had it, it was up to us to hang onto it and so for the next few minutes we were just a massive heaving scrum of bodies as the three of us fought off the blokes to each emerge bruised, bashed but triumphantly victorious.

'It was tough but good natured and of course like anything in the club there was an underlying message in the ritual that we all understood. We had to fight to get our flash at each and every stage, and to keep it when it was put in front of us; and we were never to forget it.

'Well after all that, the party that night was pretty wild as a heady mix of adrenaline, booze, drugs, pride and music combined to produce an unbelievable vibe.

'I remember standing in the dark at the edge of the bonfire, sucking deep on a joint as the dark angry, atonal, chaotically intense, and uncompromisingly brutal beauty of first the Pixies and then the Jesus and Mary Chain ripped through my brain, music that didn't give a shit what you or anybody else thought and lived life on its own terms. I could respect that. It played to something inside me.

'Here, now, with my new flash, I felt freedom. Freedom to lose myself in something elemental, animal.

'If you just looked at the partying it was like joining *Animal House*.

'But to me it was more than that, it was something with deeper meaning. It was belonging. It smelt of respect, it smelt of power and almost for the first time ever in my life, of independence.

'Looking up into the black, black, diamond dust sky that went on forever, letting the acrid smoke stream from my lungs, I had found myself.

'It was like finally coming home, home to a home I'd never known.

'And as the flames of the fires danced into the night, it was fun. Us versus them, them being anyone who wanted to get in the way of us having fun – authorities, squares, the law.

'Like school when I was growing up, like another brick on the wall. *The Wall*, the soundtrack to my first nervous breakdown.

'At some point later that night I found Maggie naked in the back of the crew bus. I don't know what the hell she'd taken that evening but she was completely wasted, so pulling the doors shut behind me, I climbed in beside her.

'That was the night Jenny was conceived.

'And afterwards there was the trip back. A slower version of the ride out, until at last we were all loitering around in the ferry terminal car park, a mass of bikers parked up on one side of the forming up area, perched on bikes, smoking or sprawled out against the fence getting some rays as holiday makers' cars with hot tired kids and massive swaying caravans took their places in neat segregated rows on the other, and a few French ferry workers sat around in a cabin by the barrier leading to the ramp.

'The boat was in and we'd heard and seen the incoming traffic disembark, so now while the sun beat down on our last French hangovers as the time ticked away to the scheduled departure there was nothing to do in the van but wait with our feet up and out of the window, light up another fag and inspect each other's bruises and bright new flash.

'Eventually a figure appeared at the entrance to the ferry in a fluorescent tabard and carrying a clipboard, so he had to be official then, we reckoned, as a sudden start of attention rippled right through the crowded car park.

'Glancing up the ramp into the ship he obviously got some kind of confirmation as he swung up the barrier and with a nonchalant and very Gallic wave of his clipboard he beckoned us all forwards.

'The carefully controlled embarkation on a lane by lane basis under the strict control of marshals we'd had on the way out? There was none of that on the way back. It was a *Gentlemen start your engines Le Mans* style start as everyone scrambled to fire their vehicle up in a mad dash for the gap where all the lanes of traffic would converge, while the bloke just left us all to it, disappearing back inside. He was probably sitting down to another long lunch and a packet of Gauloise.

'On board, to celebrate Stu and Dobbo's bottom rockers and my flash, we had a meal in the fancy restaurant, figuring our way through the French on the menu and not giving a stuff about the looks we were getting from the other tables. Maggie looked a little green but I put it down to a bit of seasickness, either that or coming down from whatever crap she'd found to smoke or snort the previous night, but true to form she perked up when the vino arrived.

'You could always rely on her to be our designated drunk.

'We were lucky really, we weren't in the van. We'd disembarked and there was some hold up on the docks so traffic had backed up and Stu, Maggie and I had got out to lounge around in the sunshine and have a smoke, while Dobbo had stayed with the van and was the only one in it when Customs waved him into the shed for a shakedown.

'Of course they'd seen the club and they'd given a few of the guys on the bikes a good going over but found nothing and then I guess some bright spark had got it into their head that as the crew bus we'd be the ones carrying the club stash; like we'd have any weight left on the way back from a party run!

'So they turned the van inside out and sure they found some hash but it was buttons, you know? Anyway they had Dobbo as the driver so busted him for it and he ended up getting three months, while the rest of us had to cadge lifts home on the back of guys' bikes as the van was impounded.

'But the thing was, it wasn't his gear. It was mine and Maggie's stash, so he didn't have to take the rap, but he did. He never opened his mouth and he took the hit. For me, just a tagalong.

'That taught me something. Something about loyalty and what it meant. Dobbo and Stu, they were blokes to look up to, blokes to learn from.'

*

Bomber had talked to Iain about the process of joining the club.

'As a tryout you stick to your sponsor like glue. Where he goes, you follow. What he does, you watch. What he says, you listen to and learn from. And you do so because he's your guide, your mentor in the ways of what's going to become your new world. Sure, he takes you round and introduces you to the all guys, but it's more than that, he introduces you to the life. He's your instructor, your guru, your rabbi.

'And I was lucky, because really, I had two sponsors. Because of the way things had worked out I had both Dobbo and Stu.

'Of course for those first few months after we were back from France it was only Stu as Dobbo was doing his time, they had him on remand before the trial and then he had the time they gave him less what he'd served before he could make it out.

'As a tagalong I came firmly under Stu in the hierarchy and at times he ran me ragged.

'I have to admit there were times in those first few months when I really did just think about jacking it in, wondering if I'd ever get on his right side.

'Stu could be a dead scary guy at times. Don't forget, back then I'd only known him since the party so it hadn't been long and Stu was guarded. He was one of those blokes who were quiet, you know? He watched and waited a long time as he got to know you and waited for you to prove yourself.

'So sure, there were times when I thought about getting out before I got in too deep.

'In the end though, it was ink and blood that settled it.

'Stu told me that if I was tagging along I needed to get the official support tattoo done. It was a sign of commitment, a first bit of blood in.

117

'I thought about it long and hard the night before. Wondering if I should go or just not pitch up? Grab Maggie and ride on back over to Edinburgh or even see if she'd go down south with me.

'Because somehow, this was going to be the moment when it became serious. Wearing a bit of flash on my jacket was one thing. It was sewn on and could be cut off again.

'This was marking my skin. This wasn't going to be something that would wash off with a bit of soap and water, it was giving myself an indelible brand for all the world to see forever more.

'The appointment at the tattoo parlour was for eleven. I was there at ten-thirty and Stu turned up a few minutes later, the old shop windows rattling to the bark of the straight through pipes on his Bonnie until he shut her down.

'As we sat and leafed through the samples book and I listened to the buzzing sound coming from behind the curtain that screened off the back room, Stu said conversationally, "There's just one thing to remember about all this and being involved with the club."

'"What's that?" I'd asked him, wondering what was coming.

'"Just don't be a grass," he said flatly.

'I started to protest in surprise, "I won't..."

'"You'd better not," he said, calmly overriding me, "because if you do, we'll kill you. You understand?"

'I looked at him blankly so he repeated his question, "Do you get it?"

'I nodded my acquiescence and after studying my face for a moment to satisfy himself, he grunted his satisfaction and went back to scanning the available designs.

'It was just like that, a matter of fact announcement. Like it was on the induction tick list.

'A mark on the skin. It changes you, more than you would think.

'As I walked out of there that lunchtime and we both fired up our bikes I was a different person from the kid who'd walked through the door earlier that morning.

'Now as we rode away to head to the pub for a few pints to celebrate

I knew a piece of club flash was part of me, and it was something that I would carry to my grave.

'I had passed a milestone, and to me it felt there was now no going back.

'And so as I followed them both in those first years on my way in, they were my upfront guides to how things worked and what was going to be expected of me if I worked my ticket and made the grade to be awarded a patch.

'And the thing was you never knew how long it was going to take. The club's etiquette on stuff like that was fierce. You never, ever, asked how close you were, how long it was before you could expect your patch. The patch was something the club and its members awarded when, and only when, they considered it had been deserved, and to show any sign of expecting to have earned it was considered absolutely presumptuous, a crime worthy of a severe kicking at the least, busting back to tagalong if you were lucky, or chucking out completely with no hope of return if you'd really managed to piss someone off severely.

'But even as I was getting further and further in, there were some things that Stu wouldn't talk about, either as a tryout, or even more so once he got his patch. It was obvious that given his interests he was clearly working his way in with the guys who were serious about business and with that went a new level of carefulness about what he said. There were things he was very tight lipped about – who was running what sort of shit – all that kind of stuff, and I just accepted these were things he wouldn't talk about. It was his business, so I didn't need to know.

'As for how he and Dobbo dealt with it between them, well, again, that was their business not mine.

'To be honest, sometimes all the secrecy gave me doubts. I guess that's part of why we have a proper tryout period. It gives a bloke time to really think if this is for him, lets guys see the absolute commitment that a patch is going to require and ask themselves if they're really up to giving it.

'For me, the doubts never lasted long. Meanwhile there was always the next party to look forward to as I was out at work spannering, or then on the trucks, while arriving back home at the squat Maggie and I had, I knew I'd usually find Stu crashed out on the sofa as he lounged around getting wasted with us, and Maggie just got bigger and bigger until eventually Jenny arrived and everything changed.

'And as a new dad with a kid to support. I suddenly realised I had some choices to make.

'Between them, Stu and Dobbo had taught me everything I needed to know. Sure they were very different guys.

'Stu was one of those blokes who always had an angle. As I worked with him on more and more deals that hectic first year, Stu became my mentor, my brutally cynical, occasionally breathtakingly so, joking guide to how the world I'd joined really worked. And I lapped it up.

'The club's great. We can do whatever we have to and whatever we bloody well like. It's a great laugh, ideal, it's up to you what you do, it's your nut.

'He told me that the club's a big machine to keep running and the guys at the top, they're always on the look out to see who can help feed the beast. So you want to shine and get ahead in the club? Well you know what you've gotta do and be seen to be doing. You help the club out and it'll help you out. It's only fair isn't it? Greed works, you know?

'Dobbo had a very different world view.

'"You know the club rules," he'd told me, "everybody works. Nobody gives a fuck if anyone wants to deal. Screw it, we all like a bit of stuff and those that have access, well it's always going to be a way to earn a bit, but there's a difference between someone doing a bit of dealing on the side and major league trafficking and gangster shit, you know?"

'"And why does everybody work?" I'd asked him.

'"Because if they don't and we're just full of crims and dealers then it just brings a whole load of polis shit down on everybody. So my advice to you, mate? Steer clear of the shit as far as you can. I know it's tempting, it's easy money, and sometimes you'll need to get involved in something just to help back a mate up, but if you want to make it in the world, keep a focus on your day job, see what you can do with that."

'So in the end that's what I decided to do. I had a kid, I wanted to provide for her and always be around for her. That was something I'd sworn to myself I'd do if I ever had a sprog and now it was time to make it real. And so I decided I couldn't take a path that might lead to going away again, not because I couldn't handle it, I knew I could, but because it would mean walking out on her. The thing I was never going to do.

'And as it turned out, it was good advice from Dobbo anyway. Because in the end it was something I was able to grow into my own business, something real, something worthwhile.

'And everybody in the club, from Mal on down was supportive, respected my choice. It was never any hassle.

'But then we all know what eventually happened in the club.

'After Mal caught it, Dobbo got the top spot with Stu as his number two which could have been a recipe for trouble in the long run if they weren't so tight a pair of guys. But then Dobbo only had the gig for what, a year or so, before we lost him that night, a hit and run not a mile from the clubhouse.

'Of course that was all a difficult time. We knew we'd had a rat and it was up to Stu to root them out which is what he did, and I'm not going to talk about that.'

CHAPTER 5   THE TOP TABLE

The big international OMGs vary in their formal structures but as organisations they tend to fall into one of two main models, they're either what I'd describe as a franchised basis, or they're a much more corporate sort of affair, and each type has their strengths and weaknesses.

The corporate ones are what you might expect of any large business organisation in that someone somewhere, although it's usually in the States, is the top man, the international president. They're chairman and chief executive rolled into one, however they've got to be there, and they'll have a board of senior officers through whom they work to issue and then enforce instructions, policies and decisions. Below them there may be regional presidents, say in other countries where the club operates, and below them individual charter presidents running their own local chapters. And while the regional and local operations may have wide areas of discretion and will guard their local independence fiercely against the centre in quite legalistic disputes about what things are in each side's jurisdiction and authority, the organisation is quite obviously run as a top down affair when it comes to strategy.

The franchise model is quite different in that these clubs don't have an international boss. Sure there'll be players who are well respected and seen as figures who have national or even international authority, standing, and influence, but that's really what it's about, power through influence rather than formal authority.

In these clubs a local charter has to demonstrate that it can dominate its territory and hold it while living up to the standards that the club culture demands. But assuming they can do that, what they then do on their own turf, the type of members they want to have, and how they want to use their position, is almost entirely up to them. So if a charter wants to be crime free and have everyone working so it's made up just of ordinary working guys, that's fine. But if another charter becomes a self-referring bunch of crooks, well that's its business too and by and large no one else's.

That's not to say they don't have some organisation above the charter level. They will often have regional groupings at the same level as the more corporate ones, but these are a bottom up affair, where local or national representatives come together to discuss and agree strategies and rules and ensure standards are being maintained regarding who gets into the club and checking everyone is holding up their end. So the regional group would need to approve any club patch-overs for example, might set limits on the numbers of members being made up to ensure quality control and, in extremis, if a charter is seen to be letting the side down or running out of control, decide to take the appropriate action to protect everyone else's investment in the club's reputation.

Iain Parke briefing from an unnamed Serious and Organised Crime Agency officer 2008

'So, why go after Bomber?' we asked DI Chambers.

'Why not just arrest Stu if that was who we were after? Is that what you mean?' he countered. 'Well it wasn't that simple...'

'Why not?' we wanted to know.

'Because Stu, and some of the other key players in the club, weren't just ordinary charter members any more.

'No, they had formed themselves a new charter, but it was more than that. It was a club within the club if you like, and one that crucially as far as I was concerned, Bomber wasn't in.

'And that was important for two reasons.

'Firstly as I've already said, it told me something about what was happening with his club career, and secondly, it helped confirm in my mind that he was one of the straight ones.'

We knew from the history Iain had left in his notes that like others, the club had always had Freebooters. Ever since the very early days, patches who had become senior enough to remain as members but for one reason or another didn't want to be tied to a particular charter had been able to claim this independent status.

But as DI Chambers explained it, in the last decade or two some of the clubs, the Rebels under Stu included, had taken the idea a stage further and formed specific Freebooter charters which generally represent very much the Top Table in the relevant club. Now, as the police understood it, if you are a Freebooter it meant you were part of the top team running the club, the board of directors if you like, and that was a big change. Before this the club had been like a collection of local franchises, each charter independent, able to do its own thing, run its own affairs, so long as they upheld the code, dominated their turf and represented the club properly. But now it was different. Now there was organisation, a plan. Somehow, with the new Freebooter charter at the top as a C suite, it had all gone more corporate and business like, with a growth plan, standards, and policies.

Bomber had described to Iain a whole new world of messages being delivered down the chain from up top about cooling it, the need to avoid bad publicity, instructions to reduce the number of parties where there might be trouble, even suggestions that blokes tidy up their image, become more presentable, stop doing stuff to deliberately freak out the citizens. The club on this analysis was travelling a long way from its thuggish roots as a bunch of bar room brawling rowdies.

And the other side of the coin of course, from the police point of view in terms of establishing guilt and capturing evidence to put to court, was that the way it was organized, Top Table was now insulated. The idea was that the Freebooters would never get their hands dirty. They wouldn't touch drugs, they wouldn't handle the money, they'd never whack someone themselves any more, although God knows, they'd done it in the past. They wouldn't even hold formal authority as far as the world, or more importantly, the cops could see, they wouldn't be the club or charter Ps. The officers could front the club, but the Freebooters would run it, the power behind the throne, able to operate safely and discreetly in the shadows, doing what they needed to do.

They wouldn't even talk about what needed doing, not if they could help it.

There would be nothing to directly link them to a crime. Not a finger-print, not a note, not a wisp of DNA because they were never going to be there when it happened, the real players would always have an alibi. And with a culture where everyone would know just what they were expected to do from a nod or a signal or a murmured ambiguous word while walking down a noisy street, trying to find evidence of instructions was going to be nigh on impossible anyway, particularly once an understanding that something ought to be done to someone had filtered down from the Freebooters to a patch who farmed it out to a tryout or an associate looking to make his grade. Try proving that in a court of law. Even if the bloke who actually carried out the hit rolled over, what did you have to put in front of a jury? Hearsay about hearsay about a nod and a wink and what that really meant.

'It's a bit like Hitler and the Final Solution,' Bomber had explained to Iain, in one of the occasionally wince inducing historical analogies he was so fond of.

'Everybody knows he did it. But has anyone ever found a direct order he issued? No. Heydrich and Eichmann directed and organized it, thousands of SS and collaborators were involved in doing it on the ground, but where was the actual definitive instruction to start exterminating the Jews? The reality was they didn't need one. Heydrich had a note from Goering saying that the boss had decided something needed to be done to sort this once and for all, and that was all he needed. They knew what was meant, they understood what they were expected to do and they got on with it.'

But to DI Chambers that was exactly the point.

'That was the way it was with the Freebooters. To make your way up the ladder, to work your way towards that inner circle meant understanding what they wanted, what you were expected to do, and delivering it, and all just from getting into the right mind set, with as few words spoken about business as possible. A conspiracy of silence.'

'And if Bomber wasn't a Freebooter after all his years in the club, after his relationship with Stu for God's sake...'

'Then that tells you something about him doesn't it?' DI Chambers nodded.

'The Top Table brought organisation to the business side of it. Before, guys who were into the dealing side, and it wasn't everybody by any means, they had their own sources, brought in their own gear, whatever. They were also in competition with whoever else was operating on their turf. The Freebooters set out to sort all that on both sides of the trade, supply and demand.

'The supply side was simple. They co-opted the best of the sources onto the Top Table to supply the club's gear centrally through the Freebooters. It was a sweet deal for both sides, the guys with the sources got a monopoly to supply anyone in the club who wanted to deal, and the Top Table got a cut of everything that got sold.

'If you wanted gear, you bought it from one of the Top Table's approved suppliers at the club rates, it was that simple. Go anywhere else and if you were lucky you'd get a warning first. If not, or if you were stupid enough to ignore it, one day, patch or no patch, you were going to wake up and find yourself dead.

'The rest of the demand side took more doing but they persevered. They sat down with each of the major competitors and hammered out a deal. It didn't happen overnight but they worked at it over a few years and eventually got to where they wanted to be. The Freebooter pitch was simple, they had at their disposal an organisation that had pretty much national coverage and could supply both dealing networks on the ground, through the Top Table naturally, and muscle.

'So the deal with the other major players was to split territories into agreed exclusive turf, with the players becoming suppliers into the club for distribution across club controlled areas and the club enforcing discipline on the streets to shut down any independents that might try to undercut or challenge either side.'

'Are you saying they created a cartel?' we asked.

'That's exactly what I'm telling you,' DI Chambers confirmed.

'Part of the deal was they also established a minimum price that everyone involved would see charged for their gear, inside and outside the club. Well if you control the market between you, you'd want to avoid price competition wouldn't you? No point in creating a grey market if you don't have to. It'd just damage profits and risk undermining the nice little arrangement everyone was enjoying, good business at low risk with minimal hassle.

'And again, everyone had to stick to the rules, patch or no patch, and charge at least the minimum price. The national deal was bigger than any one bloke, whoever they were, and so it was the same deal. No one got told twice. It was establishing a good old fashioned union to control the market. It made business sense for everybody, and with sufficient ruthlessness it could be made to work. And so, sufficient ruthlessness was applied, after all, that wasn't something that was in short supply.'

'But what about all this talk of brotherhood?' we objected.

DI Chambers just shrugged.

'For the guys at the Top Table it's a loyalty of shared interests, that's all. Sure the patch and the history is important but only to ensure you know that the next guy can be relied on to do whatever's required and most importantly, to keep his mouth firmly shut come what may. But beyond that? It's a business arrangement, no more, no less, and the moment you're not needed, then you'll be gone.'

'But if Bomber wasn't part of this Top Table, and wasn't in fact really dirty at all, why pick him up? I thought you said you didn't think Bomber was in on it?'

'No, no I didn't, but that wasn't to say there weren't people who thought he was. But anyway, whether he was Top Table or not, that wasn't the point. It was all part of the same operation...'

'This Plan B thing?' we asked.

'No, that came later. And to be fair, I could see why the blokes wanted to have a look at Bomber,' he said, counting the reasons off on his fingers.

'He had ongoing business dealings with Stu; he was in imports and exports, which had to put him in the frame for a look at whether it was all legit; and there were those calls the Spanish police had intercepted before and afterwards as part of their operation where we think Stu had talked to someone about what sounded like arranging the hit.'

'But you'd never linked either of those calls to Bomber, had you?' we objected.

'No, no we hadn't. But as one of Stu's key contacts in the UK he had to be under the microscope.

'And you've also got to remember what a hot item this was. We'd just heard that two ex-cops with definite links to the club, and Stu in particular, had been executed, so the pressure in the force was on to wrap this up and bring the killers to justice. It's the same when there's any kind of Red One, everyone on the job drops everything and piles in. There's a real ethos of, if you pick on one of us you're taking on all of us.'

'Sounds familiar,' we commented.

'Well quite,' DI Chambers admitted with a wry smile. 'So to start with, once we'd tracked Stu down it was just a matter of lifting the pair of 'em and pulling both of them in for interview.'

'And you led the interviews?'

'Yes I did. We ran both of them in series. It gave us a chance to bounce stuff back and forwards between the pair of them, at least while the PACE clock was ticking.'

'So what did your colleagues think?' we wanted to know.

'Oh well, I think I was in a bit of a minority when it came to Bomber, I have to say. When we interview we always do it in a team of two so I was paired with the junior Met officer on the taskforce, DS Timms.'

According to DI Chambers, DS Timms had a distinctly cynical view about Bomber's alleged innocence when it came to dealing in drugs.

Timms' view, it transpired, was you only had to look at Bomber's history and what he had been asked to do to see if he was really squeaky clean or not.

Aberdeen, with all the offshore lads, their money and the clubs and bars they'd spend it in made a natural patch for a serious drugs operation from DS Timms' point of view. It was prime territory that needed organising on a businesslike footing if you wanted to make a go of it and take full advantage of what it offered and the opportunities to ship serious amounts of gear. So you just had to ask yourself, after the whole Munster shambles, who had Stu entrusted with the job of sorting the local charter out? Bomber, that's who.

'I remember DS Timms saying to me as we were going down to the interview room for one of our sessions, "Now I'm sorry, but given how serious a patch it is I just don't see that job going to someone who isn't into the business end of things up to their eyeballs. Come on, pull the other one will you?"

'And to be honest, it was difficult to argue the point.'

DI Chambers was sitting back in his chair as he talked us through how it had gone with Bomber.

'The problem's as old as the hills though isn't it?' he was reflecting, 'the more capable the subordinate, the bigger the threat they potentially are to you as boss. Too good and they can be a potential rival.'

'And Bomber was a very effective fixer?' we wanted to know.

'Very, by all accounts. DS Timms was right. Just look at who Stu sent up to Aberdeen to deal with the granite city crew after the whole Munster thing. He wasn't going to give that gig to just anybody was he? No, whatever sob story Bomber spun to your bloke Iain, there was only one reason Stu sent him up there. It was so he could sort out a rogue charter, and to me that says trusted lieutenant, trusted to do whatever's necessary.

'But again, that was one of the ways the Top Table took steps to defend their position. It was good old fashioned divide and rule where they would create rivalries. If they set crews lower down the tree in competition with each other then they'd have too much to do in looking out for each other and trying to demonstrate they were the best, to worry about mounting some kind of coup or challenge to the next levels up.'

'Because?'

'Because the second string to the bow was co-option, dangling the carrot that if you had what it took to become a real player then eventually you too could potentially step up to be a Freebooter as well.'

'You sound a bit unsure about Bomber, if you don't mind us saying so,' we said. 'On the one hand you didn't seem to think he was involved in crime, but on the other you've got him tagged as one of

Stu's most trusted lieutenants. Surely you can't have it both ways, can you?'

'Well if anyone, Stu and Dobbo had brought Bomber on and into the club don't forget. He might have had Malcolm as a formal sponsor after that first run in but the day to day practicalities seem to really have been devolved to Dobbo and Stu...'

'And that forms a strong bond.'

'I'm sure it does,' he agreed.

'So what did you make of them?' we asked DI Chambers 'what were they like to deal with?'

'What did I make of Bomber? Now that's an interesting question,' he said as he gave it some consideration.

'Not evil, certainly to start with. In fact, given the right circumstances you could actually say he was or would have been one of the good guys. He was always a bit guarded when he was talking but he was relatively easy to get on with when you met him, so long as you treated him the right way...'

'Being?' we asked.

'Like a normal human being,' he countered.

'And Stu? What about him then?'

'Now I always knew he was a very different kettle of fish. He was a man who chose his path, he did what he did just as he always had to get what he wanted. He wasn't someone who was just following some kind of primrose path in innocence, no way.'

'He knew what he was doing?'

'Yes. But even he was a bit of a contradictory character.'

'Why do you say that?' we wanted to know.

'Well, it's a bit difficult to put into words but here was someone who was capable of tremendous eloquence at times, and someone who could have awesome levels of ambition...'

'Like splitting off from the Rebels internationally and setting up his own club with their rivals The Menaces?'

'Exactly. But then you have to look at what he did with all that. I mean, you put all that effort into climbing the greasy pole, and breaking and reforming a club like that in your own image, and what do you do with it? Penny ante dealing shit, I mean, it's all a bit contradictory at times.

'He goes to all that effort to set up the Top Table, insulating himself from the day to day dealing because he knows that we're out to get him, if not today then tomorrow or the next day. He knows we're coming for him so he makes his arrangements to keep clean.

'But then occasionally it's as though he can't resist getting stuck back in personally, and often for some pretty small scale half arsed crap.

'We nearly had him a couple of years ago, just a small thing but it would have been a chink in the armour at least, I don't know if your bloke Iain heard about it?'

We shook our heads, it didn't ring any bells with anything in the files.

'He was at a gig and he'd given some wraps of speed to kids on the doors, one of which we then tugged. Of course as soon as the kid realised who we were asking him to give up he changed his story. Well you'd expect that, wouldn't you? If the kid wanted to carry on walking around anyway, so perhaps Stu figured it wasn't that much of a risk to start with, but even so, with all the other serious crap he had on the go, why take the risk? It just seems insane.

'Is it habit? Is it just because he thinks he really is untouchable? Is it kicks? Is it just that he needs to keep pushing the envelope, upping the ante? What? Makes no sense to me.

'It's like he's almost wilfully blind, as though he's willing to piss away everything he's worked for, all the effort he's put in, the absolute power he's achieved, for what? The thrill of some stupid hand to hand street sale?

'Well you know what they say about absolute power.

'But you've also got to say, this is a bloke who's really created some-thing. Whatever you think about it, he's built himself a bit of an empire – businesswise, the club – both in a world where most of us wouldn't survive a week, let alone get to the very top.'

'You sound like you almost admire him.'

'Steady on, I wouldn't go that far, but you have to recognise that even a shit like him, he's got something. He's seen the opportunity to reach out and get something and he's gone and done it. He's got the ambition, he's got the drive and perseverance and he's got the smarts to have not only survived but thrived. You've just got to ask, in any other environment, in any other circumstances, what would he have made of himself? What the hell would he have been like if he'd just applied himself in the straight world?'

'Like Bomber you mean?'

'Yes, I suppose so. Although that's the downside of Bomber of course. He did all that in the legit world and yet he's then let it all be used and let's be honest, wrecked, by the likes of Stu. So he has his blind side as well, it's just that his is his inability to really get out and cut the ties.

'Oh sure he's retired and sure he says it's all legit business. Like you know, for what it's worth I believe him, as far as it goes.

'But he's still letting Stu use it and he's still letting his association with the club bring a load of grief down on him and his business, grief that's got a fair chance of completely ruining it. How successful a transport company do you think you're going to have once you're on the rummage crews' radar? Once word gets round to all your normal customers that you're getting turned over each time you ship something, how long do you think that's going to last?

'And that's before you start looking at what it's done to the rest of his life. His family, his relationships, his kid.

'DS Timms seemed to have a pretty black and white view of things. I think in his mind in making a pact with Stu, Bomber had actively chosen evil or something like it.

'To me it was more about whether Bomber wanted a way out, because if he did I was sure we could give him one.'

'Talking? Grassing?'

'Yes, well that was the problem right there. Grassing was always going to be a way out for him, but it was never going to be one he was going to want to admit to, even think about. All he ever needed to do was approach us and I think towards the end in his darkest moments he'd been thinking about doing just that, in fact I know he has from the conversations we've been having, but the truth is, it's just too alien to everything he's ever stood for in his life for him to actually do it.

'He'd have to break first before he'd turn on his mates. I know that from what I've seen of him. Each time I think we've come close, in the end Bomber has decided to stay loyal to Stu and the club rather than seek an escape, even when we were in that interview room and I was pointing out the dangers of his position and the risk he faced if Stu talked.'

'Which was?'

'Well it's that classic prisoner's dilemma isn't it? If you both stay schtum, then both of you get a reasonable amount of grief...'

'But the first one to rat wins?'

'You could put it that way, yes.'

'But whatever we tried with Bomber, we couldn't shake him. DS Timms had a go, trying to undermine his faith.

'Where's the envelope, Bomber? Where's the brief? That's part of what you paid all your subs for over the years wasn't it? Knowing that you'd be looked after when it came to this?

'So where are they now Bomber?' DS Timms demanded, ''cos I'm looking round and I'm not seeing them? Where's the help from your brothers now you need it?'

Bomber just shrugged.

'Who says I need help? Besides which I'm retired, aren't I? Have been a year or more now. I'm not paying any dues, so I'm not really entitled to that support any more, although I guess if I asked for it some of the guys might sort me out.'

'For old times' sake?' DS Timms said, sarcastically.

'Yes, something like that,' Bomber told him calmly.

'DS Timms banged on about crime but I could see he wasn't getting anywhere.

'Bomber just batted him back calmly with what was his party line, "Not me, there's crime in the club sure, but I'm clean."

'Right up until DS Timms pressed the wrong button and finally got an emotional reaction out of Bomber. "Yeah right, so what about Aberdeen then, Bomber? What happened up there? Who was responsible for all that up there then, Bomber? Your turf, your shout wasn't it?"'

'It's just a pity that the reaction he got was exactly the one I'd been working hard to avoid, because Bomber just shut down at that. He folded his arms and didn't say another word for the rest of his time in the room, not to DS Timms and not to me.

'We sat there a bit longer with DS Timms talking at him, and firing questions, but they just bounced off the lump of stone now sitting the other side of the table and eventually even DS Timms gave up. We packed our files away, turned off the tape recorder and left Bomber to sit with his thoughts in the empty room.

'Outside, beyond the thick door, DS Timms turned to me with a sour grin as we headed off down the corridor to where Stu was waiting for us, "Touched a nerve there didn't I? About Aberdeen?"'

'"Well" I said to him dismissively, I was still irritated that his steaming in had wrecked the dialogue and even rapport that I'd been trying so hard to build with Bomber just to get him talking, "what the fuck d'you expect with what happened up there?"

'We were at the door to Stu's interview room and as he reached for the door handle DS Timms just gave me a smug smirk and said, 'Ready for round two?'

DI Chambers had brought the tape and transcripts of Stu's interrogation as well and so he played the tape to us as we followed it in writing together with his expert commentary to help us appreciate what was going on.'

'Your full name is ████ ██████ ██████████, although within your club you are known as Stu, is that correct?'

'Yes.'

'And you currently live in Mallorca where your address is

Llamedos, ███ ██ ███, is that correct?'

'Yes.'

'And you also have a place in North Cyprus as well?'

'Yes.'

'Handy that, what with no extradition treaty and all?'

'Hadn't crossed my mind.'

'And you own a company, Sylob Limited, is that correct?'

'Yes.'

'And what does that business do?'

'I export soft toys.'

And after that as DI Chambers explained, to start with it was straight no comments all down the line from Stu.

'He told us at the outset that was the way it was going to be.'

> 'Because you lot are always setting us up all the time we've got a club rule, no one says anything to the cops about anything, club business or not, without the club's permission. Sorry, but that's just the way it is.'

'The only exception came when DS Timms tried to push him, telling him he might as well talk to us as, "Your mate down the hall, he's chatting away, so why don't you tell us your side of the story?"

'Stu just looked at him in disgust.

'"Well, even if I believed you," he told us, "that's his business isn't it? Besides, he's not in the club any more is he? He's retired isn't he? Just like me."

'As it happens, within reason, Stu was prepared to talk a bit about their business activities and lives outside the club.

'So much so that DS Timms actually asked Stu the same question as I'd put to Bomber earlier that day.'

> 'Why are you talking? You guys don't talk.'

> 'We don't talk about club business. This is different, you asked

about my company and that's my business, so it's up to me if I want to chat about it or not. Anyway, you know as well as I do, I'm retired these days, have been since the start of the year.'

'Out in good standing?'

'That's right. Even got the tat to prove it, you want to see?'

'No thanks.'

'Well, suit yourself.'

'So what do you do? Now you're retired and all?'

'You're going to like this.'

'Try me.'

'Teddy bears.'

'Teddy bears? What do you mean teddy bears?'

'I've got a business, I import and export soft toys.'

'You're kidding me.'

'Straight up, scout's honour.'

'Alright, I believe you but... Why teddy bears?'

'Yeah... It was toy runs, it just got me thinking one day. There you were, you had people spending 50 quid on a bear and it's what? Stuffing and a bit of sewing shit you can get done cheap in the Philippines or wherever? And I just thought, there's money to be made here. And then when I was travelling, overseas...'

'South Africa?'

'Yeah, there, and other places, I got to looking around and what do you think I saw?'

'I don't know, tell me?'

'Kids, lots of kids. There's millions of kids all over the world, particularly the up and coming bits. People just keep making 'em and as the parents get a bit more money they want to spend some of it on them, so I reckoned, there's not just a market for toys here, it's bigger than that, way bigger than that.'

'Why South Africa of all places? Is that just a coincidence?'

'Emerging markets sunshine, they're all the thing to a businessman like me. Even a copper like you'll heard of the BRICs won't you? Brazil, Russia, India, China, they're the big ones, and if you want some investment advice your starter for ten is, on which continent is Brazil?'

'When I want investment advice from the likes of you I'll ask for it thanks.'

'Yeah well, with your lot's pensions I guess you don't need to keep your eyes open the way we do out here in the private sector…'

'The private sector? Is that what you're calling yourselves these days?'

'Like I said, I'm a businessman, I buy and sell things, I pay my taxes so they can pay for the likes of you lot, although fuck knows why I bother, that's the private sector.'

'And Bomber? Is he just a businessman too?'

'Bomber? Yeah, he's straight.'

'So why do you use him to ship your gear?'

'Because he's good. He runs a great business, does everything right and I can trust him like a brother. Why wouldn't I want to put my business his way? I've known him for twenty years or so for fuck's sake. Who else would I ask to ship my stuff?'

'But when it came to anything else, anything about the club, Stu was giving nothing away. When we asked him to talk to us about it all we got was the mick.'

'Are you sitting comfortably? Then I'll begin. Once upon a time there was a big bad biker.'

'Are you taking the piss?'

'We've arrested you for questioning in connection with the murder of two retired policemen, have you any idea how seriously we will be taking this investigation?'

'Why, you looking for their stashed loot or something?'

'Only there's things about this big bad biker you don't know sunshine. You have no idea.'

'He knows something that you don't.'

'This is bullshit, this tug. You know that don't you?'

'We played him the tape of the calls.'

'This tape was made on Thursday 1 March this year.'

I need a couple of pieces of work doing.

Sure, no problem.

Let's have a walk and talk when I'm back and I'll fill you in.

OK, let me know when and where.

Will do.

'And then this one was recorded on Friday 16 March.'

You know those cleaning jobs you were after?

Yeah?

Well it's all done. Turned out on the day there was a bit of an offer on.

Oh yes?

BOGOF mate.

Bog off?

Two birds with one stone mate. Bump one, get one free.

OK, so it's sorted?

All taken care of.

That's great, owe you one.

No problem, anytime.

'So my first question is, do you recognise the voices on that tape?'

'He just sat there with his arms folded, looking bored.

'DS Timms pressed him, saying that's you making the first call isn't it? And then receiving the second one?

'He shrugged and then said, "Well, if you say so, I'd have to say I can't remember them."'

'You're saying you can't remember making or receiving those calls?'

'Nope, I'm a businessman, I'm making calls all the time. Organising this, chasing that, it's what I do, and no I don't remember every detail of every call I made a month ago or more. Do you?'

'Yes, your so called import and export business, we know.'

'There's nothing 'so called' about it, that's my business. It's what I do for a living, you ought to know, you've crawled all over it often enough.'

'You're being very careful on those calls aren't you? You never really say what they're about.'

'Well if it was me then I'm not surprised, I'm always very careful about what I say. I have to be don't I? I'm a businessman, I make deals over the phone all the time so I need to watch what I'm saying, what I'm agreeing with who. If I didn't I'd soon get myself in the shit wouldn't I?'

'So you can't help us with these calls then?'

'You don't recognise the second voice by any chance?'

'That's your mate Bomber isn't it?'

'No.'

'And you can't shed any light on the deaths of retired DI ███████ and retired DS ████ ███████ on Thursday 15 March, the day before the second of those calls we just played you was made?'

'No.'

'And as far as you are aware there's no link between either of these telephone conversations on the 1st and 16th and these deaths?'

'Oh so that's what this shit is about, is it? You're looking to hang that on me are you? Well I can tell you for starters that's complete bollocks. Whatever happened to those two shits, it had nothing to do with me.'

'So you knew the dead men then?'

'Of course I knew them. They'd harassed the club and my guys for years until they fucked off. We had a party when we heard they'd been booted out of your mob, I can tell you.'

'So you have no regrets that they're dead then?'

'They can both rot in hell as far as I'm concerned, but that's a tad different from having anything to do with arranging them being there, son. Is this phone crap the best you've got? You'll have to do better than that you know.'

'And the irritating thing was, he was right.'

'Can we go back to Bomber a minute?'

'OK if you want, it's your party.'

'So you met him at a party didn't you? That's what he's telling us.'

'I glanced at DS Timms a moment, where's he going with this, I wondered. I was nervous I suppose, at the time while we'd got some stuff from Bomber, very little of it was actually of any use and I didn't want DS Timms giving away anything Bomber had said which we might want to think about using later in some way.

'If Stu was surprised he didn't show it. "Yeah, years ago," he conceded, "so what?"

'Something about jumping a pool, some kind of challenge?'

'Yeah, shit that was funny. He tried it at night and fucked it up, got a proper ducking and stuffed his bike in Mal's pool. He was crapping himself but Mal saw the funny side, so the lads just made him get it out again the next day and have another go. So the next morning he had to drain the pool, get it out and get it started.'

'What did you do?'

'Us, what do you think we did? We stood around making unhelpful comments and generally taking the piss, but it was OK.'

'A bit of give and take?'

'Yeah, banter, but he took it alright which got him a bit of respect,

140

'you know, that he could handle shit.'

'And then we got a ramp sorted and off he went.'

'And he made it?'

'Yeah, fair play to the bloke, he did. Was a right laugh. Mal had organised a sweepstake so everyone had a bit of fun.'

'And what happened then?'

'No one was going anywhere so he stuck around for the evening, had a few beers, got talking to some of the guys, you know the sort of thing.'

'Including you? Did he talk to you?'

'Yeah, sure, why?'

'So what did you talk about, what did he tell you about himself?'

'Bits and pieces. Shit, what do you think it was, some kind of frigging interview?'

'But he told you his background?'

'He told me a bit about where he'd come from if that's what you mean, but hell, we don't usually care much about where guys are from, it's what they're about that's important to us.'

'And you thought he had the right stuff?'

'I could see he had potential, sure, right from the off. But at the time I thought he was way off being the finished article'

'So you liked what you saw, you and the guys.'

'Well it was Mal's shout, don't forget. Dobbo and me were still just tagalongs ourselves at that stage. But sure, Mal liked him, got us to sound him out about tagging along.'

'And what was his reaction to that.'

'Man he was thrilled, no question, he said it was the first thing he'd ever been invited to join.'

'And what did people think about that? Bit of class that or what?'

'Or a bit of a twat more like, but he showed he could sort his bike out, and he demonstrated he'd stand up and have another go, so I guess that told the guys something about him right from the off.'

'Fair enough.'

'What the hell's going on here? I was wondering to myself. Was Timms planning to go all the way through everything we've got from Bomber with Stu? Why really show Stu what Bomber said?

'Because as I sized up the situation and considered my options – let it run, interrupt the interview, take over myself – DS Timms was carrying on. He wanted to know more about what Stu made of Bomber when he first met him.

'As far as I could see it was all too obvious a story. Bomber, ambitious and bright but a bit of an outsider, dissatisfied with the limitations of trying a straight life the way I guess a lot of young lads with a dead-end job and few qualifications would be, had drifted into company of some bikers on the edge of the outlaw scene and then on into the scene.

'To hear Stu tell it, Bomber had come actively looking. Stu claimed he'd been trying to put Bomber off at first, filling him in right from the start on the horrors of what getting involved might lead to, acting the proper health warning the way he had it, only for Bomber to insist, telling Stu he wanted to serve the club in exchange for a chance to patch.

'So why warn him off then, Stu? If the club's such a great thing what's the problem?'

'It's a tough place, the club, and you need to be a tough guy to take part. When I first met him I wasn't sure he had the shit, you know. So sometimes it's easier, kinder even, to run guys off if they've not got a chance, than let them carry on thinking they're going to make the cut. Saves a whole load of grief for all involved.'

'But he did, didn't he? Make the cut?'

'Yeah, yeah he did. I found he was a tougher little bastard underneath than I'd given him credit for at the outset, I'll say that. There's more to him than meets the eye...'

'Still as Stu described that party and the early days of knowing

Bomber, he carried on playing down his part. He always maintained Bomber was a more than willing participant in edging towards the club and that if anything Stu's role as he saw it had been to warn Bomber off.'

'Why's that Stu?'

'I was just trying to help him avoid making the mistakes I've made. It's what you'd do for a mate.'

'And is Bomber a mate?'

'What the fuck do you think?'

'Meanwhile Stu had obviously got a bit bored with this as he glanced at the clock on the wall and did a mental calculation as to how long the trip was likely to be from his solicitor's office out to the station.'

'So fascinating as all this reminiscing is, have you actually got some crime that you're planning to charge me with so I can let my brief know what it is when they pitch up?'

'And the trouble was, he was right. We really had nothing at all on him at that stage.

'But of course, that wasn't really what the arrests had been about.'

*

As DI Chambers had already told us, while many in the police painted the clubs as purely criminal organisations, not everyone saw it that way.

No one inside the clubs or out denies that some club members are criminals.

But then club members will point out that criminals have been found in everything from the police themselves, to parliament, to the Freemasons and big banks; yet, leaving aside the big banks' recent conduct perhaps, no one seems to want to label any of these as criminal organisations.

And even though crime was in the end one of the reasons he admitted that he had decided to retire from the club, the way Bomber saw it was different, as he'd told Iain in one of his interviews.

'The thing is,' he'd explained to Iain, 'the way I saw it, you didn't have to get involved if you didn't want to. Nobody forced you to join in. So long as everybody in the club was loyal to the club and stuck to the rules about no talking to the cops, so long as no one was ratting, then it didn't matter. In fact, having some guys in the club who were clean probably suited them quite well, confused the picture, gave them more cover.

'And everybody was loyal to the club and tight. Right from the start it was a sort of self-selecting thing. The sort of guys who were drawn to the idea of the club were the sort who didn't fit in to straight society. They tended to be the rowdy ones, the troublemakers, the ones who'd had their run in with the plod, big or small. So, even if you weren't into the sort of business the Freebooters were into, you still weren't going to rat them out. You just weren't going to get involved, that's all.

'You just kept your head down, got on with your own stuff and slowly realised that if you weren't playing their game well, that was as far as you were going to go in the club. Because the promotions, they went to the guys that could help drive the Top Table's agenda. While around you, you could see the new members coming in, the tagalongs who were invited to tryout, starting to change. Like was selecting like, let's just leave it at that.

'But you still did whatever the club asked you to, whatever it was. And fuck they asked some stuff. I've done things, over the years, stuff you wouldn't believe. Things looking back now that I'm not proud of, but I did them. I did them because I was asked to and I did them because they were for the club.

'And you wanted to believe, I suppose. You wanted to stay loyal and to believe that everybody else was loyal too. I mean, this was a club I'd given my life to, wasn't it? So facing up to what had happened to it, well that was always going to be a hard thing to do. But sooner or later I just had to start asking myself, am I being played for a mug here?

'As for the newbies, the wannabes, the tagalongs, the tryouts, well they'd just get on and do whatever anyone asked them to. They just assumed it was what you did to prove yourself to the club and to earn yourself that next step up the rung towards getting your patch. Because they knew that if they didn't want to do what someone from the club was asking them to do, no questions asked, then someone else surely would, and earn themselves the kudos instead. I mean, when you're looking to get in and you're serious about it, when the club asks you to do something, you do it, simple as. Turn it down and you might as well just fuck off and do something else with your life.

'But the problem was further down the line. You didn't know whether what you were being asked to do was for the club, or whether it was just to further the Top Table's business interests, or a bit of both.

'So if the word came down that some independent club had to be dealt with, rolled up, patched up or driven out, was that club business, about ensuring we stayed top dogs? Or was it because they were potential rivals to the Top Table's trade? Or a bit of both? And so where did you draw the line? At what point were you compromised? When did you become involved, wittingly or unwittingly in helping them with their deals rather than just helping the club? And did anyone but you see the difference anymore? Because this sure as fuck wasn't the sort of thing you were going to start chatting about down the clubhouse any more.

'We used to talk about all sorts in the old days. Everything and any-thing went, back in the days when we were a bit more of a democracy than we are now. You had respect as a member, hell it was a members' club, it belonged to us, so it was up to us to decide what we did with it. But that was then, this is now, and it ain't like that anymore.

'That's why I decided I needed to get out. Because big bucks were trumping brotherhood every time.'

Then he left Iain with one of those chilling remarks he'd drop into a conversation every so often.

'It wasn't so much their way or the highway any more. It had become their way, or dead in a ditch.'

*

Of course Bomber wasn't the only patch Iain had talked to about crime and the clubs. Most famously he had interviewed Martin 'Damage' Robinson extensively in the period leading up to his still unsolved murder in jail. Iain even included an excerpt from the transcripts of his interviews in the resultant book, *Heavy Duty People*, in which Damage described his attitude towards being in the drugs business.

IP   What about the drugs?

MR   What about them? [Shrugs]

We sold whizz, coke, E, acid, basically anything that people wanted to buy and enjoy. We dealt in stuff that was fun and basically wouldn't kill them, so what's the problem?

IP   You made enough money out of it.

MR   Yeah we did. So what?

Just think, next time one of your mates has a snort at a party or your bird drops a tab at a club, someone's had to source it for you, someone like me.

This coke and shit doesn't smuggle itself in y'know? It takes a bit of good old entrepreneurial risk taking and effort on somebody's part so's you can get off your face.

There's demand, we take the risk and supply, and we get the rewards. Ain't that how it's supposed to work?

Anyway, big tobacco sells stuff that kills you and if you've got a pension I bet you own some of it.

[Laughs]

So who's got the problem to be guilty about now?

IP   OK, so you got me.

MR   Yeah. Bang to rights.

[Pause]

You know people like to think they're so clean. But really they're all dirty in some way or other. I suppose part of the difference is just that we don't try and pretend otherwise.

IP   So you're telling me you're just more honest about it?

MR   [Laughs] Yeah, I guess so. No bullshit from us.

Of course in addition to that segment, over the course of many days, and hours' worth of recordings Damage spoke quite frankly and at length about the issues around operating as a criminal.

But the extract Iain used was obviously only part of a much larger set of conversations in which Damage talked openly about many aspects of his life including his involvement in crime.

IP   But drug addicts cause crime…

MR   Oh don't give me that sanctimonious crap!

Alkies cause crime to feed their habits, and the government relies on tax from them to fund its spending.

Gambling addicts cause crime to feed theirs, and nobody blinks an eye when another betting shop opens on the high street, or is bothered when a casino starts up on some out of town business park, just so long as the tax man keeps on collecting his betting duty on every punt they make.

I sold Es, coke and acid to people who want to go out and have a good time, and I've never heard of a clubber mugging a granny to get the price of a tab. Have you?

IP   Well no…

*

MR   Respect. How old does your money and title have to be before it's respectable?

Normans, biggest bunch of thugs and sheep stealers, invaded and stole the whole fucking country at the end of a sword. Massacred, murdered, enslaved the whole people and parcelled it out amongst the warlords as their booty.

Here we are a thousand years later and their descendants are sitting in the House of Lords, still controlling whole swathes of the country in the estates they own and who are some of the richest families in the land. The Duke of Westminster. The Duke of Northumberland.

And it's not just them. I sold drugs and so I'm a criminal. But there's huge corporations like Jardine Matterson and where did they make their money to start with? Pushing frigging opium in

147

China that's where. We even went to war about it for fuck's sake.

The old trading and shipping businesses in Bristol and Liverpool. What paid to build all their fancy architecture? We'd call it people trafficking these days but back then it was old fashioned slave trading.

IP   And like you say, tobacco.

MR   Exactly, grown by those slaves back then, and just plain killing people today.

It doesn't matter where your money comes from. Stealing it, whatever. In this country you just have to hang onto it long enough until nobody seems to question it.

*

IP   Are you a criminal?

MR   Yes, I don't hide from that. I'm a criminal.

I don't live by society's laws, I break them and live by our own. That's what you're called when you do that.

IP   Are you a professional criminal?

MR   I make my living at it, yes, so that makes me a professional.

IP   So what is that like, how does it relate to being in the club?

MR   Being in the club has nothing to do with it. That's my life, my work, that's what pays the bills.

IP   But surely some of your club brothers are involved in your crimes with you.

MR   Yeah, well I'm not going to comment on that in detail, but what if they were?

If I'm doing a job and I need some help then I'm going to want to talk to guys I trust and by definition that's going to be other guys in the club. But that doesn't mean everyone in the club is involved in what I choose to do for a living. I won't have that hung around me, or the club. I made my choices a long time ago, fair enough. Yes, I've involved some of my brothers in what I've done, that was their choice, but fuck it, guilt by association, where does that end?

IP   So you're not organized crime…

MR   (Laughs) Fuck it, you've met us, you've been on runs, seen what we're like.

Do we look like organised criminals to you?

IP   Disorganised ones then?

MR   Chaotic more like.

I mean, if you wanted to be a major underworld figure, what would be the first thing you'd do? Go out and get a big patch to stick on your back?

IP   No…

MR   Well then.

Yes I am, I was, a criminal, I was in the business of crime. But don't fall into the trap of tarring the whole club with what some of us get up to.

IP   OK then, so tell me about this work of yours…

MR   You know what one of the problems is of bring a professional criminal?

IP   No?

MR   The dickheads you end up having to deal with.

You just wouldn't believe the bunch of rank amateurs, wannabees, cowboys and outright whackos acting it out large, you end up coming across when what you really want, really, really want, are some good quiet businessmen who just get on with it, do what they need to do and keep their mouths shut, don't act like arseholes, and stay under the radar.

The problem is, they're few and far between.

If you want to be professional you have to remember that it's a business and you have to run it like that.

And partly that means you find what works and you make sure

it works for you.

Violence is the thing. That's the only thing that makes my business different from any other business in the straight world. And if you're going to do violence then you need to do it right. You need an approach, a reliable language of escalation so everyone knows where they stand and understands the messages you are sending, and what the implications are of anything you are saying by what you're doing.

So, if someone is doing something you don't want them to, they get a warning. Just verbals, nothing physical mind you, not unless they go arsey or something, but then that's different isn't it? Answering back? You get what you give in my book. Give respect, get respect, give me lip or backchat, get yourself a pasting.

But a first shout wasn't about that. It was about sending a clear message. They get told direct, stop whatever it is or you're going to get hurt. What could be clearer than that? No one can complain after that can they? No one can say *I didn't know*. If you choose to carry on once I've told you to stop, well that's down to you sunshine, isn't it?

But I'll be fairer than that even. So if someone carried on doing what they weren't supposed to, interfering with my business, whatever it might be, then they'd get a second warning.

But this time it wasn't just verbals, it was physical, intimidation, a warning that we were serious people who weren't to be fucked about with. It could be a going over, it could be a knife in the ribs, it could be a sawn off shoved in their face. Whatever it was, whatever it took, the message had to be clear. This was their second warning and there wasn't going to be another.

And if they ignored that message, well what came next was on their head not mine. I'd given them their chance.

If you have a problem that won't get solved one way, well then you solve it another, permanently.

*

IP   So would you say you were a gangster?

MR   I'm a businessman, I'm not a gangster. I fucking hate people calling me that.

Gangsters are dumb thugs. Gangsters are people who want the notoriety, want to mouth it off about how hard they are. You'll see them out and about, dressed up, showing off and looking for opportunities to get pissed and wired and then cause trouble, get into fights and beat people up. And for what? Mostly it's all just to indulge an appetite for casual, senseless violence for the sake of it, and to big up their reputations in their local pub, or on their local estate as tough guys.

Gangsters are unpredictable nutcases, always looking for something or someone to give them an excuse to tee off on somebody. When there's a gangster around you can feel the tension in the air, worse if there's a couple of them as they'll egg each other on, be looking for excuses to set the other one off. *Do ya see that bloke, he's looking at your bird, what are you going to do about it?*

I mean, who fucking needs it? When I go out for an evening I go out to enjoy myself. Have a drink, spend time with my bird, all that sort of stuff.

Sure if something happens and it ends up in a ruck I'll participate, I'm no pussy, I'll keep my end up if something kicks off, but I don't go out looking for it, you know?

But gangsters will. They look for trouble.

I'm a businessman, sure sometimes in my world there's a bit of violence, I won't deny that, but it's not what I'm in it for. I'm about making money, not a reputation. That's the difference. I'm serious about the business, gangsters are serious about the show.

And if you're going to be in business then you need to be serious about all aspects of your business and that means taking the plod seriously as well.

Some of the guys have no respect for cops at all, and to be fair, there's a lot of cops who don't deserve it. Like always, it's a case of to expect respect you've got to give it and so when lots of cops treat our lads like shit, what do they expect to get back?

For me, I take 'em as individuals. There's some who are complete shits, some who are lazy bastards and some who'll fit you up without thinking about it. Do I respect any of them? No fucking way.

But there's others who are professionals, who do their job and if they treat me with respect as a bloke, then I can respect them back.

That's at a personal level.

But over and above that I'm talking about the need to take them seriously at a professional, business level and you have to treat them as your opposition, respect their capabilities.

Which means never making the mistake of thinking the blokes they have in the serious squads are dumb bunnies, they're not by any means. And there's lots of them. They've got the money, the tools, the backup, the science, the manpower, the intelligence, the touts, the bugs, the offers to turn guys facing time, so that when they come after you, you've got to recognise it's big boys' school.

Forget, ignore or convince yourself with wishful thinking that it ain't so and you and your crew are going to be facing some serious weight sooner or later.

They know who's who on the scene and to a reasonable degree, who in general does what, even if they don't know the details. So the question for them and you is, where are they going to put their time?

And thankfully, the answer to that is often about politics and bangs for their buck. The thing you have got going for you is the plod are hardly short of targets to have a pop at. So they are always going to have to make a judgement about where they want to deploy what they've got.

So, let's say there's a loud and obvious street gang that makes a lot of noise and local headlines. Perhaps they'll have a penchant for drive-bys or spraying their opposition's favourite café with a Mach 10. Well they'll make themselves a very public nuisance and public target that the cops will be under pressure to tackle, and it'll be one where the players are well known, and the associates and hangers on that could be lent on to get them are easy to spot.

Now, if at the same time you're running your business all nice and quietly, with no public snafus, fuck ups or serious incidents, where do you think the cops are going to put their resources?

The public menace that's easy to identify and go at, or the quiet tight knit firm that's operating out of sight where you know it's going to be a sod of a job to get into and could take years to get to the stage where you've got stuff to pin on guys? Put yourself in the plod's shoes, where you want results that play well with Joe Public, it's a no brainer right?

Now do you get why I don't like gangsters?

IP   OK, I see.

MR   But all that's by the by, mind you, if the plod do get a bee in their bonnets about you.

If they decide to home in on your crew, long job or not. Then while the heat is on, you've got a major problem.

The more they do, the better informed they are about your business, the luckier they get.

You can try and pull in your horns a bit if you can, depending on how much damage it might do to your business as others see an opportunity, and see if you can ride it out. Because again with the politics and bean counting, if they can't get a result then sooner or later the powers that be are going to start to question what they're getting for their overtime bill and all the rest of it. Budgets are tight all over, the plod's no different, and if you can keep it tight, sooner or later someone in management is going to start asking if the operation is really paying off, whether resources wouldn't be better placed somewhere else, particularly if there are some targets that need hitting to keep the Home Office or politicians sweet. And then unless you're facing someone who's got some real firepower and ability to defend their turf, the team will start to wind down. Officers will be reassigned, budgets for overtime and snouts will be cut, and the pressure and risk will start to ease.

But even then, you need to stay wary, stay on top of your game, stay tight.

Remember, you never know when a real operation against you is starting so you have to stay alert all the time.

And if you're relying on luck to stay outside, then you need to remember that to keep swanning around you need to stay lucky all the time.

To put you away, they just need to get lucky once.

IP   So how do you deal with something like that?

MR   It just means the first rule of business is to never, ever, under-estimate the cops.

Always, always, operate 24/7/365, on the basis that they're giving you a good look over and that way you'll always be making sure you never give them anything to see.

'But other than getting his reminiscences about getting involved with the club and stories about how great the parties were, you weren't actually getting anything of substance out of Bomber?' we asked.

'That's about the size of it,' he admitted. 'Having had no change out of Stu we thought we'd have another crack at Bomber just in case. So DS Timms started in on him again, although from the expression on Bomber's face I could see he was wasting his time.

'So if you're clean then, Bomber, let's talk about Aberdeen shall we?'

'But then the club brief turned up to see the both of them, and that was that as far as saying anything was concerned.

'It was just a matter of waiting for the PACE clock to tick out and then we had to let the both of them go.'

*

'We watched from an upstairs window as Stu and Bomber walked down the steps at the front of the building.

'We were too far away to hear what was being said but it was obvious that Bomber was trying to talk to Stu, without much success. You could see it from the body language.

'Even as Bomber's stance turned from talking to appeal, the message back was coming over loud and clear as Stu turned his back on Bomber and slid into a waiting car leaving Bomber standing on the pavement. *Not here. Not now. Not with you.*

'"Well when trust goes, it goes," Timms muttered to himself beside me, sounding satisfied at this sight. And I guess he was right.'

CHAPTER 6   BIG BOYS' RULES

So long as large sums of money are involved – and they are bound to be if drugs are illegal – it is literally impossible to stop the traffic, or even to make a serious reduction in its scope.

Milton Friedman, Nobel Prize winning economist

'So where did you go from there?' we asked DI Chambers.

'Well, it was time to report back up the line,' he told us.

*

Because of the importance of the initial arrests and our interviews on the Operation Derby strategy, the next scheduled taskforce meeting had been brought forward to the following week so as to be able to have us deliver our report.

I let DS Timms lead. It seemed like he wanted to talk so he gave the edited highlights of our interviews' progress, or lack thereof, before everyone assembled wanted to dissect the nuts and bolts of it. We distributed copies of the transcripts to give everyone some bedtime reading and we heard back from what the other teams had been up to.

So far, so normal.

The first surprising bit of news came out of the blue just after DS Timms had finished speaking. It was a tip off from one of Strathclyde Police's well placed touts which if it was right, seemed as though it was set to turn the world upside down, or at least our tiny section of it.

Because the word in the clubhouse apparently was that the club was putting it about that Stu's status had been changed.

For all his *I've got the retired tat* bragging in our interview, it sounded as though his next trip to the inkman was going to need to be to get them all covered up as the club was taking the astonishing step of casting him out into the biker equivalent of outer darkness.

It was no longer *Retired*.

It was now *Out in bad standing*.

And in the world he lived in, the difference was huge.

'So why have they decided he's *persona non grata*?' a voice asked from down the table.

Out in bad standing was a serious step, it's about as serious as it gets in the outlaw world before you get on to just dead in a ditch. As someone out in bad standings Stu would not only formally be barred from having any relations with any member of the club, but in practice he'd be shunned by most members of the rest of the biker world, whether linked to the club or not.

And for a man whose business apparently relied on his current and ex biker contacts that could be a killer blow.

'You're going to love this,' declared Strathclyde Police.

'Oh yes?'

'It says here,' he said, gesturing to the piece of paper in his hand, before peering back down at it to find the section he'd marked in yellow highlighter, 'it's for bringing the club into disrepute…'

When he wanted to continue he had to raise his voice to be heard over the tide of laughter and astonishment that had spontaneously rolled around the room, '…through criminal activity…' which redoubled the noise, '…and involvement in drugs.'

He waited, looking at the Chairman, who eventually called the meeting back to order as the mirth and sarcastic commentary died away, before he resumed, referring to the report in front of him.

'Our source says that the official announcement is going to be made tomorrow but a special meeting of club officers was held yesterday to ratify the decision. The club is going to be saying it's been done as part of the club cleaning up its act and modernizing its approach. They're going to be putting it out that it's got to be a club where everybody works…'

'We've heard that one before,' someone muttered away to my right, receiving a murmur of assent from others around the table.

'Meth use or dealing are going to be made patch pulling offences,'

Strathclyde Police was saying, 'and it's ending up with something about making sure that people won't be able to hide behind a club patch to commit crimes and cause trouble for their brothers,' he concluded.

'It that it?' the Chairman asked.

'That's the bones of it.'

'And this source, how reliable is it?' someone asked.

'Reliable enough, I understand.'

'Well, thank you for that,' said the Chairman, and Strathclyde Police nodded in acknowledgement before the Chairman threw the discussion open to the room.

'So then, gentlemen, what do we make of this development?'

It provoked a fierce debate I have to say, and for all the obvious reasons given who Stu was, and what he had been.

'I just don't buy it that he's out in bad standing,' Surrey was saying, 'It's not like he's just some low level muscle. This is someone who knows where the bodies are buried...'

'Literally,' added the senior Met man grimly.

'Quite,' Surrey said, acknowledging the interjection with a smile, 'he was one of their top guys for years. He was critical in growing them and their operations to get to where they are today. If nothing else, the stuff he must have in his head, you'd think it was worth a fortune to anyone who wanted to go up against them. And given how ruthless he was while he was at the Top Table, you know he'd have no compunction in doing whatever he decided he wanted to.'

'And he'd be a risk to the guys still there if he decided to cut a deal in the light of this and spill his guts,' agreed the Met.

'So why do something like that, so publicly?' someone objected.

'Or they know something else about him?' suggested another from further down the table.

'Yeah, you'd think they'd arrange something else if they wanted him out,' observed Timms' boss.

'A shiv in the showers you mean?'

'Well it happened to your bloke Damage, didn't it?' Timms said, looking at me.

'Yes, you're right.'

'But then if it was real...' Greater Manchester Police started to speculate.

'If?' Surrey objected.

'Yes I know it's a big if,' GMP conceded, 'but let's think it through for a moment shall we, to see where it goes? If what Strathclyde here has just told us is really what they want to do, then just having Stu topped wouldn't get them what they want would it? The point is they want to make the statement, they want this to be a press thing, the message that the club is cleaning up its act, it's expelling the crooks. That's the publicity they want and they're not going to get that if he's just snuffed are they?'

'Just the opposite really.'

'Yeah, *we've murdered him because we're cleaning up our act*, it doesn't really fly does it?'

'No, but that doesn't get away from the question, is it really what they want to do?'

'What, the club cleaning up its act? Don't make me laugh!'

'So it's all just cover then you think? Or is there more to it?' intervened the Chairman.

'It could be. What if it's just to make a show of expelling him – because he's on the outside now and because he's out, he's no more use to the current guys?'

'Just 'cos he's not wearing a patch any more doesn't mean he's necessarily stopped working with them. These are blokes he's been dealing with for years remember. Why would he stop, patch or no patch?'

'So why do this to him then?' Surrey challenged, 'bit of an odd way to treat someone if you do want to keep working with him?'

'It could it be a case of sorting a few birds with one stone possibly?' GMP suggested. 'It's all very well talking about the guys he's known for years but things change don't they? They're not the Rebels any more for one thing, they've merged, so what's come out of that? Then there's the guys coming up through the ranks, the next generation all eager and ambitious and looking for their shot. How loyal are they going to be to a retired bloke like Stu? He's an old timer as far as some of them're concerned isn't he?'

'Time to put him out to grass you reckon?'

'Time to get him out of the way more like,' muttered Timms beside me.

'So you think this might just be someone taking out an older rival so he can't come back...?'

'And as he's out it also undermines any remaining powerbase or relationships he had within the club? I see what you mean,' the Chairman mused, considering the implications. 'While at the same time the new boys can be pinning the blame for crime on him and his ilk while they present a shiny new image that gives the new team cover? Yes I could see that as a plan.'

'Unless it's actually a scheme to help him?' suggested Strathclyde.

'A ploy you mean?' asked the Chairman, switching his gaze to him, unused even now to having Strathclyde volunteer any information without the judicious use of sodium pentothal. 'So how would that work?'

'Well it's obvious that we're looking to put him away big time isn't it?' Strathclyde asked, and looked around the room to see a few nods.

'We've taken apart all Stu's shipments we could find over the last few months and then we picked him up more or less the moment we could once he was back over here, so they all know the microscope is on him. And with two dead ex-officers now in the frame, we aren't going to be stopping anytime soon are we? They know as well as we do that once we've got blood in the game, even retired and even – yes I know you're all thinking it – possibly dirty blood, then we're going to stick with it until we've nailed the bastards who did it, right?'

There were more nods and a murmur of agreement as the table waited to see where Strathclyde was going with this, while beside me I could almost feel the intensity with which Timms was staring at him.

'And, given the taped calls we had, and which Timms played to him, it'll be pretty clear that we've got our eyes on Stu for ordering it and Bomber for making the arrangements, agreed?'

'So what's your point?' the Chairman asked, moving him towards a conclusion.

'Well there's two ways to read it, I'd say,' Strathclyde summarized, 'the first is that the club has decided he's becoming too hot, so they really are cutting him loose to fend for himself...'

'They're worried what he might bring down on them?' the Chairman asked on behalf of the group.

'Well if he and Bomber are linked to the murder of two retired police officers from my force then they should be shouldn't they? The last thing the club wants is Stu and Bomber traipsing that mess back to the doors of the clubhouse.'

'And the other way?'

'This is where I think it might, just possibly, be to help him,' Strathclyde paused, as if gathering his thoughts on how to present what he wanted to say. 'Look I know it's a stretch, but if they say they've chucked him out, then as someone publicly in bad standings we obviously wouldn't think he's actively connected any more, would we? After all, we all know what it means, right? We all know how dangerous it would be for him if he ever crosses their path again?'

What was Strathclyde up to? I wondered. He was getting at something, that much was obvious, but for the life of me I couldn't see what his angle was, other than trying it seemed to keep Stu firmly in the frame.

'If it's real...?'

'If it's real.'

'So you think their plan is to throw us off the scent?' the Chairman was reflecting on what Strathclyde had been suggesting, 'To lead us to think he's now exiled with no connections back into the club...?'

'Which is the major taskforce target here, let's not forget,' Strathclyde emphasized, 'not Stu as an individual, certainly not Bomber, and these two retired officers aren't even our case...'

'Officially,' the Chairman nodded.

'Officially,' Strathclyde agreed, 'Or jurisdiction either. They're the *Policia Naçional*'s jobs aren't they? And as far as I'm aware they've not asked for our assistance, have they?'

Which was odd, I thought. Given they were from his force, why was Strathclyde trying to distance us from the two killings? Was it because they were dirty and he didn't want their muck, whatever it was, tainting him? Or was there more to it than that? Oh well, I decided, not my problem.

'So you're suggesting they want us to lose focus on him as we concentrate on the club, which allows him to slip under the radar?' concluded the Chairman, 'Hmmm, an interesting idea that.'

'But anyway,' Surrey interrupted, seemingly impatient with all this speculation, 'whatever's going on, the reality is at the moment we've got nothing on either of them. That's why we had to let the buggers go last week.'

'How did he describe himself again?' asked the Chairman looking across at me.

'Who, Stu?' I checked, 'Retired, as of the turn of the year.'

'Oh bollocks,' the senior Met man couldn't contain himself any longer, 'I just don't buy that at all. Even if he wanted to be, could he really retire? In that world? Really? Look to step out and away from the club and the rest of the crims? Oh come on, you have to ask, are they actually going to let that happen? Let him just wander off into the sunset with what he must know? The dirt he must have on people? All locked away in his head?'

'You know what they say, boss,' DS Timms chipped in, backing him

162

up.

'Exactly!' and the senior Met man glared around the room darkly as if challenging anyone to pick a fight with him on it.

But each for our own reasons, no one took him up on it.

As the discussion went on around the room I found my attention drifting.

I was more interested in the mechanics of the Top Table as we had been fitting the pieces together from our various sources than debating how many angels could dance on the head of the *what the club might be planning* pin.

At least I had that much in common with the senior Met guy, even if nothing else.

There was no doubt about it, the Top Table thing was clever, really clever, and not just because of the way it was intended to protect the guys at the top from being implicated in any of the day to day stuff.

But at the same time, it had its weaknesses. In reality, there's always a limit to how far you can make that work in practice.

When you're talking about serious money and serious jobs that needed doing, there was only so far down the chain you would want to push some of that shit.

I mean, you're not going to want to give some low life that you only know through a mate of a patch the job of picking up your key chemicals are you? Once they know where the stuff comes from, who you're getting it from, then that's valuable information. Something to trade, either with us if they're busted, or just out on the open market, that's if they don't just decide they want to start up for themselves.

It'd be like handing out the keys to the castle, and you wouldn't want that, now would you?

So even when they're trying to stay clean, you sometimes still get the big fish getting involved in some of the key nitty gritty. The really sensitive bits, the ones they feel they really need to keep control of, like arranging a chemical pick up, that sort of stuff.

Sure you can compartmentalise, that's one of the things Damage had been good at, but even so, once someone's inside the circle, even if out on the edges, you never know how many parts of the picture they are going to start to pick up. A word here, a joke there, hanging round the bar one night and seeing Tom or Dick or Harry come in. Putting two and two together, working out how the jigsaw fits. It's always a risk, you know?

So there's some stuff that however much you want to push it out, you need to keep it inside and have it done in house. You just can't help it.

And if you're doing that, well there's only so many blokes in the inner circle. So however much of a kingpin or untouchable you think you are, chances are you will have had to get your hands dirty more often than you might like, and be closer to the action with fewer cut-outs than might be ideal from an insulation point of view.

And of course, the insulation thing is all very well but you also have to remember where some of these guys have come from and how they've got to where they are. If they've been dealing they've got used to operating at that sort of thing and some of them seem to find making a switch from doing to just directing more difficult than you'd think. It's like it's just a business decision. They've been used to being hands on so sometimes they just can't help but keep at it. I don't know, perhaps their experience of moving up through the ranks, the status they build for themselves, the reputation they accrue, perhaps it starts to make them think they can get away with anything.

So that's when you find senior guys being caught doing really petty shit. Why the hell would a senior officer like Stu have let themselves end up getting tugged on a crappy little street level burn for a few quid?

Guess you can take the guy out of the street but you can't take the street out of the guy.

Anyway, I digress. Like I was saying, the Top Table idea was clever for another reason which I suppose does link back to what I was saying about the guys they could trust to execute things that needed doing.

Because as a senior guy to be successful in the drugs trade, or any other criminal business, you need to have a capable and ruthless crew to do the necessary whenever required, which meant a group of individuals with, let's just say, limited moral scruples or reluctance to use violence when it comes to getting what they want.

But as a boss that gives you a problem, doesn't it? Because if you're heading up that sort of team, sooner or later someone's going to get ambitious, or greedy, or both, and the job they are going to want is yours isn't it?

And the problem with that is, as we've discussed, the better they are to have working for you in your business, the bigger the threat they are when they decide to turn on you.

But with the Top Table idea, suddenly the whole dynamic's changed, because the Top Table's not a single post. There's no fixed number of players and it's not a one in, one out kind of deal. So, if you are good enough and play your cards right there's no reason why you can't expect in due course to have a chance of joining your boss at the table instead of having to replace him.

Better still from the boss's point of view, you would let it be well known that the rest of the members of the Top Table would take a very dim view of anyone who tried the traditional promotion route of creating a vacancy with a dose of lead poisoning. For their own protection and standing they would make sure that wouldn't work. So the group of bosses at the Top Table became a sort of mutual insurance society.

Which the more I thought about it, made the idea of them chucking out a player like Stu all the odder, and which brought me right back to the debate that was winding up around me on that very subject.

As I turned my attention back to the discussion, beside me DS Timms was responding to some comment saying with a heated, 'Don't forget, this is a bloke who took out two cops...'

'Except we don't know that for sure,' came the protest from the

165

other end of the table.

'Oh come on!'

And so it went on.

The consensus seemed to be that the plan to sow dissent was working.

The SOCA representative was reporting on the telephone monitoring that was in place.

'He's been trying to make contact, you know.'

'Who?' I asked.

'Bomber, he's been trying to call Stu on and off for days now.'

'And?'

'Nothing doing,' the SOCA man shrugged apologetically for not having more to bring to the party, 'Stu's not picking up on him at all.'

But this lack of actionable evidence wasn't a disappointment to everybody around the table. Beside me I saw DS Timms rubbing his hands together in satisfaction and I caught his whispered comment to his boss sitting on the other side of him, 'Looks like the poison's starting to work doesn't it?'

Until eventually later that afternoon someone around the table finally asked the question, and put the concern that had been coalescing in my mind for the last few days into words.

'So what if he just ups and offs Bomber?' the Devon and Cornwall DI asked from down on my left. 'We all know what they're capable of, so it's got to be a risk hasn't it?'

At last it was out there.

*

'And what was said about that?' we asked.

'Well you've got to remember the context,' DI Chambers told us, 'this is a group of blokes, experienced officers. We all know the score, how the game is played, what the rules are and where the boundaries lie. But at the same time we're like any team. There's a degree of banter, bravado, people saying what would be the unsayable in a more public environment, so it's not like some of what was said would be meant to be taken seriously.'

'So what was said?' we insisted, 'surely people had views?'

'Well, someone said, and I can't remember who it was, "What if he does? If it gives us a chance to get him, that's great. And if not, well it's just one less of the buggers out on the street."'

'And no one objected to this?' we asked in a shocked tone.

'No, far from it, like I said, it was said in jest, everybody knew that was something we could never countenance, so it was treated as a bit of a joke, with others joining in.

'Yeah, could be two birds with one stone. One down and the other to blame? It could even get them fighting amongst themselves.

'Sounds like a win-win to me. Less bad guys, less trust, more overtime. Really, what's not to like?

'This wasn't serious stuff you have to understand. I was there at the time and as far as I was concerned nobody in the room meant it, it was just professionals kidding around.'

'Except that from what you've told us so far, there seemed to be more to it than that wasn't there?'

'Well I wasn't to know that at the time, was I?'

'Like I said, to start with it was all a bit of a joke, but then when first DS Timms and then his boss chimed in, the tone subtly changed.'

'Changed, how?'

'It was difficult to put my finger on it at first, but it felt as though some of the guys in the room were more serious about it than they were letting on. At first I thought it was just me, you know how you over-read something, think that something is going on for no particular reason.'

'So what was different?'

'That's just it, nothing really, not in what was being said, it was more the way it was being talked about. Oh sure, it was all still a bit of a joke, but to me there was now a definite undertone, as though people were saying things as a joke just to be able to test how others would react, to see who else in the room might be thinking what they're thinking. But because it was all just a laugh, and because most of the people in the room had joined in at one stage or another, it was one of those things that you could never call them out on. Just there, just then, with what had gone before, it was out in plain sight but completely deniable at the same time. *What are you talking about mate? It was just a piece of fun? Everybody was talking about it, I was just joining in like everyone else, having a laugh, you know, what's your problem with me?'*

'And the trouble was, it was just a feeling. I couldn't be sure.'

'You thought you could be putting two and two together and getting five?'

'Possibly. What was particularly worrying me was the suggestion in what DS Timms was saying that Bomber was in danger. There seemed to be a general presumption around the room that he had arranged the killings in Mallorca. Worse, there was an almost palpable undercurrent of feeling from DS Timms and those who sympathized with his view that this almost made him fair game.'

*

'Why do you think he could be in danger?' Greater Manchester Police was asking.

'It's the need to tidy up loose ends, right?' said Timms. 'Know what I mean? Stu's very security conscious, has to be to have stuck it out at the top that long hasn't he?'

'Kill the killer?' suggested GMP.

'Yeah well, hey, once we've got his testimony...'

'If you get his testimony,' I cut in, objecting.

'We will...' Timms said smugly.

I locked eyes with Timms but he just returned my gaze with a nonchalant sneer. God, I could see why everyone hated the Met so much.

'You seem very sure. Do you know something the rest of us don't?'

I asked.

'No, I can just join the dots can't I?' he replied.

'Meaning?'

'Meaning that just as soon as Bomber gets the message Stu is turning on him, then he'll turn to us. That was the plan wasn't it? Or part of it at least. Where else is he going to go?'

Timms looked around the table to see how this line of argument was going down, before turning back to face me brazenly.

'And then, if he's not around to be cross examined on it,' he said with deliberate casualness, 'well so long as we can still use it, it's hardly a loss really is it?'

'More a win I'd say,' his boss muttered.

'Quite,' came a distinctly Scottish voice from down the table.

'You know what they say themselves, Sir,' and there were a whole host of meanings behind the challenging tone of that 'Sir', Timms said quietly to me as he harped back to his earlier comment, 'three can keep a secret if two of them are dead.'

*

I wasn't the only one who'd noticed the undercurrents either.

The Chairman had obviously started to get uncomfortable with the turn the conversation had taken and pulled us all up sharply with, 'Gentlemen, let's all just remember what our duties are, shall we? A bit of banter is all very well amongst professionals but I'm sure we all recall the oaths of office we've sworn to cause the Queen's peace to be kept and preserved and prevent offences against people and property, don't we?'

DS Timms just grinned at me but he did shut his mouth. Whether it was because he felt the joke had gone far enough or whether he'd realised how what he was saying was going down, I just didn't know.

But then the Chairman was continuing to reassert order before it got completely out of hand and looked to move us onto a new topic with, 'Gentlemen, gentlemen, please...'

And all the while as I watched casually out of the corner of my eye, DS Timms, his boss, and Strathclyde Police exchanged glances between them that said clear as daylight, *To be continued.*

*

The Chairman could see it had been a long afternoon, people were getting tired and tempers were fraying so he decided to begin to wrap it up as he called things to order on our discussion about Bomber and the next steps in the campaign.

'So that's agreed then, is it?' he asked rhetorically, while everyone else in the room let out a mental sigh at the thought of that first cold beer of the evening waiting just down the hallway, 'We're going to arrange to re-arrest Mr Harris at the earliest available opportunity next week to maintain the pressure?'

'On what basis?' I murmured, but didn't actually ask properly out loud. This close to beer o'clock no one was going to thank me for sticking my oar in like that, or for starting to raise questions of reasonable grounds, PACE, harassment, or an interference with the Right to Liberty and Security under Article 5 of the European Convention on Human Rights as set out in Part I of Schedule 1 to the Human Rights Act 1998...

'Oh, I'll think of something, don't you worry about that, Sir,' muttered DS Timms again in a voice just one stop short of insubordination directed at me but just too low for the Chairman, who was summing up, to catch and I shot him a poisonous *drop dead* glare in return.

And with that we broke for the evening and there was a general dignified stampede for the bar.

By nine or so we were all feeling much more relaxed. Amazing what a decent bite and as many pints as you want can do in that department. Most of the blokes had been drinking steadily all evening, before, during, and now after visiting the restaurant, and they were settling in for a long session. That was one of the good things about the bar here in the police college residential training centre we were using for our meetings, there was no such thing as closing time, not until the last diehard drinker had called it a night, or more accurately, a morning.

But even having been at it all day, some of them were still going, chewing away at Stu and Bomber like dogs with a favourite bone. And the more pissed some of them got, the looser the talk became.

'I don't get it. What has Stu got over Bomber? Why's he staying so loyal?'

'Because he is and because they've got history. You've heard the tapes we've got of the interviews. The two of them go way back, right to the start. They even had that bird in common.'

DS Timms was in the thick of it I noticed, working the room.

'Seems to me it was a bit of a deal,' he was saying, 'Stu said to Bomber I'll give you your world, you can have what you want in it, including the girl, or whoever else he wanted, but only if Bomber and his whole world then belonged to Stu. Seem about right?'

'Maybe,' someone agreed.

By half ten, eleven or so, we'd all been putting it away steadily and I don't know what your mob's like but when it's just you as a bunch of coppers letting off steam together, politically correct doesn't enter into it.

'Of course his wife divorced him, well it was always on the cards wasn't it?'

'I thought she just disappeared?' someone objected.

'No, that was his first bird, he never married her.'

'Oh well, you know what they say,' the senior Met man observed coolly, 'it's just like a game of cards. You start off with two hearts and a diamond, but by the end it's more about a wanting a club and some spades.'

'Christ, you're a cynic, sir,' DS Timms was laughing at his boss's wit and wisdom, 'you know that?'

And I'd wondered where he got it from, I thought to myself.

And by midnight some of the blokes were getting rat-arsed.

By this stage those in the bar had broken up into little groups. There was a small brown-nosing cluster laughing at the Chairman's jokes as you never knew where and when having a line into an ambitious and upwardly mobile Assistant Chief Constable could come in handy, or even where they might turn up in years to come, but that wasn't for me. No, there was no doubt about which group I was interested in.

The two Met officers were ensconced around a table on the far side of the room. They were deep in conversation with Strathclyde, while the Surrey bloke who was with them seemed much the worse for wear by now. In fact, it looked for all the world as though the Met boys had parked him on the seat between them so they could keep an eye on him.

So, picking up off the bar what was left of my pint, I wandered over.

'Mind if I join you?' I asked, as the conversation broke off and they looked up at my approach.

DS Timms' expression told me his answer to that clear as day, but his boss and Strathclyde were made of more diplomatic stuff and made the appropriate noises as I pulled a spare chair up to the table.

There was one thing I wanted to understand. I wanted to dig out what they really thought about the impact of our tactics of spreading mistrust between Bomber and Stu as a way in, and what they thought about the risks.

'What were you talking about back then in the room?' I asked DS Timms. 'The plan is to push Bomber to try and turn him to put pressure on Stu, right?'

DS Timms glanced across to both his boss and Strathclyde for a clue as to how to handle this but they were both blank faced. *You made this mess by running off at the mouth back in the room* seemed to be the message, *don't come looking to us to sort it out for you.*

'Sure it is,' he said, 'but if that doesn't work, then there's always Plan B.'

What the hell was Plan B when it was at home, I wondered? Only one way to find out I decided.

'Which is?'

DS Timms seemed to have decided this was case of in for a penny, in for a pound and I suppose I could see his rationale. After all, if I ever decided I wanted to make something of it, here we were at just gone midnight after an evening's boozing and he'd have his boss and another senior officer from another force as witnesses to dispute my version of events.

'Break Stu's trust in Bomber to send him over to us,' he said, with a trace of sulk in his voice.

'So that's why you were so keen to fill Stu in about what Bomber had told us?' I wanted to know.

'Sure, that's right,' he shrugged in acknowledgement, 'I just wanted to get Stu convinced Bomber was talking. Come on, you know that's how the game works. Get them thinking they're ratting on each other. First one to rat properly wins remember?'

'Yeah I know,' I nodded to keep him talking, 'it's just…'

'Just what?' he asked.

'Well you know, it's a dangerous game that…'

'For who? Bomber?' he wanted to know.

'Yes. Like they said back in there, Stu could end up coming after him.'

'Yeah, like any of us care,' DS Timms shrugged.

'S'right… why shud we givva shit?' Surrey slurred.

The senior Met man rolled his eyes and looked as though he was doing a good job of mentally counting to twenty.

'Another round?' I suggested, lifting my glass and nodding my offer to go to the bar, 'Same again?'

'Go on then,' Strathclyde said, and after a moment's hesitation the two Met guys followed suit. Surrey didn't seem to have noticed which was just as well as he'd obviously had a skinfull.

I'd offered to go because I needed a moment to think. To try and sort out in my own mind what I was hearing here.

So what was going on here? I tried to work it out.

As far as I could make out this was some game plan by the two Met officers who had used the afternoon to suss they might have a commonality of interest with Strathclyde as well as the now sozzelled Surrey and were now what? In negotiation? Was that it? Stitching up some deal?

No one had made an explicitly stated decision to put Bomber's life in danger, but that was definitely the implication of how it seemed to be being steered. It seemed careless at best, and at worst? A deliberate conspiracy?

It was all unsaid, but it was all there, wasn't it?

Using this sort of disinformation, running a disruption operation was legitimate as far as I was concerned. But it was about when it went beyond that. When it crossed over a line and in my mind if I was right, that line was now way behind us and fading fast in the rear view mirror.

The problem was, was I right?

Was I just getting paranoid?

And what would I do about it anyway? Take it up the line? With what I had? It wouldn't work even if I ever saw myself doing it, which I couldn't.

Warn Bomber?

And it wasn't as though he was any angel anyway.

I couldn't prove it but as far as we could tell, whether or not he'd been involved in the death of these coppers, he'd have been responsible for some bones of his own over the years, I was sure of that.

Besides which, even if I was convinced, I thought, as I glanced at the blokes fawning over the ACC, what was I really contemplating doing here? Snitching internally? Grassing up some other officers? On what, some suspicion, loose talk, bar room chat? Even if I thought I had enough, which was far from the case, I knew I just couldn't do that. No bloody way.

I got the drinks on a tray and headed back to the table.

The senior Met officer had obviously decided that the Surrey DI and *in vino veritas* weren't really what was required here so I saw him gesturing urgently to DS Timms. Even from across the room the message was evident, the Surrey DI had to go.

'Think it's about time our friend here got off for the night, don't you?'

DS Timms knew how to take the hint, 'Fair enough boss…'

As I got back to the table DS Timms was getting the slightly bemused Surrey DI to his feet with a 'Time for bed, big fella…'

'Here,' I insisted, setting the tray of glasses down on the table, 'I'll give you a hand with him.'

DS Timms tried to shake me off, protesting he could manage, but as I was standing just the other side of where the Surrey DI was swaying and in danger of falling at any minute, it was difficult for him to do so and I caught the Surrey DI under the arm as he suddenly staggered sideways towards me.

'OK, OK,' I said, as I took his weight, 'I've got him this side, come on, you're right, let's get him to his room. With the two of us it won't take long. You got his key?'

There was a muttered 'Yes,' from the other side of the body slowly rocking back and forth between us, and we were off, lurching across the room towards the door as DS Timms decided that if I was coming, I was coming, so the only option was to get on with it and get Surrey ensconced in his own room as quickly as possible.

And so we were off, with me content to take my time and continue some innocent conversation with the Surrey DI, and DS Timms trying to hurry us along and shut the pair of us up.

Surrey was slurring but emphatic. 'OK, they think therr untuchabullls, but 'ats all juss bollocks. 's far as I'm concerned after dead cops, they're juss fair game. You start on cops and it's a big boys' game. You know that and they know that… am I right?'

'Come on now, sir,' hissed DS Timms, desperately fumbling in his pocket for the plastic card, 'let's not say anything we'll regret in the morning, shall we?'

But Surrey was having none of it. He was rolling now with righteous drunken indignation, 'We've gotta make a stand or where'z it gonna end? You tell me that? Hit a cop that's Red One, gotta hit back or all scumbags'll think they c'n walk all over uss, simple as...'

'So what're you saying?' I asked him, as we finally arrived outside the door to his room, 'You wish the buggers would take each other out, is that it?'

He turned and looked at me with one of those grins a drunk gives you when he thinks he's being clever, holding up an unsteady finger and wagging it in the air to emphasise his point.

'Now thash un idea isn't it?' He swayed cheerfully, before DS Timms slipped his key card through the reader and with a push on the handle his door clicked open and Timms bundled him inside, slamming the door in my face behind him.

I stared at the blank door for a moment, wondering what to do next, and then I turned away.

*

'So what was Plan B?' we wanted to check.

'We'd picked on Bomber as our way in. Plan B took this a step further and put him in play.'

'Which meant what in practice?'

'OK, let's roll back a moment.'

'The basic plan had always been to pick up Bomber and Stu and see if by putting pressure in Bomber we could get anything on Stu, right?'

'OK.'

'So Plan B was in theory just taking this a bit further and using it to sow mistrust between the gang members we were investigating to see if that would give us a means to get in. Effectively it meant suggesting to Stu that Bomber was co-operating with us as a witness.'

'So it was to just stir the shit and see what came out of it?'

176

'On the surface, yes, you could put it like that.'

'But you can't do that surely?'

'Oh couldn't they just? You haven't heard anything yet.'

'You said "in theory". What did you mean by that?'

'Plan B was a legitimate tactic, but the real Plan B was that DS Timms and his mob were looking to take it further. One of the risks of stirring the shit, as you so delicately put it, is that with a mob like this it can easily lead to violence, we all knew it. None of us were naïve, but as far as I was concerned it was just one of the factors we had to manage so nothing got out of hand. No one wanted bodies all over the shop as a result of anything we'd done, or at least that's what I'd always thought.'

'But now you were having your doubts weren't you?'

'It wasn't just doubts. By now I was pretty bloody sure bodies were exactly what DS Timms and his crew were after.

'If he couldn't nail Stu for killing the two ex-cops, setting up Bomber as a target for him to knock off was the next best thing as far as DS Timms was concerned if it gave us a chance to catch him on it.

'And even if we still couldn't stick that on Stu, it was just one less problem on the street as DS Timms saw it, so he didn't really care either way.'

'Jesus, you can't be serious?'

'Deadly, to coin a phrase. And like I said, there's worse. Much worse.'

'What's worse?'

'Plan C.'

*

As I walked back down the corridor away from Surrey's room I was wondering what to do.

I needed a smoke before I called it a night, so pushing through one of the doors off the residential wing corridor, I headed out into the dark and walked along the bush lined path round the side of the building towards the patio outside the bar.

As I turned the corner, against the light of the windows I saw the two of them standing, silhouetted as in turn each cupped their hands around the sudden bright yellow flame of a lighter.

'...asset? Don't make me laugh. Liability you mean, has been for years...'

There was a grunt of agreement. 'Memoires my arse. That's just straight blackmail. What the hell d'you think he wants, for fuck's sake?'

'God knows. But whatever it is, no one wants it or can risk it.'

I stopped stock still and held my breath, hidden from their sight by the blackness on the edge of the area, the bushes, and their night blindness from the flame.

As I strained my ears to listen to their still careful conversation I could see why they'd decided to take it outside.

'So how do you think it's going?'

'What did your lad call it? Plan B?'

'Yeah, he's keen that one. Will go far...'

'Only if he learns to keep his mouth shut.'

'Fair point.'

'So you're happy with how it's going?'

'Well as everybody can see there's two dead cops on the table.'

'Fair enough. Big boys' rules and all that.'

'Fine, but what are we going to do?'

'Well I've been thinking about that. And as far as I can see it's just a matter of pushing Plan B to its logical conclusion, isn't it?'

'Plan B? You think it's going to go that far?'

'So it's an eye for an eye?'

'As I keep saying. Big boys' rules, laddie. Big boys' rules.'

Which to me, listening in the darkness, confirmed it. DS Timms' so-called Plan B was actually a deliberate attempt to set Bomber up.

They were looking to either give Stu a reason, or give him a motive with which to fit him up if someone else did it.

But as I listened there was more. Much more. This wasn't just an operation that was on the tracks. This was something that was completely off piste.

'What if he doesn't play ball?'

'Well then, we might just have to set it up for him ourselves.'

'You mean?'

'Plan B might have to become Plan C. If he doesn't do it, then we do it. Those two guys are still out there if we wanted them again you know. And they can do one or both, just depends what we want. I'm thinking both would be better?'

'OK, let's wait and see about that as an option, shall we?'

'Sure, but let's just remember, if all else fails, it is an option.'

'OK.'

'And on that subject, your boys' logs?'

'All burnt. We had quite a bonfire. You don't have to worry about that.'

'I do worry.'

'If you think my bosses want any evidence left lying around, you're off your rocker. No, it's all had to be completely clean all the way ever since the big lads found out which way was up.'

'Good.'

'No one will ever be able to trace this stuff. Don't worry about it.'

'And you're not worried about anything he might have squirreled away?'

'We've thought about it, yes, but with him gone and not around to talk to anyone about it what would there be really? Some papers and wild allegations by a dead crook? That's why I'm thinking both. It's the safest way all round.'

'For you maybe...'

'Well let's not forget where he came from, shall we?'

'OK, OK, point taken.'

Hidden in the darkness I was having difficulty taking in what I'd just heard.

Plan C was a death squad.

Two professional hit men.

A death squad that had already been used for some reason to take out the two ex officers in Spain.

Where the debate was not only whether to use them but also how many targets to give them, just Bomber, or him and Stu.

So my immediate problem was who the hell could I trust?

These were senior officers, working together on their own agenda across a range of forces.

I didn't know why Strathclyde and the Met would be working together on this. That was unusual enough, everybody hated the Met after all. But here there was some screw up they, and presumably Surrey, had a mutual interest in putting the lid on, that much was clear. But what that might be I had no idea.

And that was when I realised the truth.

We had our own Top Table.

And I wasn't on it.

*

'So what did you understand them to mean by big boys' rules?' we asked.

'Big Boys' Rules was one of those expressions which had come into use in some policing circles. It's origins were in Northern Ireland and the military, specifically the SAS who'd been operating there against the Provos but it had spread first to some of the let's just say more aggressive policing units deployed over there and then here across the water.'

'And what does it mean?'

'It was a sort of shorthand about the way the SAS described their attitude to using guns. As soldiers, they maintained that when it came to weapons they were trained to shoot to kill, that's what getting involved with guns was about in their view.

'And so they had this simple mantra in terms of justification when it came to any armed engagement with the Provos like the operation at Loughall where they ambushed an active service unit who'd arrived to attack a police station and killed all eight of them.

'The SAS view was very straightforward. *Big boys' games, big boys' rules*, which roughly translated as, if you go out with a gun or a bomb, then you can't complain if you get shot.'

'Play with fire, expect to be burnt?'

'Exactly.'

'Doesn't sound much like a police approach to dealing with criminals?'

'No, it sounds like a justification for executions.'

'Shoot to kill?'

'Did you ever follow the Stalker enquiry? What do you think?'

So what did you do?'

'What was there to do? I had a real problem.'

'It wasn't like I'd heard an actual order, or even anything very definitive that I could stand up in front of anyone else. Lots of people had said lots of things that afternoon and evening. If I started to complain about one particular set of words I'd claimed to overhear, late in a bar, how far was that going to get me, do you reckon?

'They'd all have just denied it, they could back each other up on that couldn't they? Or even if they'd admitted what they'd said, all they had to do was point to what everyone else was saying to muddy the waters about what was banter, what was blokes in their cups running off at the mouth, and what might actually just be serious. Do you think anyone up the chain would thank me for pulling everything that had been being said around the table or down the bar into the harsh light of day for them to have to pick through? No sodding way.

Anything I'd tried to raise at that point would have been squashed pretty bloody sharpish I can tell you, and me with it.

'Besides which, you don't snitch on another copper in this job. Grassing someone up? It's just not done. Get a jacket like that and your career's over, it's that simple.'

'So what did you do?'

'I went back to my room and spent the rest of the night thinking about my options.'

'Which were?'

'Well, when it came down to it I only had one. I had to go up to Aberdeen and talk to Bomber direct. I knew I had to give him an Osman Warning that his life was being threatened.'

'By Stu?'

'No, by us.'

CHAPTER 7   ABSOLUTE TRUST

West Mercia Police Guidance Note

Subject: *Osman Warnings*

File reference: *Policies / 176-3-5*

Version: *1.03*

Approved by: *Superintendent – Central Authorisations and Policies*

Approval date: *10 Sept 2009*

Review date: *10 August 2011*

Associated docs: *Threats to Kill Procedure Ref: Policies / 176-3-5a*

Threats to Kill Risk Assessment Ref: Policies / 176-3-5b

Standard Osman Warning Format Ref: Policies / 176-3-5c

1. **Introduction**
    a. *This guide outlines the basis of and officers' responsibilities in respect of Osman Warnings concerning a threat of imminent danger to an individual through criminal action, in particular a threat to kill.*
    b. *It should be read in conjunction with the Associated Guidance documents listed above.*
2. **Legal Basis**
    a. *The right to life is protected under the Human Rights Act 1998:*
        i. *everyone's right to life shall be protected by law. Part 1 of Schedule (2.1)*
    b. *To fulfil their responsibilities under the Act, the Police are obliged to:*
        i. *consider any serious threat to life that they become aware of*
        ii. *examine the facts objectively at the time of the existence of a threat*
        iii. *take appropriate action in respect of the threat*

and

    iv.   *keep the situation under review whilst a life is at risk from the criminal actions of another.*

c.   *This provision has been the subject of case law, specifically Osman v UK 1998, EHRR 245 which gives rise to the Osman Warning obligation.*

d.   *In the Osman case the Court held that the obligation arises when:*

    i.   *the authorities knew or ought to have known*

    ii.   *at the time of the existence of a real and immediate risk to the life*

    iii.   *of an identified individual or individuals*

    iv.   *from the criminal acts of a third party.*

e.   *The test is therefore a stringent one requiring the Police know (or ought to have known) of a real and immediate threat.*

f.   *The Court also recognised:*

    i.   *the difficulties involved in policing modern societies*

    ii.   *the unpredictability of human conduct*

    iii.   *the operational choices which must be made in terms of priorities and resources. and*

    iv.   *[the need not to] impose an impossible or disproportionate burden on the authorities.*

g.   *The Courts therefore recognise that dealing with the requirements of the obligation needs to be viewed in the context of a range of policing operations and calls on resources.*

3.   Process

a.   *In the event that a threat to kill is identified the <u>Threats to Kill Procedure</u> should be followed.*

b.   *A <u>Threats to Kill Risk Assessment</u> should be completed by the Senior Investigating Officer and submitted to an officer of Superintendent rank (at minimum) for consideration as the authorising officer.*

c.   *In general where an individual is considered to be in real and imminent danger from another's criminal actions the police should warn the intended victim by delivery of a written warning using the <u>Standard Osman Warning Format</u> unless there are reasonable grounds not to do so.*

d. The purpose of an Osman Warning is to:
    i.   allow a potential victim to take precautionary steps to protect themselves and/or
    ii.   consider any protective measures the Police may propose.

e. Osman Warnings are not intended to:
    i.   take pre-emptive action against the alleged criminal, or
    ii.   identify Police intelligence sources.

4. Issuing Considerations

a. When considering whether an Osman Warning should be issued the following matters should be considered (see _Threats to Kill Procedure_ and _Threats to Kill Risk Assessment_ for further details):
    i.   Is a warning likely to result in, or exacerbate existing, violence against the criminal identified, or any group they are associated with?
    ii.   Is a warning likely to expose a police intelligence source, and will this revelation have a serious impact?
    iii. Are there any pre-existing special police relation-ships that are of relevance to the decision?

5. Issuing Process

a. Authority to issue:
    i.   A request to issue an Osman Warning should be put to an on-call officer of Superintendent rank (at minimum) by the Senior Investigating Officer accompanied by a completed Threats to Kill Risk Assessment.
    ii.   The Superintendent should make a written record of their decision as soon as is practical.
    iii. If in exceptional circumstances, having regards to the urgency of the situation, it is not practical to seek authorisation using the process noted above, then the Senior Investigating Officer may issue an Osman Warning, but an officer of Superintendent rank (at a minimum) must be informed as soon as is practical thereafter.

b. Decision not to issue:

> i. If on consideration of the _Threats to Kill Risk Assessment_ the Senior Investigating Officer's decision is that no warning should be issued,
>> 1. the decision must be endorsed by an officer of Superintendent rank (at minimum)
>> 2. the reasons for the decision must be recorded in writing on the _Threats to Kill Risk Assessment_ and be counter signed by the endorsing officer, and
>> 3. a Threat Management Plan created setting out the alternative strategies being adopted to minimise the threat to life.

6. Form of Warning

> a. The Senior Investigating Officer is responsible for drafting the wording of the Osman Warning with reference to the _Standard Osman Warning Format_.
> b. The warning should contain:
>> i. sufficient information to allow the recipient to understand the risk and decide what steps to take for their own protection; and
>> ii. any protective proposals the Police wish to propose.
> c. The warning should not contain any:
>> i. unnecessary detail which could compromise police intelligence sources or operations; or
>> ii. raw intelligence data.

7. Delivery of the Osman Warning

> a. All Osman Warnings must be delivered:
>> i. personally to the recipient, (under no circumstances should such a warning sent by post)
>> ii. by the Senior Investigating Officer.
> b. In the event the Senior Investigating Officer is not available and the urgency of the situation warrants it, this may be delegated to the most senior officer available but they must be personally briefed by the Senior Investigating Officer on the circumstances of the case and any sensitivities with regards to the source of the intelligence.
> c. It is critical that the recipient fully understands the

    warning given and the use of interpreters or other
    suitable intermediaries may be required in some cases.

  d.   *Delivery of the Osman Warning should be recorded as a*
    witness statement noting the circumstances and form of
    warning given which should be signed by the recipient.

  e.   *If the recipient cannot or will not sign the witness*
    statement then the delivering officer should record the
    fact and circumstances.

  f.   *The delivering officer should:*

    i.   *notify the recipient of protective measures*
    proposed, and

    ii.   *record in the witness statement any measures the*
    recipient advises they intend to take on their own
    behalf.

8.   ***Further Actions/Review***

  a.   *As set out in the <u>Threats to Kill Procedure</u>, the Senior*
    Investigating Officer must establish in all cases a specific
    case review timetable for reassessment of the risk for
    approval at Superintendent rank (at minimum).

9.   ***Recording***

  a.   *In all cases where the issuing of an Osman Warning has*
    been considered the following documents should be
    copied to Divisional Intelligence for filing:

    i.   <u>*Threats to Kill Risk Assessment*</u>

    ii.   *all associated assessments, statements*

    iii.   *Osman Warning issued (if applicable)*

    iv.   *witness statement re delivery (if applicable), and*

    v.   *the Threat Management Plan and all subsequent*
    updates.

Internal Police guidance note on the use of
Osman Warnings obtained by Iain Parke

'I rang the bell and stood back a pace to look up at the house and see if there was any sign of life.

'The house was a relatively modern one on one of those executive housing estates which had sprung up around surrounding villages like Bridge of Don and Newmachar on the back of Aberdeen's oil money; all cul-de-sacs, paved drives and neatly presented front gardens commuter belt.

'All except here at number 16, where the grass was knee high, what looked once to have been carefully tended borders had gone to wrack and ruin, and a few overflow black bin bags of rubbish were slumped against the side of the overfull wheelie bin that obviously hadn't made it out in time for last week's collection.

'The neighbours must bloody love you, I thought, as I stepped around the rusting body of a sports car, its wheels chocked up on blocks with a fine crop of thistles erupting from between the pavers either side of it and up to the solid blank front door.

'The intercom buzzed for a metallic voice to demand, "Yeah?"

'Inside it was dark. Once upon a time the place had been nicely kept, stylishly decorated even. Now the place looked a tip. As I glanced into the living room in the gloom of the curtains still shut against the late morning daylight, all I could see was crap strewn everywhere. I was a bit surprised to be honest, from everything I'd heard about him and from all I'd seen, his business affairs, the paperwork, he'd always seemed very organised, very neat, always on top of things. So to find him living here in an utter pigsty like a complete slob was a shock really.'

'Cleaner's day off is it?' I asked, as he led me into the tip of a kitchen where every surface was piled with dirty crockery.

'Fuck off copper,' was his succinct response.

Fair enough, I shrugged. I wasn't here about *Homes and Gardens* after all.

'So what's this about a warning then?' he asked, sprawling onto a chair at the kitchen table.

He hadn't offered me a seat but I pulled one out anyway and sat down opposite him, clearing a space in front of me by lifting a pile of unopened post and depositing it on a larger pile of old newspapers and magazines further down the table. I guess he hadn't been in the mood to check his bills and statements for a while.

'Well,' I started, as he pulled a packet of fags out of one of his work shirt pockets and lit it with a flick of a Zippo lighter, 'I have duty to tell you your life is in danger…'

'Oh, who from?' he asked nonchalantly, blowing a stream of smoke up towards the ceiling where the smoke detector hung open, battery-less.

'Stu,' I told him.

'Oh really?' he gazed coolly at me.

'And if he is, why not tell me officially? Because this is unofficial I take it?' he said, noting my lack of any paperwork to show him.

'Because I can't tell you this somewhere official,' I acknowledged. 'I can't tell you where there may be witnesses because I don't know who I can trust…'

He barked a laugh at the thought, my obvious discomfort seemed to have amused him.

'You don't know who you can trust?' he sneered. 'Can't you trust a copper?'

'On this?' I countered, 'No, I can't.'

'And why's that?' he asked.

'Because you're being set up by people on the force. They're fitting you up with a snitch jacket and trailing you in front of him, that's why Stu is going to be coming after you. And if not him, then somebody else.'

He seemed completely unmoved by the idea.

'What do you care?' he wanted to know, taking another drag on his fag.

I'd been asking myself the same question all the previous day on the way back from the taskforce and then all the way up here, and I still really didn't have a good answer to that other than what I told him.

'It's not the way the game should be played, in my book…'

'The game?' he snorted. 'So that's what you think this is? A game?'

'Still, for all his derision as we talked, we were at least still talking.

189

'Here in his home as we sat in the mess and the dimness of the shaded off room, there was something changed about him, I could feel it but not quite put my finger on it.

'I thought I saw concern, a fading sense of certainty. A feeling underneath his prickly exterior he was at least starting to think about his situation, to weigh up what I was telling him first about Plan B and then Plan C, against what he was experiencing on his side of the street and perhaps, just perhaps, he was putting two and two together for himself, beginning to consider if he hadn't already been thinking about it, what were his possible ways out of this?

'Not that he was really showing that much willingness to co-operate with me.

'And of course I couldn't really blame him for being suspicious.

'I'd just told him that our mob, the cops, were looking to paint him as having come over to us just to put him in bad odour with Stu.

'He'd seen in his life how we'd tried to work the clubs in the past. He'd known about the rats and touts we'd turned and how they were treated by either side. He'd have heard the promises, the blandishments, the threats before, I was sure in his career as a club officer and therefore *de facto* police target, and they'd all just washed of his back. Had to have, otherwise we wouldn't be here now.

'And yet, here I was, a cop, someone he'd only ever met once before and that was on the opposite side of a hostile interview room, asking him to trust me against not only my own mob but also Stu and the men he'd known as his brothers for over half his life.

'It was a tough sell, I knew that. But what worried me was how reluctant Bomber was to buy.'

*

We were confused, it has to be said. What else had he been expecting, we wondered, pitching up at Bomber's door out of the blue like that?

'Why did you think you were going to be able to get through to him?' we asked. 'What made you think he would trust you? Listen to you even?'

190

'I don't know,' he told us, shaking his head slowly, 'I knew it was a long shot, but I thought we had made a connection...'

'Back in the room?'

'Yes. There was a moment, just something, but I thought it was enough.'

'Funnily enough, it was off the back of one of your bloke Iain Parke's pieces.

'It had been published in one of his *Guardian* features on an anonymised basis, presumably one of the conditions under which it had been given, particularly in view of its somewhat incriminating content. I'd had it flagged to me as part of my intelligence gathering role for the force on anything to do with the biker scene, so it had been sitting in my files for a while, but it had struck a chord you know when I'd first read it, and so it had stuck with me, right up until I got involved with the taskforce and first pulled Bomber's file.

'And then, well, I just knew.

'I couldn't prove it was Bomber of course, but in context I was pretty bloody sure it had been him talking in the piece. So as he sat there in front of me in the interrogation room I told him I was going to read him something.'

DI Chambers had it with him and as he showed us the piece he meant, we knew he was right. We'd seen it in Iain's files and we'd also seen his notes about how it had come about.

A few weeks after talking about his time in Aberdeen, Iain had met Bomber again. Bomber had called, asking for a meet and so Iain had travelled up the following weekend.

Bomber picked him up from his hotel on the Saturday afternoon.

'So what's this all about then Bomber?' asked Iain, as he climbed into the car.

'Just wanted to show you something,' Bomber told him cryptically, as they wound their way through the city traffic and quickly out into the countryside, heading towards the hills inland.

As they drove Bomber wouldn't say anything about where they

were going, what it was he wanted to show Iain, or why, but as Iain asked questions anyway, he did talk a bit more about his background as far as he was ever prepared to go.

'I had a fucked up childhood. It wasn't anyone's fault, my parents cared about me and wanted the best for me, but it didn't work out that way. That's just the way it was, I wasn't protected from some horrible shit that shouldn't happen to any kid.

'And so, when it came to be my turn the one thing I knew was that I was never going to let anything like that happen to a kid of mine.'

As he spoke, he kept coming back time and time again to Jenny.

'The club had been my life and it still was even after Jenny was born you know?

'It was my family and when I needed support because of Jenny's situation, the club stepped up, unquestioningly. Whatever I needed, time, money, whatever, it was taken care of, Stu made sure of that. I was family and so was she.

'So I just always felt I owed the club a debt of loyalty, and the way to repay that was to make sure everyone else was as loyal to the club as I was.

'All I ever wanted was to look after my kid.'

*

'And that's where we kept coming back to as we interviewed him,' Chambers told us.

'It's a bit early for *Listen with Mother* isn't it?'

'Maybe, Bomber,' DS Timms said, 'you tell us.'

'Now I'm just going to read this to you,' I continued, 'and then I'm going to ask you what you think about it? How's that?'

He just gave a shrug.

'Read what you want copper,' he told me, and so I started.

'This is a piece that Iain Parke published not long before he was last seen which would put it about the time he was known to be talking to members of your club, is that right Bomber?'

'No idea mate,' he told me affecting a bored tone. 'He talked to lots of people.'

'Did he talk to you?'

'Might have done. I really don't remember.'

'Well why don't I read this to you and let's see if it jogs any memories?'

'Knock yourself out...'

*

The car park was a clearing, nothing more than a circle of pock-marked rough ground carved out at the foot of the hill down a bumpy, just about tarmacked, track from the main road.

Opposite the entrance, a scruffy patch of grass bore its sole amenity, a grey faded wooden picnic table and benches, etched with the hearts, forevas and illegible names of some penknife-wielding local kids who'd obviously not managed to find anywhere better to go.

There were no attractions to draw people here on a cold spring day. No places to go, no sights to see, just a selection of rutted packed rubble, and earth logging tracks heading up into the hills in a few different directions as places to walk in silence, for no particular reason.

A place for dog walkers, and these days for all I knew, possibly doggers. If any of them could be bothered to make it way out here.

There was a map printed on a board at the foot of the trails. It showed three marked routes in dashed primary colours against the dull green splodge of the forest, while some optimistically specula-tive photographs and notes illustrated alleged local wildlife like rural wanted posters.

I glanced at the map although even now I didn't really need to. I knew which way I had to go, more or less. Well, it's not the sort of thing you forget is it?

It was the first time I'd been back for what? Let's see, my daughter was only four at the time, upstairs asleep in her bed, so that makes it what, fifteen years? Has to be, since we were here.

At the leading edge of the woods it was all local trees, a piece of natural woodland, fronting for the organised and regimented affair lurking behind it.

As I strode in, light filtered through the leafy cover in bright greens, dappling the ground, while occasionally sudden shafts of surprisingly hot sunlight for this time of year caught me where the trail opened out to the noon sky, while in the cool shadows between the trees, a mysterious floating mist of bluebells kept catching the corner of my eye.

All was silence, human silence anyway, as the occasional road noise faded away into the background, absorbed by the trees and drowned out by the roaring chirp of the birds singing, Fuck Me or Fuck Off.

The path was climbing steeply now, and so was my heart rate. Years and the flab were catching up with me at every step.

I was well in and the trees were pressing closer together beyond the rotting vegetation-filled drainage ditches leading downhill on either side of the path. Even with today's bright sunlight, peering in under the bare grey lower branches it was soon pitch black between the walls of trunks marching off into the gloom.

This wasn't idyllic pretty woodland.

This was ugly Forestry Commission land, as industrial as a factory and about as romantic.

Row upon tightly packed row of commercial conifers stretching up across the hills in great dark green oblong blocks, silent now except for the crunch of gravel underfoot and the odd chilling cry of a cuckoo echoing through the trees.

And the thing about this type of place was, you knew that young trees, like there were here fifteen years ago, weren't going to be disturbed or cut for decades.

They were just going to be left to grow taller and thicker as they raced upwards in a silent continuous Darwinian struggle against their neighbours for every scrap of available light. High above their thick prickly branches closed together amongst their densely packed stands, reducing the forest floor to an inky drift of silent fallen needles, covering everything year on year in an ever thickening blanket.

I passed by the entrance to an old long-abandoned boggy quarry buzzing with insects and thought, yes, I remember that. It can't be far now.

And then a hundred yards or so further I crested a small rise that let me steal a rare glance out down across open heathery moor-land and eventually all the way to the towns on the coast and the flat grey line of the sea, before the path swung sharply left to cut further back uphill. Closing my eyes against the bright sunlight I remembered our breath steaming from our exertions in the chill night air, and back down towards the coast a dirty glowing bruise of reflected light in the sky.

This was the place, I thought, looking around again. Somewhere round here. It had to be.

I knew there was no point in looking. I knew I'd never actually find the spot. I didn't even really know why I'd come.

Sometimes I miss you so much I wish I remembered exactly where we buried you that night.

Thank God for my mate was all I can say. I don't know what I'd have done without him that night.

But he knew exactly what to do.

He knew about this place.

He knew his way around it, leading the way up the hill and then off the track to find a suitable spot.

I didn't ask how, I didn't ask why. It was his businesses, I didn't want to know.

It had been such a shock. Coming back in late that night and finding her there, like that, all the gear strewn around her on the floor, the gear that had obviously killed her.

We'd fought, again. No surprise there, and it had all been about the gear, about the way she was off her head all the time, about how it wasn't right, not with our young kid around. But the truth was, she couldn't help it, she was an addict, I could see that, and no amount of pleading or arguing or talking was going to change that. Speed for uppers and smack for downers and speedballs as a mix, she'd graduated from snorting and smoking to jacking up a long time since, so I guess looking back it was really only a matter of time. She'd promised to go straight a few times, she'd done it that week, which is why we'd rowed when I'd come home to find her spaced out of her gourd and a set of works abandoned amongst the half empty coffee cups and overflowing ashtrays on the coffee table while she was curled up on the stained sofa.

Like I said to my mate when I saw him that evening down the club-house as I nursed a drink and brooded on my problems, I didn't even know where she was getting the shit from. It wasn't like there were any dealers around that we didn't have a handle on and I'd leaned on a load of 'em to make sure they knew I didn't want her being supplied, but somehow, through someone, she was still getting this gear, and after having been off it for a week or so she'd have been gagging for her hits. She was losing it, I told him. I was worried. She was so far gone these days I didn't know what she would do, or say, about anything, just for her next hit. So one of the things I was determined to get out of her was where she was getting her stuff. I needed to know who her dealer was so I could sort them out once and for all, I told him.

'It's none of your guys, is it?' I asked him. I knew my mate ran a string of distributors and always had access to whatever he wanted.

My mate just shook his head, and he'd have known if it was.

He was sympathetic, but as I laid my trip on him that evening I knew there really wasn't a lot he could do to help other than lend an ear as I complained that I hadn't realised I was entering some point scoring competition when I'd gotten together with her.

She was my woman and my problem, and anyways he had some business of his own that he was off to that night so he left early after I'd said I was just going to hang around the clubhouse that evening, let things cool down at home.

My mate said that sounded like a smart move, he even offered to have a word with her sometime if I thought it might help, and I said yeah that would be great. I mean, she'd known him longer than she'd known me. If there was anyone who could talk some sense into her it would've been him.

'What I don't get,' I told him, 'is where she gets the dosh to buy the gear? I'm the one who's bringing in the cash, I know where it goes, what we spend it on with the kid and all, so how's she paying for it?'

I shook my head as my mate had the tryout at the bar stick another pint in front of me.

'Who the fuck knows, mate?' he said, putting a huge comforting hand on my shoulder as he stood up to go. 'Look, don't worry about it for tonight. You just have a few pints, get your head down here and we'll try talking to her tomorrow. How's that?'

'Cheers mate,' I said, as we hugged.

'No worries, it's what we're here for isn't it? To look after each other? Yeah?'

'Yeah.'

And with that he was off, striding over to the door while I turned back to the two pints that were now stacked in front of me at the bar.

And I'd intended to spend the night. I really had, but by about eleven-thirty or so I'd wound myself up so much about what I wanted to say to her that fuck it, there wasn't any choice but to grab my lid and head back out into the night.

The sting of the cold night air brought tears to my eyes which I blinked away while the wind chill of the damp night air was a mind-clearing shock against my exposed skin and soon began to penetrate the denim of my jeans as I rode through alternating pools of yellow streetlight, the rumble of my exhaust echoing back at me from the darkened terraces beyond the silent rows of parked cars on either side.

Pulling up outside our front door I killed the engine and stepping *off I lifted my lid and looked around. Elsewhere along the street the houses were shut up but I could see light peering around curtains or leaking through front door windows of the row of red brick two up, two downs. Our house however was dark, completely dark.*

Unlocking the front door I flicked on the hall light. I didn't call out as I knew our little girl would be asleep upstairs and the last thing I wanted to do was wake her, so I crept down the hallway, pushed open the door into the front room, and reaching across, fumbled for the light switch.

She was lying on the floor, as if she'd simply rolled off the sofa, and as soon as I went to lift her I knew she was dead. There was no question of that.

Her body had gone as limp as a fish as she flopped across my arms, and all the colour had drained from her face leaving it a grey against the purple blue of her lips, or what I could see of them beneath the smeared vomit.

She was cold, not breathing, and as I felt and then listened, had no heartbeat, and so I called it.

And then I called my mate.

He was round like Mr Wolf.

He must have dropped everything because he was with me in, well, it can't have been more than quarter of an hour, although as I'd sat on the armchair opposite where I'd lain her out on the sofa, I don't think I'd taken my eyes off her long enough to glance at a clock, let alone take in what the time was until I heard the tap on the window and went to let him in.

He agreed with me. An overdose, had to be. It happens. Going clean and then falling back's one of the most dangerous times for junkies as they can have lost some of the tolerance they've developed, so their previously normal dose becomes a dangerous one.

'You can't let her be found mate, you know that don't you?' he said quietly, 'you can't have the plod poking around anywhere near this before you've had the chance to sort it out?'

I knew he was right. Her shit was everywhere and the moment the cops turned up they would be having a good old rummage and no doubt would stick all this crap on me. Well I'm a biker aren't I? So the speed and shit's bound to be mine isn't it? Stands to reason, doesn't it, and take the prisoner down.

'Think what it'd mean for you. You don't want to risk losing your kid, do you?'

No, I couldn't afford to let her be found, not here, not anywhere; not before I'd had a chance to do some thorough cleaning, not if I wanted to stay free and not if I wanted to keep my daughter.

Christ, what about her?

She was still upstairs. We had to get this organised and sharpish.

But my mate was one step ahead of me already. From the moment I'd called him and in a guarded way told him I had a major problem, he'd been planning. Why else had he turned up driving his van and why else had he already slung a sleeping bag, some ties and couple of shovels in the back?

While he nipped outside to fetch in the stuff, I raided the kitchen for a bin bag to start scooping up everything out of the living room that was going to need to go. Butts, works, lighter, baggies; working methodically I cleared the table's surface.

'The furniture and carpet'll have to go as well, you know,' he advised, as we zipped her into the sleeping bag.

'No worries though, I'll bring some of the lads over tomorrow and we'll get it all down the dump in the van. We can sort you out some stuff as replacements. Unless you want to torch the place?' he suggested practically. 'Might be better, gets it completely cleaned and makes it a full insurance job?'

I didn't know what to say. This had been our house. We'd lived here together. We'd had good times, we really had.

'Just think it over,' he said, seeing me hesitate. 'OK, you ready?'

We lifted her up. She didn't seem to weigh anything, and with a quick scout around outside to make sure no one was stirring in the street and no curtains were twitching, a moment later she was safely in the back of the van.

'You'll need a story,' he said, as we drove.

I shrugged.

'She was a junkie. I kicked her out to protect our kid, told her not to come back until she'd cleaned up her act, and I've not seen her since,' I said in a flat voice.

'Could have been her then with the petrol through the letter box,' he suggested. 'Revenge maybe? Could work for the insurance.'

'I'll think about it,' I said, and we drove on in silence.

And so we buried her that night. We dug a hole in the ground in amongst the trees a way off the track and dumped the sleeping bag into it, together with the bin bag full of crap I'd scooped up. Some weird set of grave goods for someone to puzzle over if she's ever found, which I doubt she will be.

We shovelled the earth back in over her and kicked around piles of needles to disguise the site, not that anyone was ever going to come looking here. Then we walked away without a backwards glance, ducking to push through the whippy lower branches until we reached the trail again, and headed down towards where the van was waiting, shovels over our shoulders.

We knew an all-night café, a truckers' place tucked away on an industrial estate on the outside of town, so we drew in there to grab a brew and a bacon and egg sarnie each just as the sky was beginning to lighten.

As I stirred sugar into my steaming mug he was stuffing the first half of his breakfast into his mouth, washing it down with a great swig of NATO standard tea.

'So, have you thought about it?' he asked.

'Yeah,' I told him, 'so here's what I want to do.'

He dropped me off at the end of my road, no sense in having the van seen more than was needed we'd agreed, and I walked down the pavement in the chilly dawn as the sky cleared to a range of fresh pinks and blues. Around me the street was waking up, curtains being drawn back, the sound of radios floating out through part open windows.

Above me birds were chattering on the wires and a solitary jogger old enough to know better came sweating past in a T-shirt, shorts and trainers, while on the other side of the road an early commuter, all suited and booted and ready for another challenging day in the office, was pulling his front door shut behind him and fumbling for the keys to his car.

I reached the little iron gate and taking the two steps needed to cross our front yard, I let myself back into the house and listened.

All was quiet.

It was time to get her up, breakfasted and ready for school; knowing that, and it was all thanks to my mate, I'd managed the problem.

I owed him one. Again.

And I was going to owe him more I knew, from now on, with no one to look after my girl but me, my life had changed forever.

There was silence in the interview room as I finished and put the paper down on the desk.

'So, Bomber, what did you think of that?' I asked.

He said nothing, just shook his head, his eyes locked on mine.

'No views at all?' I asked, and left it hanging there for a while.

Some blokes can't handle a silence. They have to rush to fill it, but Bomber wasn't like that. He could be still when he wanted to be.

I glanced over at DS Timms and gave a bit of a sigh.

'Alright then, Bomber. Why don't I tell you what I think?'

And still there was silence from across the table as he stared back at me.

'Well, Bomber, I think that piece was about you.'

No reaction.

'I think that was you telling the story of how you came home to find your Maggie dead of an overdose and your daughter Jenny asleep upstairs in bed.'

No reaction.

'I think the mate you called was Stu, and think the two of you took her away and buried her that night just the way it's described here.'

No reaction.

'And you know what?'

No reaction.

'I believe it. I believe that's what happened and I believe that's why you hid the body, which as I'm sure you know is a serious offence, so as to protect your kid from being taken into care. And I can understand absolutely why you'd do it, why you'd have had no choice as you saw it.

'I believe it, as far as it goes...'

'And did you believe him?' we asked.

'Yes, yes I did,' he told us.

'But with just this as evidence?' I held up the piece of paper, 'the next question is what am I, what are we,' I added nodding at DS Timms, 'going to do about it?'

Still no reaction.

It was my turn to shrug as I put the paper back down on the desk.

'And probably nothing, is the answer,' I told him. 'What can I do? Go and ask the local chief constable if we can dig up every forest in Scotland to see if we can find a body? Don't worry, with just this there's nothing we can do, is there?'

And still no reaction.

'Which is all very well, Bomber, except for one thing...' I said, and left it hanging there in the air.

He gazed at me as the silence stretched out between us until at last with a bit of a snort he said unfolding his arms, 'Alright then, let's play if you want, so what, you've read your story and I'm not commenting. Now where do we go?'

'Stu, mate,' I said.

He gave a frown and a shrug as he raised his hands in a mock question, 'So, what about him?'

'You never knew when or how she got the stuff, did you?' I said, ignoring his response for a while. 'All her gear, you've said so your-self. She didn't have the money to pay for that sort of habit so where was she getting it from? Was someone giving it to her?'

He was folding his arms again but I could sense he was listening.

'A mate perhaps? Someone she'd known a long time. Someone with ready access to gear? Would have to be wouldn't it, given the shit she liked to do?'

He was slumped back in his chair now, his eyes narrowed to slits as he waited to hear what I was saying.

'Even so, even for a mate, that's a pretty generous thing to be doing day in day out for what? Months? Years on end? Feeding her habit? I mean, what's in it for them?'

He was in lockdown by now.

'Stu and Maggie went way back didn't they?' I pressed on, 'And of course Stu supplied drugs didn't he? That was the business he was in, wasn't it?'

I paused.

'So you've got to ask, haven't you, Bomber, was Stu giving it to her?'

'Stu wasn't giving her shit,' he growled through gritted teeth.

'So you say,' I shrugged, 'but it's odd though isn't it? What happened that night?'

Just the glare again now from the other side of the table.

'You're out at the clubhouse and you cry on Stu's shoulder about what a state she's in and how you don't know what she's going to do, and that you're going to lean on her about her dealer, and then you're late home because Stu's left you with some beers in the bar as he goes off to sort some business of his own.

'You walk in, you find her dead, and you call Stu.

'And Stu's right over, isn't he. Stu's got all the gear organised, a van, bags, shovels. He knows where to go, what to do. It doesn't sound as though he's overly surprised when you called him.

'It was Stu that convinced you she had to just disappear wasn't it?

'It was Stu who was concerned about what our mob might find if we'd been called round, if she'd had a post mortem, if we'd searched the place. And what do you think that might have been, do you wonder?

'Bomber, you've got to ask yourself, whose side, apart from Stu's, has Stu ever really been on? Who has he ever really looked after apart from number one?

'He's played you for a sucker, Bomber, hasn't he?'

'Face it Bomber, he has been for years,' chimed in DS Timms.

'You've got no fucking idea, copper,' Bomber shot back fiercely, 'he's always looked after me like a brother. We've been family.'

'Family? Sod that for a game of soldiers. Patsy more like,' DS Timms was on a roll now, 'He's been exploiting you for years and unless you wake up he's going to carry on using you right up to the moment when he's got no more use for you and then you know what's going to happen don't you, Bomber?

'Anyone who ends up being any kind of threat to Stu, anyone who's a rival, anyone who's a potential rival, or anyone who just knows too much, they all have a way of ending up the same way. Dead.'

As we sat there and argued the toss in the room, Bomber was having none of it.

But at the back of his eyes I could see a nagging terror of doubt starting to take hold.

'OK then, let's get back to Stu,' I suggested, as we didn't seem to be getting very far on anything else. 'So what do you really do for Stu?'

'You know as well as I do, you've seen the paperwork,' he said, with an edge of irritation in his voice, 'I transport his sodding bears.'

'And that's it?'

'That's it,' he said firmly.

'You know,' he added, leaning forward again and resting his elbows on the table, 'all this fixation on Stu's business and his soft toys reminds me of something a bloke in a Polish club told me about once at a party.

'There was this guard at a factory, this was way back in the Commie times, and every day come quitting time he sees a bloke come out of the factory with a wheelbarrow full of rubbish pushing it through the gates. He does this day in, day out until the guard becomes really suspicious.

'*Right,* he thinks to himself, *who wheels a load of crap out of a factory every evening and trucks it on home?* So the guard reckons, *Aha! I know what's going on, the bloke's stealing stuff. He's hiding it in the crap and that's how he's smuggling it out of the factory!* So the next day the guard stops the bloke and searches through the crap.

'And it's all shitty stuff, a real mess, but since he finds nothing he's got no choice and he has to let the bloke go. The next day it's the same story, and the next and the next.

'By the time it's been a week, it's personal. The guard just knows he's being had over so it's a point of pride that he has to search through every bit of shit because one day, one day, he's going to find what the bloke is nicking. Days turn into weeks, weeks turn into months, months turn into years and still he keeps going at it every day, never finding a sodding thing.

'Time passes. The Wall comes down, Communism collapses, the factory gets privatized and still it keeps going every day regular as clockwork until eventually, it's the guard's last day at work before he retires. Just as usual at five o'clock the factory whistle goes and the bloke with the wheelbarrow comes rolling along towards the gate.

'The guard searches it from top to bottom for the last time and once again can't find anything in the heap of crud in the barrow. But this time before he lets the bloke go he just has to know, so he says to the bloke.

'Look this is my last day, so you just have to tell me. What have you been stealing all these years?

'Oh that's easy, says the bloke as he shrugs, picks up the handles and starts to wander off home again, *Wheelbarrows.'*

'And your point is?' asked DS Timms as he finished.

Bomber grinned at him in satisfaction that he'd had him in some way. 'Well you know copper, sometimes shit is just shit.'

We kept going of course. Between DS Timms and me we tried all sort of tacks. DS Timms pushed him on a range of things. I remember at one point he was asking things that I just didn't understand.

'Such as?' we wanted to know.

'Like, *What's your man Stu got over Strathclyde Police?* I remember wondering at the time about that and whether there was something going on I didn't know about.'

But while we weren't getting anywhere in terms of real responses, I did think we were starting to get through to Bomber a bit. That he was starting to think about his situation.

'Fuck me, Bomber, it's been quite a price you've paid over the years for the life isn't it? Family. Relationships. So I've got to ask, what's the payback?'

'Freedom's not free.'

'Oh bollocks. So what do you do with this precious freedom of yours?

'You've given your life for it, fair enough, but what has it got you? What have you actually achieved with it?'

'Respect...'

'Respect? Is that what you call it? According to you you've got this freedom, but do you use it to do something worthwhile? No, I'll tell you what I see you lot doing with it. I see you using it to do petty ante shit, to bully people, throw your weight around, putting the frighteners on people knowing that your mates in the gang will always be there to back you up. Is that what your precious freedom amounts to? The freedom to act like arseholes whenever you want and get away with it? That's not being respected, that's being feared, or don't you know the difference anymore?'

'You don't know what you're talking about, copper.'

'Oh? So tell me then.'

*

'As Timms saw it, in actively choosing to join the club, Bomber had made a pact with the devil, or Stu at least. I didn't have quite the same view, but we both knew there was also always a way out for him.'

'Becoming a tout?'

'Grassing on his buddies. All he ever needed to do to get out would have been to approach us, and for all I knew there'd been countless moments in which Bomber might have considered doing just that.'

'But he never had, had he?'

'No. He'd always stayed a loyal soldier. Even now, with all the grief we were showering on him he was still staying loyal, rather than seeking a way out.'

DS Timms had one last go, just before the end.

'You're being played for a sucker, you know that don't you?

'Look, you're loyal, we know that. Hell, in some ways I can understand that, admire it even. You stick to your mates, don't want to let them down. And in most circumstances that'd be a great thing.

'But not now Bomber, not in this.

'They're just using you and your loyalty, you can see that can't you? They're using you and your business for their own ends.

'Not yours.

'Not the club's.

'It's them and their cash, that's all their looking out for, that's all that matters to them, isn't it? You can see that in what they do, can't you? How they act, what they want, what really matters to them when the chips are down?

'It's not about just being out there and riding your bikes with your mates any more, is it. Deep down you know those days are long gone, aren't they?

'And you know what's killed them, don't you?

'Drugs and money. That's right isn't it, Bomber? Drugs and money?'

'You know what? No comment.'

After that and our switch to have a go at Stu, it wasn't long before the club appointed lawyer was in the room after which Bomber had no choice really but to keep up the act. But to me, it seemed something had changed. Something in what we'd said to him had hit home, I was sure of it. There was a look in his eye, an indefinable something, an acknowledgment that he would meet and talk outside, somewhere where he wasn't under caution, somewhere he could start to speak freely.

And of course, eventually the PACE clock had ticked out and we had no choice but to release him.

'So I can go now?' Bomber asked, standing up as we entered the room.

'Yes, you can go,' I told him.

'Well that was lovely,' he smiled, 'we must do it again sometime.'

'Count on it, arsehole,' DS Timms muttered under his breath, just loud enough for me and Bomber, but not his brief to hear.

'And that was it? That was the basis on which you decided to approach Bomber direct in the hope he would talk to you?'

'Yep, that was it.'

'Bloody hell, that was taking a risk wasn't it?'

'But now at Bomber's house, it was me doing the talking.'

*

'You've got to listen to me, Bomber. They're going to be coming for you. Next week they're going to re-arrest you. They're going to take you in for questioning and they're deliberately going to leak it to Stu that you're helping with their enquiries.

'And what do you think Stu is going to do then?' I asked, pointing out the noose which was tightening around him. 'He's already suspicious isn't he?'

'Says who?' he grunted. But at least he's talking to me, I thought.

'Says the fact he's not answering your calls,' I told him. 'They're setting you up, Bomber. They're going to get your best mate to kill you, you can see that, can't you? And for what? To get him, not you. And if they can't do that, the chances are they're going to do the both of you.'

I waited to see what his reaction would be to that but he was just watching me carefully. Letting me make the running. Well I wasn't too happy with that.

'Oh yes,' I challenged him, 'you know what I'm talking about here don't you? And yet, what are you doing about it? Are you just going to sit there and let it happen?'

'So why are you so concerned then, copper?' he challenged, 'Why do you give a shit? What's in it for you to want to warn me? I know what you think happened to Maggie remember? You told me so when we were sitting in that cell.'

It was a fair point, I guess in his position I'd have been suspicious too. There was nothing I could do but tell him the truth.

'You're a biker but you're straight. You do the right thing, see the way you looked after Jenny – it can't have been easy given the circumstances...'

'Maggie leaving, you mean?' he said, eying me shrewdly as though he was looking to see if I was trying to catch him out in a confession of some kind.

'Well yes, that as well if that's the way you want to play it...' I started, but he interrupted me.

'As well as what?' he wanted to know.

'Oh come on, Bomber,' I said with a tone of frustration in my voice. I wasn't interested in some bloody fencing match with him. This was a matter of life and death as far as I was concerned and one where I was putting my career on the line just by being here for all I knew.

'You know what I'm talking about. We do the tests you know,' I told him.

He shook his head and looked vaguely annoyed, 'I haven't got a fucking clue what the hell you're on about. What tests?'

'DNA,' I told him bluntly, 'we swabbed you when we tugged you remember. It's routine, we do everyone. You, Stu, anyone we lift, Uncle Tom Cobbly and all. You get nicked, or become part of an investigation, you go on the database. Come on, you know that's how it works.'

'So?' he insisted.

Did I have to spell it out for him?

'What?' I asked him, 'You didn't think we'd find out?'

'Find out what?' he asked. To my utter astonishment he seemed completely at a loss, 'Where the fuck are you going with this?'

'Jenny,' I told him simply.

'What about her?'

'Well you know she wasn't yours, don't you?' I asked.

And she wasn't. As he collapsed in front of me I realised that he hadn't known and I had just destroyed the last illusion of his life.

Because the DNA evidence was quite clear, not that anyone other than me had bothered to look at it.

Jenny wasn't his daughter. She was Stu's.

The man who was now arranging to kill him.

But we didn't have time for that now, I thought, as I launched into an urgent appeal for him to let me help him.

'Look, work with me here, Bomber, will you? I'm the only one who can help get you out of this. I know the only thing you can do that has a chance of keeping you safe...'

I kept expecting some response from him but he said nothing. So I plunged on regardless.

'I've been thinking about this a lot and the answer is you need to go public. It's the only way. You need to make yourself fireproof, too high profile a target for anyone to pop their head above the parapet and have a go at. And I know how you can do it.

'I know who you need to call, I know what you need to say to them, I know what you need to be able to show them, and I'm the only bloke that can give you what you need from our end to back up your story...'

But just at that moment I could tell from his thousand yard stare he wasn't here, he wasn't listening to a word I was saying.

And then he muttered something to himself, it was too low a mumble for me to hear so, giving up on my exhortations for the moment, I realised I had to let him deal with this new reality, work through who and what he was now, before I'd have any hope of him engaging with what I was saying to him.

So quietly I asked him, 'Sorry, Bomber, what was that? I missed it.'

It was difficult to make out. He was mumbling, it was as though at first I wasn't there at all.

'I swore to look after her, protect her, always be there for her.'

And then as his eyes slowly focused on me and he seemed to register where he was, his voice came as though from someone wearily climbing out of a pit, 'I never wanted anything to happen to her.'

'I know you didn't, Bomber, I know,' I told him in absolution, and he closed his eyes and nodded, at that moment, a broken man.

Which only left one question

'So what did happen, Bomber,' I asked softly, 'up there in Aberdeen?'

*

'And that was it?' we asked. 'You were why he called us?'

'Yes that was it, and it was my idea. It was the only thing I could think of that might possibly work.'

'So did he talk? Did he answer your question?'

'No, not really. Hell, there was so much more I'd wanted to ask, about him, about Jenny, about everything really. I wanted to know what had really gone down in Aberdeen, but he was too far gone to press him on it then, I could see that.'

Which was where we had something to bring to the party as our managing director pulled up one of the files he had stacked on the floor beside him and slid it across the table to DI Chambers.

'Well I think we can help you there,' we told him, as he opened it with a wary look and began to skim through the pages with suddenly increasing interest. But of course we already knew the answer to his questions.

Because Bomber had told Iain and it was in the file he was now holding.

CHAPTER 8   CONSEQUENCES

Think you know who your friends are?

Fuck up and find out.

Biker saying

'It wasn't long before I got a call,' Bomber told Iain.

'Maz, the Enforcer, was on his way in with Dodo, one of the tagalongs.

'I don't know what Maz had said or done to him but by the time the tagalong stood in front of me at the clubhouse, he was a babbling wreck. It took me a few minutes to get it out of him. He'd seen a patch going in to the undertakers.

'I hit the fucking roof. All I wanted to know was who the fuck had had the balls to take us on like this?

'The tagalong was squirming so Maz had to sort him out a bit until he was talking straight, but eventually he spat it out. It was Stretch.

'I asked him if he was sure and he just nodded, he was.

'And of course it was fucking Stretch, I thought to myself. They were just alike those two.

'Maz asked me if I wanted him fetched and I sat there for a moment as I thought about the best way to handle this.

'But really there was no choice, so eventually I gave him the order he was waiting for, to bring Stretch in.

'Of course I'd always known it was going to be Stretch, if anyone. I mean, who the hell else would it be?

'The problem was Stretch and Tazz were Pete's brother and step brother, both club and blood.

'And Stretch faced with his brother in the funeral home…?

'Stretch did just what you'd expect him to do. Whatever the hell I or anybody else said, he was never going to ignore Pete lying there, or leave Pete to be buried alone. Fuck that. He was going to bury him right and to hell with the consequences.

'The thing you had to remember about Stretch was, well he was young.

'Was he too young to have made a patch? Well I guess, looking back, maybe. We only tend to make up older guys now, you want to be sure they've got the nous and the staying power to make the commitment. But back then we'd taken some younger guys in. Fuck, I even argued for it. Said we were all getting on and if we didn't do something about bringing on new young blood, well we'd end up just a bunch of old farts.

'So for a while we'd been deliberately recruiting younger guys. And it wasn't just our charter either, it had been across the club. Hey look, Dobbo and Stu weren't exactly crumblies when they joined were they? I mean we weren't taking in kids, you know? This is a blokes' club and you had to be a solid bloke still to make it in, but for a while we had new guys coming in in their twenties.

'And Stretch was one of those. But it wasn't like he was an unknown quantity or anything. His older brother Pete was already in, and so was his half-brother Tazz, so he was almost like a legacy pledge.

'But by Christ you could tell he was Pete's brother. Just like Pete, Stretch was one of those blokes who didn't think, he was someone who acted; he didn't reason, he just felt what was right and did it. And if that meant going up against me and the club, or taking on the whole fucking world alone, well so be it. He knew that facing up to the club could get his patch pulled, or worse, but he just didn't care about the consequences. If it was what he needed to do, he did it and that was that.

'And he was going out with my daughter, Jenny. Now she was a wonderful kid. Good looking, bright, kind, she was going places, you know? Kath, my wife, used to joke she was the apple of my eye and she was right?

'I'm tired, fuck it I'm tired. I could just sleep for a thousand years.

'When I was younger, when Malcolm was P and Dobbo and his mate Stu and me were just the new patches in the club, I was different. I was wild then, larey, I had a short fuse if you crossed me; mad, bad

214

and dangerous to know.

'But Malcolm died. Then Dobbo died. And Stu stepped up, taking those of us in his circle in his wake.

'And so my moment had come, and Stu had me take over up there as P so there was no choice really, I had to roll up my sleeves up and get on with it.

'You think it's going to be great, being P you know? You see the status, you think it's about being respected and all, but the reality, it's very different. It's all about responsibility, being a leader, being the one people come to who'll sort stuff out, being there to support everyone who needs it while nobody really gives a moment's thought about the grief they're giving me or how much shit, whatever it is, they are doing is going to land at my door for me to clear up. I tell you, sometimes when I got to the end of the day and I crashed out in bed knackered with it all, I'd just lie there and wonder whether it was all worth the hassle.

'Sometimes I used to think sod it, I ought to jack it all in, step down, let someone else take all the crap and be free to go back to being a party animal.

'And the only thing holding me back was my sense of duty to the club. Otherwise, responsibility and shit, who needs it?

'But I was kidding myself really. The fact is I loved being P. It was what I'd always wanted to do ever since I'd first come across the club, and however well or badly it was going, I knew I just had to make a decision and get on with it. That was what the job was, problem solving and fuck it, at least I was never going to get bored.

'The trouble was, what for me was just a bit of political necessity, a decision made so we'd have a united front while the shit was hitting the fan and the plod came crawling over everything, for Stretch it was something very different.

'For him it was simply about Pete being family. What I'd done without thinking about it was set his family and club loyalties against each other, and all about something as basic as burying his brother. I mean, looking back, what was I fucking thinking? Everybody buries their dead. Even wars stop occasionally to let the dead get collected

215

and dealt with right.

'But the problem was, once I'd said that was what needed to happen, I couldn't very well go back on it straight off, could I? Not without looking like a twat, not without looking weak.

'There was a knock at the door of my office at the clubhouse and Maz put his head around it.'

'You got him?' I asked.

'We've got him, Maz nodded, 'I've put him downstairs in the bar.'

'Any problems?'

'No, he was fine.'

'What's he saying?'

'Him? Nothing. Looks like he's just going to front it out.'

'Is he bollocks! We'll see about that. Alright, then,' I told him as I got to my feet, 'let's get down there and get it over with.'

'Downstairs in the bar Stretch was sitting calmly on a chair which had been pulled out from one of the tables round the side of the room, while two of Maz's crew were standing sentry quietly by the doors.

'I nodded to Maz and with a gesture he instructed the sentries to disappear outside while I pulled up another chair and set it down straight in front of Stretch but with its back to him. He watched me, his face impassive as I sat down straddling it. I rested my elbows on the back, clasped my hands in front of me almost as though I was praying, and stared levelly back at him.

'I broke the silence.'

'You know why you're here?'

'I know,' he nodded without surprise, his gaze never wavering.

'You were seen at the undertakers. You going to try and tell me you weren't there?'

'I was there.'

'So tell me this,' and I shook my head in a mild warning, 'and I'm not interested in hearing any speeches about the rights and

216

wrongs of it, you knew the order was out, that no one was to have anything to do with it?'

'Sure I did, you had this bastard here,' he jerked this thumb in the direction of Maz, 'call me specifically, you know that.'

'You'd heard what I'd said? What the club was doing.'

He just shrugged at me and said he'd heard.

'And you ignored a club decision? You still went?' I pressed.

'Of course I did. He was my brother, what else was I going to do?'

'So what, you thought just because you're shagging my daughter that the rules don't apply to you. Is that it? Thought you were fireproof?'

'No.'

'Thought you could get away with it, did you?'

'Screw you, no, but I can tell you one thing...'

'Oh yeah, and what's that?'

'I'm going to be there when they put him in the ground tomorrow.'

'And I said no club members are going to be there.'

'Well then...' he said, staring straight at me.

'So you're saying you've got the balls to go against that rule tomorrow as well?'

'Well if you call that a rule,' he sneered. 'I'll tell you what the rules are. They're what this club was built on. They're about loyalty, brotherhood and standing by your mates, whatever the hell happens. And you think I'm going to break those rules just because of something you've decided? You want to know why I did it? He was my brother, he was your brother whether you liked it or not, whatever you did to him in the end, and I was, I am, going to do the right thing by him. End of.'

'And I have to say I lost it a bit at that. Had a bit of a rant to be honest. I mean, here I was trying to hold it together and sort this shit out, and there he was, a bloke who'd shown he'd just go off on his

217

own doing whatever the fuck it was he felt was right, with no thought for anyone else, just facing me down.

'So I let rip at him. I was frustrated, I guess.'

'For fuck's sake, what is it with you guys up here?' I yelled, 'Is this what Munster built? A charter full of nutters? Are you all out of your fucking heads or what? It doesn't matter what the club wants, what it needs, it's all about you, isn't it?'

'He never blinked at my tirade.

'But I'm telling you mate, those days are over. The club has a right to a P who's got both feet on the ground, someone who's been put in here to do what's in the club's interests.'

'So I've got news for you sunshine. I'm not Munster, I'm me, and so long as I am P I'm going to get a bit of order and discipline back into this bloody club if it's the last thing I bloody well do, and no little toe rag like you is going to get in my way!'

*

'Don't ever make the mistake of thinking that being a P is something romantic. People see the flash and think it's about status, being the big man, but it's not.

'Being P's a job, and a bloody tough one at times too. Oh I'm not knocking the upsides, yeah it's great that you get the respect that it can bring. But fuck it, if you want the respect, you have to earn it. You have to work at being P every day; and like every other trade, it isn't all beer and skittles.

'But since it is was my job, it was something I took very seriously, that's the sort of guy I am, if I'm going to do something, I want to do it well.

'I take it seriously and I put my job before my personal feelings because that's what you have to do to do the job right. As P I knew I couldn't afford to indulge myself, even if ignoring all this shit and grief he was giving me, I actually quite liked the bloke. Well, I wasn't going to let any little shit take Jenny out, now was I? He had to have had something about him for me to let that happen, so I reined myself in to give him one last chance.'

'Listen Stretch, I can't let the fact you're chucking this in my face get to me,' I told him. 'You and your brother are good people, I know that, so I'm going to treat this as a warning. You toe the line from now on or...'

But he interrupted me even before I could finish.

'Sorry mate. Can't do that.'

'You what?'

'You heard, I can't do that.'

'So what does that mean?'

'It means his funeral's tomorrow, that's what I was checking, and I'm going.'

'You are, are you?'

'Yep.'

I just sat there looking at him after that, chin resting on my hands.

'You think I'm being an idiot don't you?' he asked eventually.

I just shrugged.

'Well, takes one to know one I suppose.'

'You think you're tough don't you?' I asked him quietly, not expecting or receiving a reply. 'You think you're above it all, that the rules don't apply to you? Isn't that right? You think what you want is more important than what the club needs? Is that it?'

He just sat there and looked at me.

'Well I don't care that you're his brother,' I continued coldly, 'I don't care that you're shagging my daughter. I wouldn't care if you were Stu's best buddy, this time you're going to get what's coming to you. You and that brother of yours. Oh I know he'll be in it with you.'

Turning my head to where Maz was standing by the doorway, I asked 'Why don't you get Tazz in here as well, I thought I saw him hanging around outside earlier on, face like a wet week, you could see him giving himself away.'

Maz slipped out of the door on his mission.

'I hate it when guys plot and conspire in the club, try to hide their dirty little secrets, their disloyalty, but you know what I hate even more?'

He just shrugged his shoulders and shook his head.

'Guys who want to put on a self-important little show, guys who want to parade their conscience, put on a little psychodrama. Want to be the centre of attention once they've been caught. Well you know what? I don't give a shit, I'm not interested...'

'So what do you want then, Bomber?' he interrupted, 'you want to take my patch as well, is that it?'

'Yes, I want you out, in bad standing.'

'Then can we get on with it? Then at least I won't have to listen to you whining on and I guess you're not interested in what I've got to say. But I know I've done the right thing. I know I'm doing what real brotherhood means whether I'm wearing a patch or not, and the rest of the guys here would say the same if they weren't all shit scared of you and Maz. Shit, what's your brotherhood worth if you have to enforce it through fear? But then dictatorship has its advantages I guess, if you like that sort of thing.'

'No one else is thinking like you...'

'Yes they are,' he interrupted, 'it's just they're too scared of losing their patches to do something about it.'

'And you're not?'

'I'm not scared of anything. Not you, not anyone who works for you.'

'You're not ashamed then, that I'm going to chuck you out?'

'Me? For doing what's right by my brother? Not a chance!'

'Even though he wasn't a brother, he was out, in bad standing.'

'Says you.'

'Says the club.'

'Says you, and you know it.'

'He was out, alive or dead.'

'He was a brother, alive or dead.'

'Whatever, well now you're going to be out too, so you can fuck off and join him as far as I'm concerned…'

I heard the door open behind me and the sound of two people entering.

'Well now,' I said without turning my head. 'So you've been sneaking off too have you? Down the undertakers, crying over the casket, betraying your club, betraying your brothers? Are you going to deny it?'

Tazz walked into my line of vision and took up position standing by his step brother's chair.

I cocked my head and stared at him, but Stretch hadn't bothered to look up or even acknowledge his presence.

'Yes, yes, I did. I'm as guilty as he is,' he said, indicating Stretch, who was turning in his seat to stare up at Tazz as he began to speak, 'just ask him.'

And that got a reaction from Stretch.

'No!' he roared, jumping up furiously to get in his brother's face, 'Not on your life! You had fuck all to do with it, you didn't have the balls then, so don't try and pretend you've got them now.'

The two of them were face to face now and Stretch was snarling.

'You did nothing. You wouldn't come. Remember? I gave you the chance and you bottled it. Your precious colours and your business meant more to you than he did, so you can fuck off now.'

'It's not too late, I can still come to the funeral…'

'It is too late. You didn't want to get involved, so it's organised now and we don't want you there. You wanted to keep in with the club so you can stick it out here.'

'Please Bro, don't be like this. We're his family, we're all he's got. Don't let us fall out like this…'

'You made your choice…'

221

'For fuck's sake, you really are as pig headed as he says you are. Why are you being such a shit? What good does it do you?'

'You're right, it doesn't do me any good at all.'

'So why not let me help you?'

'Because I'm not dragging anyone else down with me.'

'But I told you and you just wouldn't listen...'

'Yes, because it might have made sense for you but not for me.'

'You really don't want me there? You're really not going to let me join you?'

'You chose to follow the rules, to stay, I chose to do what I thought was right, to go. I made my choice, so did you. I'm not complaining about mine or trying to change it. I'm a bloke, I stick by my choices, I think you should too.'

'You're both bloody mad, the pair of you,' I pronounced wearily into the silence that followed.

'He's been bonkers ever since I first met him,' I said to Tazz, nodding at Stretch who had slumped back down into his chair, convinced I think that no one else now was going to spoil his glory and share in his martyrdom.

'Yeah well, treat people like crap long enough and who knows how nuts they'll go in the end,' spat Tazz.

'Well you went nuts the moment you decided to side with this idiot,' I told him.

'He's my brother, what else am I going to do?'

I'd heard that already today.

'Him? You can forget about him. He's out, so if you're in, he's not your brother any longer. He's dead to me, and to you as well. That is, if you're still with us?'

'And what about Jenny. Is he dead to her too?' Tazz asked.

'He will be once I've told her.'

'You can't control her like that.'

'No? You think she won't listen to her old man?' I snapped back.

'On this?' he sneered, 'Not a chance.'

'Don't you worry about her, she's not your problem. You've got a decision of your own to make now,' I told him. I just need to know whether Maz here is pulling one set of patches today, or two?'

'The irritating thing about it was that I knew Stretch realised it wasn't anything personal. He knew this was club business, but he just wasn't prepared to put the club in front of his personal feelings and agree he wouldn't attend the funeral.

'He was such an absolutist, you could see that in the way he'd given Tazz the brush off when he'd tried to join him. As far as Stretch was concerned, Tazz had had his chance to do the right thing and had blown it.

'And that was the problem we, I, was now left with. If Stretch could just be a bit flexible, then we could avoid all this shit he was going to force me into. But no, he was such a stubborn bastard and once he'd made his mind up, he was stuck on it. Irresistible force meets immovable object.

'So in the end I had no choice.

'As P I simply couldn't let anyone get away with insubordination like that, whoever they were, whatever the cause. It just couldn't be allowed to happen, and so I had Maz and his crew strip Stretch of his colours while he and I stood there in silence.

'And when all his flash was off he was told that Maz's boys would be round to his flat to collect all the club gear at the weekend, and he had forty-eight hours to remove his ink or it would be done for him.

'Then we booted him out of the clubhouse.

'To an extent I even admired him for his whole fuck you attitude. I might not like it, but I had to respect the fact he'd made his choice and he followed it through to the bitter end, stuck to it like a man.

'The boys left me alone in the bar.

'I don't know how long I sat there but eventually I went back up to my office. I didn't particularly want to see anyone for a while and I

223

certainly wasn't in a hurry to go and see Jenny, which as it happened, didn't matter, because she decided to come and see me.

'About an hour or so later I heard a knock at the door. It was Maz to tell me that she'd pitched up at the clubhouse and did I want to see her?

'I'd have to get it over with sometime I supposed, so I told him to show her up.'

'You've heard the news, I guess,' I asked her, as she walked in and I shut the door behind her. 'So, you come to have a go at the old man or what?'

She'd been crying. I could see her eyes were puffy and she just hugged me, burying her face against my chest.

'Oh Dad!' she wailed.

I got her sat down and she curled up next to me on the sofa I've got in my office the way she used to when she was a little girl.

'You're my dad,' she said.

'You know how much that means to me. You've always been there for me, ever since...' she sniffled again, 'ever since mum left us. You know I know that.'

'I know,' I reassured her.

'You mean the world to me...'

'I know love, I know. We've always been here for each other haven't we?'

'So why does it have to be like this?' she asked. 'What's wrong with Stretch going to his brother's funeral? Why do you have to fall out over something like that?'

'Because it's not about that,' I told her softly.

'So what is it about then?' she asked, her red rimmed eyes looking up at me pleadingly.

'It's about him challenging me, love. Challenging the club. You know I can't let him get away with something like that.'

She looked about to burst into tears again. She was only young.

Nineteen remember.

'I've got a job to do love, and I've got to do it whatever I feel...'

'Whatever the cost? Whatever I feel?' she demanded.

'Let something like this go, and then what?' I explained patiently. 'Pick and mix? I let the guys do what they want and only keep to the rules when they fancy it? Fucking anarchy, that's what that would be, and what would be the point of even having the club then? It'd be the end of it and we might as well all go home.'

I started to try another tack.

'Look, I know he's your boyfriend, but there'll be others, you'll see...'

But she wasn't to be diverted.

'Dad, you know I've never tried talking to you about club business, and I know you know what you're doing as P here, they wouldn't have given you the job if they didn't think you could handle it. I'd never try to tell you your job, I wouldn't know where to start...'

'But? I think I hear a *but* coming,' I told her.

She had obviously worked herself up to something, so I sat back waiting to hear what she had to say.

'But nothing, Dad, well not really,' she said with a shy smile.

'You going to try and persuade me out of it?' I asked, folding my arms as I looked at her, 'cos I can tell you now, love, you're wasting your breath.'

'Look, I know you've got a tough job here,' she said, sitting up on the sofa and swivelling round to face me. 'I know that you need to make sure you keep the guys' respect and I know to do that you can't just listen to all the guys and just do what they want. You can't be going round all day being swayed this way and that by whatever they want or worrying about who thinks what of you. You've got to be a leader.'

God there were times, I thought, when she looked just like her mum had, before, you know, she went.

'Someone's got to make decisions, take on the difficult choices and get things done when they need to be, whatever people think, and you can't afford to be worrying about whether you're popular or not. I get that Dad.'

'But?' I grunted.

She shook her head. 'I'm really proud of you, dad. I see what you've made of yourself. I see the trust that's put in you to come here and sort out this club.'

'But?' I insisted.

'But sometimes, oh, I don't know, sometimes just being strong isn't enough, is it? You've always said that to me, that you need to be smart as well...'

'And I'm not being smart, is that it?' I demanded.

'Oh Dad, don't be like that. I just want to help...'

'Help what?'

'Help sort this mess out. You're losing one of your top guys, you know that, you've always rated him, and over what? A stupid argument about his brother's funeral?'

'And you think having my nineteen year old daughter come in and sweet talk me round to letting Stretch off is going to help me keep the guys respect? Is that it?'

'No dad, hear me out! Please? OK, I'm young I know. OK, I've not got your experience, I know, but aren't you just pushing this too far? Can't you be a bit flexible?'

'You telling me how to do my job?'

'No, dad, you know I'd never do that...'

'Well what are you doing then?'

'I'm just...'

'Who's in charge at this club? You? The guys? Or me?'

'You're P, dad...'

'That's right.'

'But that doesn't mean it's your club does it, dad? The club is about all its guys, you told me that…'

'But someone's got to run it for all of them…'

'For them, dad. That's the point, it's for them isn't it? So you have to listen to what they say. You have to take into account what they want…'

'They want to do what they're told, that's what they want.'

'Is that what it's about? Is that what you believe?'

'It's what's necessary…'

'It's insane!'

'We were shouting at each other by then, our faces ugly with rage. Looking back I still don't know how we got to that point. I just see her jumping up, I see the look of scorn and hatred on her face as she pulled the door open, and then the slamming of it behind her and the clatter of her footsteps as she ran away down the corridor and disappeared.

'Looking out of my office window a few moments later I caught a flash of blue and silver as her car peeled out of the yard and into the road, engine revving as she slipped the clutch.

'And she was gone.

'I didn't know where at the time, although it didn't take much to guess she was off to find Stretch.

'I was right. She was straight on the phone to him at his place, well it was almost their place really as she'd all but moved in by that stage, the plod had it all on tape, it turned out later.

'Stretch was evasive at first with her. I guess to start with he'd have been wondering where her loyalties were going to lie, with me as her dad or him as her bloke. But from the transcripts of the cop's bugs I saw later, any uncertainty in that direction didn't last long.'

DATE: 10 June 2008

TIME: 16:57

TAPE TRANSCRIPT

What are you going to do?

227

Do? What do you think I'm going to do? I'm going to bury my brother.

Then I'm coming with you.

There's serious shit going on here.

I know.

You know?

Yeah, I've just had a blazing row with my old man about it, about you, about how he's treating you. I can't believe he's doing this to you, to us.

Yeah, well he is. Him and the guys.

You can't be serious. The rest of them can't think this is right?

Who gives a fuck what the rest of them think?

What about Tazz? Surely he's there for you?

Tazz? Don't make me laugh. He's just like all the rest.

Well, I'm going to be there.

There could be trouble you know, your dad...

Oh screw my dad. You're going to go, so I'm on my way over now, and tomorrow morning I'm going with you. End of.

Love you babe.

Love you.

TAPE TRANSCRIPT ENDS

'I didn't know who to talk to.

'Well I did. There was only one guy I could call, but I guess to start with I just didn't want to.

'I thought back to the advice Stu had given me when he was sending me up here.

'"It's a balancing act being P," he'd told me.

'On the one hand you've got to make decisions, it's what you're there for. Someone has to take responsibility; and when you make a

228

decision there's usually going to be some guys who agree with you and some who don't, particularly if a decision goes against something they want or hurts their interests.

'Hell, if everybody agrees on what needs doing then it's not really much of a decision, is it?

'So on the other hand you need to be able to take all the guys with you when you've made your choice, including those who're against it in the first place or have lost out somehow as a result.

'And that's quite a trick to pull off, particularly with our mob. They're no shy bairns you know, they're all stand up guys who'll stick up for what they think is right or what they want, whoever the fuck you are.

'Sure you can just rely on enforcing a decision for a while, just wield the big stick and make sure everybody toes the line. It can work in the short term, and believe me, I know there're times, when it's a crisis or something, when you do just have to act, and worry about the questions after. But to be honest, those sort of deals are really much fewer and further between than you might think. In life there's rarely anything that really, really needs to be done *right now*, that can't wait a few hours, days even, so you can speak to the guys and take a proper decision.

'Because make no mistake, at the end of the day it has to be your decision and you're going to be judged on it. No one's going to respect a P who tries to duck out of deciding what to do and then stand by it. The guys will be looking to you to lead, it's what you're there for and if you can't or won't step up to do the necessary, then sure as hell somebody else will.

'You're where the buck stops.

'So if you want to be P, get used to it, but get used to doing it right so you don't have to keep worrying about it.

'Because all you really need to do to make a success out of taking even the really difficult decisions, is to make sure you're seen to do it fairly.

'And all that means is that to start with you need to consult, and be seen to really be consulting everybody before you make your decision. And I mean really be consulting, not some *I've made up my mind already but I'm going to make a show of listening* crap. You need to go at it with an open mind. You need to talk to all your patches. In any charter there's not going to be that many of them so how difficult can it get?

'Ask each of them what they think, what their ideas are, what options they see, what they'd like to happen. You might be P but it doesn't mean you've got the monopoly of smarts, so why would you think you're the only one who can come up with the right solution?

'But even setting that aside, the really important point is the club belongs to all the guys. Even though you're the P, it's not yours, you're working for them. So if there's a decision to be made that affects their club, they all need to feel they have had the chance to properly have their say and to have been listened to.

'So speak to all your guys individually to get their ideas. Put what they've got to say to church where the different points of view can be discussed, challenged, talked through. You need to give them time. Some blokes will want to mull things over, not be rushed, otherwise even if you think you've let them have their say, deep down they'll feel you railroaded them into something and they won't buy in the way you want them to.

'But once they've had their say, and enough time to think and talk it through, then it's up to you. You've got the flash, so now it's your turn to show you deserve to wear it, because you have to take away all the stuff the guys have given you and make your decision.

'If it's a particularly difficult or serious problem you might consult a bit more with your senior officers, but only so as to help you think through your choices and weigh up the options. They are there to advise, be a sounding board perhaps, but they're not there to make the choice for you. That's down to you and you alone.

'So yes, consult, but don't confuse that with putting everything to a vote, we don't run this club as a democracy or by having a referendum every five minutes. We run it by having good officers who know what they're doing and who the guys respect.

'And once you've made your decision then you don't just announce it like it's been delivered on tablets of stone.

'While once the decision has been made, it's made, and you've the right to expect everybody to knuckle down and go with it whatever their views, you've got to show respect for the varying opinions that your guys gave you, otherwise they might just feel that you've ignored what they had to contribute.

'So when you've made your decision, don't be shy, tell them why you've made it. Give the guys your reasons, make sure they know it's not for debate, that part's over, the decision's been made, but by way of explanation.

'You want to show you've made a balanced choice that has taken into account all their views. Sure it's had to be a judgement call but then what would you expect? Like I said, if everyone already agrees then there's not much of a decision to be made is there?

'And the other thing you need to do is make sure that everybody is quite clear what the decision means, what everyone is to do, or not do, so there's no ambiguity, no wriggle room or scope for argument. If the rules of the game have changed then all the guys need to know what the new ones are, who's responsible for what, what's expected of every patch, tryout, tagalong, associate, whoever, and what happens if someone screws up.

'Do it that way and everyone will feel they've had a fair crack of the whip. They'll feel they've been able to contribute their ideas, that've been taken into account in making the decision and they all know what it is and what it means. You can't say fairer than that.

'Do it like that and the guys'll go with you almost every time, even the ones that have lost out, so to speak.

'And why?

'Because it's seen as fair. It's that simple.'

*

'I'd fucked it up, I realised.

'I'd had his advice and I'd blown it right from the start on this thing.

'I'd made a decision in the heat of the moment and just thought I could impose it on the guys because I was P.

'And now it was coming back to bite me on the arse.

'So eventually there was no choice but having to make that call.'

'Look Bomber,' I heard him say, 'it's your charter, I'm not going to tell you what to do.'

'Sure I know that...'

'I'll talk it through with you, help you think through your options, even God help me, give you some advice, if you want it that is, but the one thing I'm not going to do,' he said firmly, 'is tell you what to do.'

'That's OK, I appreciate it,' I told him, 'it's my charter, it's my call. I can live with that.'

'F2F?' he asked.

'Yeah, it's gotta be hasn't it?' I agreed, and he said he'd be up that evening.

'Appreciate it,' I told him.

'No worries, bro,' he said, 'for you, anytime, you know that.'

'And of course I did. He'd always been there for me, ever since the get go.'

'The thing about Stu was, he was honest, a real straight talker. And he also came into it without any baggage so he could take a clear view of how things stood, be objective in a way that was fast becoming very difficult for me. So, as we walked and talked it through on a stroll down to the chippie through the chill night air with Maz tagging along behind as security, he helped a hell of a lot.

'The problem as he saw it, and I could hardly argue the point, was that some of the club had seen my bust up with Pete and then his brothers as becoming personal. As being about me and my authority as P, rather than being about what was good for the club. As though now it had become a face thing, which to be fair, it probably had.'

'So what do I do about that? I can't back down now, not without making myself look weak. I don't want to look like some kind of a tosser,' I asked him.

'We took our fish suppers down to the park. We'd hit an offie for a six pack of Tennents to wash it down and we sat on a bench opposite a kiddies playground, deserted at this time of night.

'Like I said,' Stu told me as we munched, 'I can't and won't tell you what to do, but don't tell me this is really what you wanted? Always remember you've got choices, you know. Don't ever let yourself get boxed in, trapped into just following some course of action for fear of changing tack if that's the right thing to do.'

'How do you mean?'

'Pete's dead, so let him go. You can't kill him again. You didn't want to in the first place did you?'

I thought about protesting but all I said was a reluctant, 'No...'

'And you know you've always said you thought Stretch had the right stuff.'

'He's been a bit of a wazzock at times, but yeah, he had it alright.'

'So what are you letting the shit blow up like this for? Who's in control here? You or some runaway train?' he challenged.

'So how do I get out of this then?' I retorted. 'How do I avoid ending up looking like a complete wet or a complete dickhead or both?'

Stu looked at me appraisingly and behind his eyes I was sure I could see the cogs spinning as he worked it out, what I would need to do. He wasn't going to tell me, to order me what to do, but I knew that if he could help me find a way, he'd share it with me. That's what he'd always done. Whatever the situation I'd found myself in, he'd always been there to help me out again and again over the years.

'If it was me,' he said eventually, as he considered the options, 'I think I'd play the respect card.'

'Respect?' I asked warily.

'Yeah,' he said, nodding, as he rustled amongst the scraps in his greasy paper for the last of his chips, 'respect.'

Satisfied that he'd had all he wanted he screwed the wrapper up and reaching across chucked it into the bin beside the bench.

'Look mate, there's nothing wrong with changing your mind if you think you've made a mistake. Fuck it, I've lost count of the things I've screwed up over the years, and there's nothing wrong in admitting to the guys that you realise you've dropped a bollock, so long as you do it the right way. Everybody's human, everybody makes mistakes, everybody realises that. So if you've cocked something up you can either go on denying it out of fear of losing face and who's going to respect that?' He was sat head turned to face me as he spoke.

'Or,' he continued, 'you can front it out. I cocked up, I made a wrong call, and now I'm correcting it 'cos I'm big enough to stand up for my own mistakes. You show you're strong enough to do what's right whatever happens.'

'You sure about this?' I asked, as I mulled it over.

'Sure I am,' he said. Well it was easy for him to say. He wasn't the one who was going to have to climb down off their high horse and admit to having acted like a pillock, but as I listened to him, deep down I knew he was right, and that he was giving me the way out if I wanted to step up and take it.

'Look, no one could have foreseen what would happen and what those little tossers were going to do. But when it did, you felt you had to make a call in the heat of the moment in the best interests of the club, and well, that's fair enough. But that was then, this is now. It was your call at the time and now things have moved on, the situation's a bit clearer. You can even show that you've heard Stretch out and taken account of how he feels and what he has to say.

'In other words, bro,' he said, tapping the bench seat to emphasis his point, 'you show you've been listening and you get back into consultation mode sharpish.'

He paused, looking at me to see if I was on board.

'When's the funeral? Tomorrow? What time?'

I nodded. 'It's at two.'

'So, you get Stretch brought back in, and you do it tonight so this is all sorted and the guys know for tomorrow. I'll call down and

Sandy can organise a contingent to run up here in the morning so there's a decent club turnout. You OK with that?'

I nodded.

'Stretch won't want to come,' he added, reaching into his pocket and pulling out his mobile. 'But you can tell him that you've thought about what he said. You've had a chance to consider it again now the heat's died down a bit. That you've listened to how strongly he feels and you respect what he's had to say and how he's said it. So, now the immediate crisis is over you recognise that the circumstances are different, and so you've made a different, a new decision and you're going to set aside the spat with Pete and treat it as a full club funeral. You can tell him you're pulling guys up from my lot so it's going to be a good show. There's no loss of face, no loss of authority, not as I see it. You might even gain some if it plays right.'

'So as he called Sandy to arrange a posse, that was what we'd decided to do.'

'Kath was concerned, I could see it in her face as I walked in through the door.'

'What's up love?' she asked straight away, peering into the hallway from where she was standing with a mug of coffee in her hand.

'Is it this thing with Stretch?' she asked, as she put it down on the worktop and stepped into the hallway to meet me as I went through the routines of deadlocking and bolting the door.

How the fuck did she know about that, I wondered, although it really didn't take much working out.

'I knew something was up,' she told me as I turned to face her, 'Jenny called by earlier today and she was looking so upset I asked her what was going on. Do you really need to do this?'

'You too?' I asked, an edge of sarcasm in my voice.

'Why?' she asked taken back a bit, 'Who else is talking to you?'

'Who isn't?' I said, 'Jenny. Stu. They've all been talking to me.'

235

'Stu? What does he say?' she wanted to know, as she trailed me through to the kitchen.

'Do you want a brew?' she added, 'I've had the kettle on, or a cold one?'

It was tempting, but I just felt knackered and was more interested in the prospect of getting my head down than another beer.

'Nah,' I shook my head and slumped down in one of the kitchen chairs. 'He's telling me he thinks I need to row it back and get the boys back on board.'

'Including Stretch?' she asked, with an enquiring look on her face.

'Yeah, him in particular,' I nodded, stretching and yawning.

'That's great, love,' she said brightly, obviously pleased with the result.

'Is it?' said Mr Grump.

'Well yes, of course it is. If it makes this mess right with him and Jenny, then that's got to be good all round hasn't it?'

'I suppose...'

'He's usually right, isn't he? Stu?' she told me approvingly. 'He's always looked out for you and given you good advice so far, hasn't he? You've always said so.'

'Yes...'

'Are you going to let Jenny know? She'll be worried.'

'Yeah, I'll give her a call,' I agreed in a weary voice.

'Well then. You look all in, love,' she said decisively, turning to pour the dregs of her mug down the sink and reaching for the phone to pass over to me, 'so you make your call and let's go to bed shall we? We can sort everything else out in the morning.'

'Yeah, you're right,' I said, scrolling down the list of numbers for Jenny's mobile.

'You know what else he said?' I asked, as I found it and dialled.

'No, what?'

'When all else fails, we can always try doing the right thing...' I heard the line pick up, 'Hi Jenny. No, don't hang up, I've got some news you're going to want to pass on to Stretch...'

*

'So I'd given in. With Stu's help I'd realised I'd been wrong and decided to, in his phrase, do the right thing. To be big enough to say fuck it, Pete was a brother and Pete was Stretch's brother.

'It would be a full club funeral and Stretch would be reinstated, have his colours back, and actually, probably more. Like I said, I'd seen the way he'd stood up for what he thought was right and he'd impressed me with his guts. It had been some mud test and he'd passed it with flying colours so I planned to recognise that somehow, I still hadn't quite made up my mind with what.

'And so as I headed out first thing the next morning I thought I was on the way to getting it all sorted.

'Of course it wasn't sorted yet, so as Kath was at home I had Maz detail a tryout, Peanut, to come round to the house and babysit.

'It's a just in case, love,' I told her as I kissed her goodbye, 'I'm not expecting any trouble but just until I've got all the loose ends tidied up on this thing.'

'"Well OK then," she said, as she watched me climb onto my bike and fire it up.

'And the thing was, I wasn't expecting any trouble. Sure there was a fair amount to do. I had to let all the guys know about the change of plan so we could ensure a good turnout this afternoon but I'd get Maz straight onto that as soon as I was in the clubhouse.

'Jenny had got Stretch on the line to me eventually yesterday evening to tell him the good news. It had taken some persuading on her part to get him to listen to me, and then a hell of a lot more on my part to get him to agree to come back in and get made up. Christ he was a stubborn bugger, but eventually he agreed to return and we arranged he'd drive over first thing. I said I'd give him his colours back and stand him a good fry up at the café down the road.

'The sun was shining and the roads were clear as I headed in.

'It was going to be a good day.'

*

'It was Maz who told me.

'At about eight-thirty Stretch and Jenny left the flat and headed down to where he'd parked his car on the street the previous evening.

'They both got in. Jenny had decided she wanted to come along to the clubhouse. I guess she'd wanted to be there to see her boyfriend and her old man make up, see him get his colours and flash back, and probably get a full Scottish as well.

'They never made it.

'It turned out that Dodo, the tryout who'd reported back on Stretch being at the funeral parlour, had seen what Nugent and Muttley had done to Pete, and had made the same calculation about how it might help them to get patched.

'So he'd decided he needed to step up and grab some of the action himself to show what he could do on his own initiative to help his prospects of being made.

'And so during the wee small hours this genius had snuck over to Stretch's place and wired a bomb to the ignition of his car.

'The moment Stretch turned the key, the car erupted into a ball of flame, the blast blowing the vehicle into the air and scattering debris, twisted metal and shattered glass a hundred yards down the street.

'As shocked residents dialled 999 and car alarms went off simultaneously across a half mile radius, Stretch and Jenny, sitting side by side, were killed outright.

'My decision, and the doing something about it, had come too late.'

*

There was a silence around them. To Iain, Bomber seemed lost, miles away with what Iain described later as a thousand yard stare in his eyes.

Iain hesitated, for once unsure as to what to say, or what to ask, before finally proffering a pathetic sounding, 'Christ mate, I'm sorry.'

Slowly Bomber swung his head around to face him, as though only just starting to remember he was there and that he had been speaking out loud.

"Salright mate,' he said at last, with an effort, 'It's not your fault. It was down to me, I've got to live with it. I do live with it, every day.'

He downed the last of his pint that he'd been nursing as they'd talked.

'So, that was what started you thinking about getting out?' Iain ventured after a moment.

'Yeah, well,' Bomber said, finishing his story in a voice flat with weary pain and resignation.

'The cops had picked me straight up from the clubhouse. They'd pulled in everybody they could find associated with the club to pile the pressure on and find out who knew what. A car bomb was a big public deal and the plod were in a complete flap thinking it was the start of some biker war shit, like they'd know their arses from their elbows.

'It was a bad time, but everybody played it right, just kept schtum, no-commented them to run the PACE clock out. They held us all for as long as they could but they didn't have anything on anyone with which to justify an extension so eventually everybody just walked.

'The house was dark and empty by the time I got home. Empty apart from a note.

'Peanut had told Kath the news while I was being held in the nick.

'And the note Kath left me said it all.

'About how it was all my fault, me and my flaming club; how she'd had it, how she never wanted to see me again, how she was gone.

'And you know what the strange thing was? Even though Jenny hadn't actually been her kid, she'd been mine, I still couldn't blame Kath. Couldn't resent the bitter things she'd written, couldn't argue the points.'

As Bomber sat there in the silent kitchen, alone with his grief, he knew that she had simply written the very words, the accusations, that he was torturing himself with... and he really couldn't blame her for that.

*

'And that was it?' Iain asked, horrified, 'She left you?'

'Yes. We never spoke again. She didn't want to see me. She filed for divorce and I said fine. Look I said, I couldn't blame her. Shit I deserved it, for what I'd done, what I'd put them... her through. That was on me.'

Iain recalled later that Bomber's eyes were blank as he was speaking, as though the events of those few days had burned the soul out of him.

'And that was me done,' he was saying in conclusion, and ticking things off on his fingers.

'The charter was screwed, with the cops crawling over everyone and everything, trying to fit anyone they could up for Pete, Stretch or even the missing toe rags.

'My daughter was dead, my wife was gone, and my club career was fucked.

'So you were wondering why I was thinking about jacking it in?'

*

'Christ,' DI Chambers said as he finished reading. 'He told me some of it but not all that. Poor bastard, no wonder he was in such a state by then.'

'So what did you say to him, about what he had told you?' we asked.

'Well I was sympathetic to a degree I suppose. I mean, whatever the circumstances he'd brought her up as his own and she'd been killed in tragic circumstances so it was a bit difficult not to feel for him as he sat there.'

'I told him:'

> 'You didn't mean it to happen I know that. You did it out of loyalty, loyalty to your club, your brothers, I can see that.'
>
> 'But what about my loyalty to her?' he asked me, his voice almost breaking, 'To my kid? What about her?'

240

'Sorry Bomber, I can't help you there. They're just choices you made, you couldn't always see where they were going to lead but decisions have consequences, you know?'

'Just like you've got a decision to make now. And it'll have consequences. Some you can see, some you can't, some will come out of the blue. But you still have to make a choice.'

'Unknown unknowns.'

'If you like.'

'I was going to need to go I realised, I couldn't stay here all day. I'd got him to say he'd think about it and I was guessing that was about as far as I could expect him to go at this, a first meeting. But before I left I asked him how he felt, and I'll never forget what he said.'

'Fragile. Like I'm made of glass. Like everyone can see right through me and that at any moment I'm going to shatter into a million tiny pieces. I've failed, you know. I've failed at every fucking thing I've ever done in my life. Husband, dad, business-man, and now brother. If you look back at it I've fucked up every single thing that ever meant anything to me.'

'And so, as I walked out of the house and pulled the door shut behind me, I left him there in the kitchen, sitting in the dark.'

CHAPTER 9   PAYBACK TIME

La plus belle des ruses du diable est de vous persuader qu'il n'existe pas.

The finest trick of the devil is to persuade you that he does not exist.

Charles Baudelaire – *Le Spleen de Paris* 1862
way before Roger 'Verbal' Kint & The Usual Suspects

'As we reassembled after lunch at the following week's taskforce meeting, the Chairman turned from where he was standing by the screen next to a young man in a city style suit and watched as the assortment of mainly older officers drew up their seats for the afternoon session.'

'Thank you gentleman,' he said, as the last of them shuffled into the room bearing a slopping cup of coffee and balancing a salvaged stolen biscuit on the saucer as he pulled the door shut behind him.

'Thank you,' he said again, 'and now to kick us off this afternoon we have Inspector Galpin from the Financial Crimes Unit who some of you will have just met in the canteen. Inspector Galpin has been with the unit for three years now and is going to give us a briefing on current developments in money laundering. So without stealing his thunder I'll hand over to him.

'Jim, if you could do the honours with the lights please,' he added to the figure sat closest to the switches.

'The curtains were already drawn, and as the room plunged into gloom the youngish presenter clicked his remote control to trigger the first slide and rehearsed in his mind once again how he was going to introduce himself and his presentation to this group of potentially career enhancing contacts.

'He knew he had the graveyard shift, the easy starter after lunch, but he was five minutes in to his allotted ten plus twenty minutes for questions and open forum discussion, and it was going well.'

'Now, as we all know one of the key problems all drugs dealers face is how to manage the financial side of the operations.

'Dealing in drugs generates money for the dealer when goods are sold and they have to pay out money to buy the goods in, and these are all going to be transactions they want to avoid being seen.

'It may also be an obvious thing to say, but drug dealers deal drugs to make money and they want that money so as to be able to buy things. So to enjoy the profits of their crimes they have to have ways of being able to access their cash in a way that they can explain where it has come from.

'Going all the way back to Al Capone who famously went to jail for tax evasion rather than his racketeering activities, we have long seen this as an area where criminals are vulnerable to detection and prosecution.

'Whether it's trying to bank, transfer, withdraw or simply explain large sums, the sort of money involved in the drugs business brings its own problems, particularly where individuals otherwise seem to have little or no sources of legitimate income with which to explain their financial transactions.

'This is particularly important when it comes to managing international transfers and payments as will inevitably be the case when drugs are being imported from other countries such as cocaine and heroin.

'So modern financial reporting rules covering everything from the know your customer requirements imposed on banks and professional advisers, through to notification requirements in respect of cash transactions across most jurisdictions in excess generally of the equivalent of around ten thousand pounds, or fifteen thousand Euros, are designed to both disrupt criminal activity and to make it easier to identify for investigation.

'The so called KYC or Know Your Customer rules are there so that the real sources and beneficiaries of any money can be traced and identified so as to avoid criminals using front men to disguise their involvement in any transactions. The reporting limits are there to make it difficult to move large enough sums of cash in or out of the financial system with which to facilitate dealing in cash.

'And undoubtedly the improved controls instituted over the past decade and longer have had an impact on criminal activity. We can see this in the ways that criminals have changed how they undertake this sort of financial transaction.

'At a lower level we have seen the development in some places of what might be considered alternative currencies which can be used as a form of barter. Upmarket watches such as Rolexes, for example, are items with a known tradable value which can be easily carried and traded and so can be used as a form of currency as both a store of value and a means of exchange outside the normal financial system.

'In some cases and communities criminals will tap into using the traditional *hawala* or *hundi* system to move money overseas. These are long standing ethnically based transfer systems covering large areas of the Middle East, Indian subcontinent and parts of Africa. They are based on codes of honour across large networks of money brokers and they operate as a parallel informal banking system outside all formal channels. As an entirely trust-based system most varieties of *hawala* systems operate without any documentation being exchanged between the brokers handling the transfer, and so its usefulness to criminals looking to move sums around without leaving a paper trail is obvious.

'On the other hand, at the highly technological end, we have seen criminals moving onto the dark web and using virtual currencies such as bit coins which are unregulated and virtually untraceable to undertake transactions.

'But sometimes the ways found to disguise these transactions are simply ingenious in their simplicity, such as the so called alternative trading approach, I'm here to brief you on this afternoon which neatly deals with a number of issues for any criminal involved in international transactions.

'The way it works is simple. The drug dealer, or people acting on their behalf, sets up a trading company dealing legitimately in goods and it doesn't really matter what these are – car parts, food, machinery. What's important is that they are things with a commercial value in the country where the drugs are coming from, where their drug supplier sets up a trading business of their own...'

Which was when the interruption came.

'These goods that you're talking about, came a gruff older London voice from out of the dimness. 'Are you saying they can be anything?'

'Oh yes, just absolutely anything at all can work, so long as they can be sold in the country they're going to...' he answered brightly.

'How about toys? Would they work?' the voice cut across him.

'Toys?' he gave it a moment's thought, 'Why yes, I think they would do very nicely. They'd be easy to sell on in most countries.'

He paused, wondering whether to follow up on the muttered *Oh shit!* that he was sure he'd heard from the back of the room. He could feel a change in the atmosphere, a sudden tension in the air as though everyone had suddenly sat up and taken notice even though he didn't have a clue why. But then the Chairman came to his rescue with a, 'Gentlemen, we have time scheduled in at the end of this for questions and discussion so I suggest we wait until then unless there's anything particularly pressing?'

He looked around the room with a gaze that told everyone exactly what response he was expecting to receive and there was a compliant silence.

'Thank you gentlemen, please Inspector, do carry on.'

'Yes, yes, sir,' said the Financial Crimes Unit officer, slightly thrown as to what if anything had just occurred, but swallowing and gathering his thoughts, he turned back to the slide he had up with its arrow covered map of the world and, with his laser pointing tool, picked up the thread of his talk again as he outlined step by step how the process actually worked in practice.

'Once the businesses are up and running then the actual transaction is simplicity itself. The company in the UK arranges to export a consignment of goods to the drugs supplier's business, whether it's in South America say, or Turkey, and the goods are shipped.

'They also send an invoice for payment and so far, it's all a completely legitimate transaction, the sort of thing that's happening thousands if not millions of times a day across the world as goods are traded and shipped across borders.

'The difference is that instead of the company receiving the goods paying the bill, the drugs dealer arranges to pay it himself using his dirty cash. So now the drugs dealer has a source of income and he can show where his money is coming from – his successful export business.

'Meanwhile, his drugs supplier now has a supply of goods he can sell in his own country either directly or to wholesalers who are to all intents and purposes, entirely legitimate. He's actually paid nothing for the goods, so all the cash he gets is straight profit paying for the drugs he has sent to the UK operator, and again this gives him a legitimate stream of income and cash.

'Better still, he can use the invoice he's had from the UK, or a copy of it with suitably amended payment details, to arrange to remit cash out of the country to "pay" their bill, which needless to say, never goes anywhere near the UK supplier but instead ends up in a suitably secret bank account in Switzerland or somewhere else equally accommodating.

'So the suppler has the cash for the drugs, a clean income stream and a mechanism for getting money into an overseas bank account; while the drug dealer here has paid for his gear and has turned dirty money into an apparently clean stream of income.'

As he came to the end of his slides and the single word, Questions? appeared on the screen he heard the swell of voices in the darkened room.

'How sweet is that?' came a younger voice in an Estuary accent, while another he was sure had been the gruff older voice could be heard venting, *'Oh for fuck's sake!'* about something, as by the door someone was scrabbling to get up and hit the lights, *'And we let the fuckers go...'*

To his right, opposite where the Chairman was just rising to his feet, he recognised the representative from Strathclyde Police he'd been introduced to at lunch. He wasn't saying anything, just sitting there smiling up at him.

*

'Me, all I could think about was Bomber and wheelbarrows.

'Because the truth was, after everything we'd done, all we'd actually established was that he did really run a legitimate transport and logistics business. Sure, he'd been taken advantage of by Stu to ship, well, not even hooky gear. But as far as criminality went? It was nothing to do with him.

'Much like I knew the two ex-cops deaths were nothing to do with him or Stu either.'

*

'What do you know about Mallorca?' I'd asked Bomber, back there in the interview room.

'It's a holiday island, why?'

'Don't play games,' I told him, 'You know what I mean. Those two dead ex-cops, that was Stu wasn't it?'

Bomber just shook his head.

'So is that's what's got your mob so steamed up at us about? Well sorry, mate but you're barking up the wrong tree on that one.'

'No?'

'No, it wasn't us. Wasn't me certainly, and as far as I know it wasn't Stu.'

'Well who the hell else was it going to be?' I'd demanded, and he'd just shrugged and shook his head.

'Whoever else had a problem with them,' he suggested. 'Who said we were the only ones who might have a beef with them?'

*

'But of course I knew better now.

'Like Bomber had said, it was just a matter of who the hell else could have a problem with what they knew, and of course as soon as he put it like that, it made absolute sense.

'Thinking back to Strathclyde Police's ringing non endorsement, I'd known it right at the outset.

247

'*As far as I know, as a force we have no official view*, he'd said very carefully indeed, *about the death of these two ex-officers*.

'Shit, I'd all but called them dirty myself.

'Who knew what sort of blokes these two ex plain clothes cops had been on the force? Particularly ones with a well-funded retirement to high walled villas in the Med?

'No full pension at fifty and on to a boring security guard outfit for these bods. No, it had been a life of luxury in the sun until it had all been cut short in a few bloody moments that bright spring morning a couple of months ago.

'And if you were dirty cops, what dirt would you have made sure you had on your own to make sure you could safely enjoy your retirement. The stuff that would make it too embarrassing to go after you. The sort of thing that no force would want to have come out the way it would in an open trial?

'But then it wasn't as simple as just protection was it? If you had stuff that dangerous, you were also an ongoing threat weren't you? An ever present risk to the powers that be of blackmail.

'*Don't play games*, I'd told Bomber, and somebody hadn't.

'They'd played for keeps instead.

'And the only ones who seemed to really know anything about the two hit men who'd done the necessary were Strathclyde Police and my friends in the Met.

'Who knows what the hell happened.

'Something must have disturbed the equilibrium.

'Perhaps they turned, started to get into the drugs business themselves but then got over their heads, were threatened, turned to trying to blackmail Strathclyde Police, or Stu, to get them out?

'Or perhaps they were just too big an unexploded bomb to have floating out there, and someone decided a controlled detonation on their own terms was preferable to an explosion out of the blue?

'Whatever it was, it had made them a problem, and one which it was worthwhile getting rid of completely, dealing with once and for all.

'And if that gave an opportunity to have a go at fitting Stu up for the job at the same time as a way of covering their tracks?

'Well, that would just have been a bonus, I guessed. Given respected cops or outlaw bikers as the choice of suspects, for most people there wasn't going to be much of a choice was there?'

'And now after I'd met him at his place, Bomber knew what was going on. He knew what the wheelbarrow was.'

'"I wanted out," he'd told me, "I wanted to be legit, he knew that and he still used me…"

'And at last he was able to admit to himself what he'd known deep down for a long, long time now. The realisation that Stu, and his association with Stu, had fucked up everything good in his life.

'His business.

'His relationships, Maggie, Kath.

'And worst of all, Jenny.

'And once Bomber had started talking, it seemed he wouldn't stop.'

'And so he's agreed to go public?'

'Yes. That's why he called you.'

'So what's next?' we asked.

'Next?' he answered with a snort, 'Oh that's simple. You need to meet Bomber and he'll give you his side of the story. I'll set it up.'

*

And so three days later, very nervously, following the instructions we'd received from DI Chambers, we made our way to the arranged place for our initial meeting with Bomber.

The venue was an out of the way pub, north up the coast road from Aberdeen towards where the old port of Peterhead jutted out into the cold unforgiving North Sea. We were told to be there by nine-thirty.

We got up there late afternoon, five or six perhaps, and so we drove past just to make sure we knew where we were going and checked it out. It looked to be a traditional roadhouse, complete with half a dozen big screens for the satellite sports and karaoke on Fridays and Saturdays. We had time to kill so we headed further up the road to wait until the appointed hour.

But by the time we arrived back there was no way we could get in. The place was lit up with blue flashing lights as the police were creating a cordon and sealing off the car park to the rear as a crime scene.

We caught sight of DI Chambers by the entrance. He was obviously looking out for us and as he saw our car he just shook his head at us and made an unmistakable gesture for us to drive on.

So we never did get to speak face to face with Bomber after all.

Axe murder in pub car park
'Blood everywhere' says witness

Local businessman John Harris, aged 51, was discovered at a quarter past nine last night slumped on the ground in the car park behind the ███████████ in ████████████.

The alarm was raised by a patron of the pub who had gone outside to get in their own vehicle and spotted Mr Harris's body.

'It was a horrible sight, there was blood everywhere,' said Mr Aiden Thomas, one of the bar staff who came out to see if he could help.

'This is a particularly vicious murder,' said Inspector Taylor of Grampian Police who is leading the investigation, 'We believe Mr Harris was attacked by a number of men using what we believe to be hammers, axes and other weapons and we're appealing for witnesses to come forward.'

According to a witness from the pub clientele who wants to remain anonymous, the body was lying in one of the parking slots at the far end of the car park, furthest away from the doors in one of the darker areas. The witness claims to have seen the body quite clearly before the police had secured the scene and told us that Mr Harris was lying face down, and while he could not be identified it was clear he had suffered a large number of wounds to the head and neck, with a small hatchet having been left embedded in his skull.

In particular Inspector Taylor urged any members of the motorcycling community who may know something to come forward.

'We know that Mr Harris had extensive links within the community, some of which may be relevant to this enquiry, so we would request that anyone who has any information that can be of assistance to us to contact the enquiry room.'

Mr Harris, a well-known member of the local biker scene, is understood to have retired last year from his long standing membership of the Rebel Brethren MC. It's not known precisely why he had decided to hang up his colours although he is understood to have left the club on good terms and at the time he was quoted as saying that he was simply becoming too old to participate fully in the club's activities the way he would want to and that he needed to concentrate on managing his growing and very successful international transport business.

There is speculation in some quarters that he'd been talking to the Police who confirmed simply that he had been interviewed recently in connection with an ongoing investigation and that he had been helping with their enquiries. The police have refused to speculate on whether there is any connection between Mr Harris's death and his prior membership of the club.

No one from the Rebel Brethren MC was available for comment.

*

Three months later DI Chambers called again. He wanted to meet. He had something to show us that he couldn't discuss over the phone.

By this stage we were part way through our research into Iain's papers that eventually gave rise to *Operation Bourbon* so we were beginning to have an inkling about what might lie behind the whole situation.

As he sat down, there was really only one thing we wanted to talk about.

We'd seen the reports in the press at the time but things had gone quiet since. As far as we could tell from what the police were saying publicly, the trail seemed to have gone cold.

'So, what happened that night?' we asked.

'He'd called me to arrange the meeting with you,' DI Chambers told us, 'but then he'd said not to come early as he was going to be seeing someone else first.'

'Stu?' we guessed.

'Yes,' he said wearily, looking up at the ceiling as he composed his thoughts, 'I tried to persuade him out of it of course, but he was insistent. He wanted a face to face with Stu before he did anything else.'

'So was it Stu?' we asked.

'Officially the case is open...'

'And unofficially?'

'The view is of course it was Stu. That's what they all wanted wasn't it? A chance to stick something on him? I mean it wasn't Stu personally even though the lads tugged him for it. He's capable of it sure, but like I've said about the Top Table and cut-outs, the untouchables want to keep their dabs off things directly these days.'

He shook his head, 'No it was a couple of mopes, typical wannabes, useful idiots. Strathclyde Police seem fairly sure, allegedly, they know who they are but as ever it's been about finding them and then getting proof.'

'Finding them? You mean...'

'Surprise, surprise, they seem to have disappeared into thin air but as far as our lot are concerned it's just the usual MO; kill the killers. Helps plug any potential leakage back up the line at source doesn't it? It's just basic security. So of course they got no change out of Stu when they pushed him on it.'

TRANSCRIPT

So that's your story? That I'd tell or use those total muppets? Do you really think that's going to stand up for a moment? You lot need to get your stories straight, don't you?

I mean, well come on, you can't have it both ways. Either we are some kind of tight knit organized crime mob, or we're a bunch of thuggish yobbos who'd use twats like that. So what's it to be? Make your minds up.

END OF EXCERPT

'You said allegedly,' we noted, 'and *that's what the view is*, so what are you saying? What's your view?'

He gave a bitter smile. 'Who's got any proof it was Stu?'

'Well no one from what you're saying…'

'So then, as far as I'm concerned the enquiry's a completely open one…'

'Wherever it leads?'

'Wherever it leads,' he nodded.

'You're thinking Plan C?'

He took a moment to choose his words carefully.

'I'm not thinking anything at this stage. I'm, just let's say, keeping an open mind, about all possible lines of enquiry, and let's leave it at that shall we?'

And there didn't seem any more to say in that direction.

But we were still curious.

'Why did he go do you think?'

'I don't know.'

'He must have known he'd have been in danger, surely?'

'You'd have thought so, he wasn't daft.'

'So he must have known what he might have been walking into?'

'I guess so,' he agreed, 'Suicide by biker maybe?'

'Do you really think so?' we asked.

'He was depressed certainly…'

'What made you think that?' we wanted to know.

'His house for one thing.'

'You said it was a mess…'

'Yes but it went way, way beyond that. This was like the place had just been abandoned, let go to rack and ruin all around him, and that was what got me thinking.

'I've seen it before.

'You know, sometimes with depression people just sort of give up hope, think nothing is worth the effort.

253

'You stop trying to do stuff because it's not it. Why try to keep the garden tidy because the weeds and crap keep growing back, faster than you can keep on top of them? It's a never ending task and eventually you think, I'm fighting a losing battle here, so why waste the effort? So you stop.

'Only then of course it becomes self-perpetuating, because the thing that really you could have managed if you'd put a bit of time in to keeping on top of it, once it's left to rot becomes a real problem, that will require more effort to get to grips with.

'And the longer it's left the more intractable it becomes, the bigger the problem and effort required.

'You know you sometimes come across old folks who have ended up living in complete squalor? Old houses, sometimes in quite posh areas. There was one round the corner from us where I lived as a kid. An old bloke, on his own. In our area his house would have been worth a bomb but by the time I was riding around on my treadder, you almost couldn't see his place through the overgrown bushes and trees in the front garden. The sort of place where you know that when he eventually dies they're going to be carting skip after skip loads of rubbish out of the rooms to clear the place out.

'I used to wonder, how do people get like that? I don't any more.

'People talk about letting yourself go. That's exactly what it's like. Giving up the fight and just thinking *Sod it, what comes, comes.*'

'It makes you wonder though, doesn't it,' we said, without really expecting an answer 'What drives somebody to be like that?'

'He was always bright, but I thought he was always a bit of a loser. He was like a kid, if he couldn't have it all then he didn't want anyone to have it. There could be a savage purity in his hate, and if you ask me that went way back.'

'He never told your bloke Iain though, did he, not really, about what was in his background? About who he was?'

We were confused. We had no idea what he was talking about.

'What do you mean?'

'So,' DI Chambers said, 'it all comes back to asking that question, if it

254

was about finding a new family, why had Bomber wanted one?'

He reached into his briefcase and pulling out a manila file he placed it gingerly on the table in front of us, in about the same way as you would handle some sweaty dynamite.

It contained a mass of photocopies of ancient hand written and old fashioned close typed police reports, together with a clutch of fragile looking yellowed newspaper clippings.

Which was how eventually, we got to read about the last secret of John 'Bomber' Harris.

Or to be more precise, James Anthony Pickering.

*

Jim Pickering was a bright lad. Born in August 1962 in Catterick where his dad was stationed as a captain in the army, his early years were hugely unsettled as the family moved from post to post in the UK and overseas as his father's career was fast tracked. By the time he was six he found himself shipped off home to a boarding school so he could at least get a consistent education.

So he wasn't around for the next few years as his parent's marriage disintegrated and by the time he sailed through his 11+ it was over. His mum had stayed in Germany with the new bloke she'd found, and his dad had upped stocks and relocated to the States with his new partner where he was making serious money in telecoms and the early days of IT. But neither new family had any place for him as a reminder of the past, effectively abandoning him to begin life as the lowest form of pond life in yet another forces family friendly boarding school, this time in Jedburgh, just over the Scottish border.

As a summer child he was the youngest and weediest in his class. He came in with a readymade chip on his shoulder and what his teachers described as poor impulse control, and the older kids promptly made his life hell. He was bookish, crap at sports, always last to be picked for any team, almost wilfully, even at that age, not interested in what the other boys were into, and every time he tried to join something or make friends, it always ended in failure, humiliation, rejection.

He was bullied at school, tormented, teased, beaten up all the way through his first year, He brought it on himself. Even though he couldn't fight for shit, he couldn't let anything go either. Couldn't or wouldn't rise above it when anyone had a go or poked fun at him. He was so insecure that anything anyone said could touch a raw nerve and set him off, and the more easily he was provoked, the more the other kids took to doing it as fun, getting a reaction that gave them the chance to get physical again and gather round to give him another going over. It was nothing serious, not physically. Not at that age. No broken bones, just Chinese burns and bruises, kids' stuff, but mentally, well, the scars went deep.

Even back then it seemed he was starting to build his own world to live in. One where he was in control, beholden to no one, and could fantasise about his revenge on anyone who'd ever crossed him.

So this went on for the best part of a year until one day, it stopped dead. It was games time one afternoon, cricket, something he just loathed, an afternoon of being sent out to the boundary as a useless fielder who couldn't catch a ball if he tried, which he probably wouldn't, to stand or probably sit around getting bored in the sun and waiting for the whole thing to end so he could get changed and go back to his dorm, or even better, squirrel himself away in the school library to hide away in a book and escape into another world.

Given his whole lack of enthusiasm it wasn't much of a surprise that he was the last one left in the changing hut, well, last but one.

Peter Bath was one of his chief tormenters. Almost nine months older than him and about twice the size, he and his little group were always picking on Jim as one of their favourite victims; tormenting him, poking, prodding, provoking, twisting his arm, his ears and his tail in equal measure to get a reaction that they could then sort out.

No one actually knows what went on that day.

Jim Pickering was never telling, and Peter Bath never could. The best guess is that Peter, alone with his favourite target, was up to his usual tricks of some sort. But this time, for whatever reason, young Jim didn't just fantasise about his revenge, he got it.

It made headlines at the time, well it would, wouldn't it? It's not every day that an 11 year old beats a 12 year old to death with a cricket bat at school is it?

From the evidence it looked as though having had his fun Peter turned to go and was heading out the door when Jim grabbed a bat from off the bench next to him and smacked him straight across the back of the head with it, fracturing his skull.

The PE teacher found them both when he came back in to see what the delay was. In court he described the sight of Jim standing there, smiling silently as Peter lay twitching his life away in an oily seeping pool of dark red blood.

Jim never spoke about it. Of course he was lucky in where his school was. The age of criminal responsibility was twelve in Scotland as opposed to ten in England so he just scraped in under the bar, while his parents and their brief played up the bullied card for all it was worth; everyone knew that he'd been being picked on, and so they pitched it as self-defence.

But at age 11, what could the system do?

*

'I looked into his background,' DI Chambers told us, as we read. 'I went digging through the reports of the time to build up a picture.

'Even though he was underage there still had to be a trial which lasted two weeks in what for the time was a blaze of media interest. Despite attempts by the authorities to make the experience less overwhelming for the defendant, the public and press galleries were packed throughout and he spent the entire time being watched with an air of morbid curiosity and horror.

'Observers at the time had mixed views, some saw him as cunning and manipulative, others as emotionally blank and shut off from the world, yet others as the slightly immature victim of the circumstances of his bullying.

'There was little dispute about the facts of the case. The forensic evidence and indeed his own statements made to police immediately after his arrest made what had happened very clear to all.

'The prosecution attempted to position the killing as a deliberate act of premeditated murder and him as a monster, an evil child, one who was unable to control a vicious temper, incapable of remorse, whilst at the same time being intelligent and possessed of a terrifying degree of cunning in how he had planned and executed this crime in such a way as to try to get away with it by blaming the victim for his own lashing out.

'By contrast the defence painted a wider picture, focusing on the circumstances that had lead up to the event, the torment and pressure that he had been subjected to over the months and years leading up to him snapping, this moment of madness as the defence put it, while they asked the jury to consider why it had happened, what had made him do it, and what might have been if the school had stepped in to sort out the bullying sooner.

'It was easy, they suggested, for the prosecution to paint this child as a murdering monster. But the real question was how and why this terrible death had been allowed to happen.

'At the end of proceedings however, he was convicted of manslaughter on the grounds of diminished responsibility, although whether the jury was swayed more by the argument of provocation, or by a diagnosis of the classic symptoms of psychopathy from one of the psychiatrists appointed by the court, it has never been clear.

'Whatever the reason, the presiding judge's views were clear as Mr Justice Carlton sentenced him to be detained for life at Her Majesty's pleasure, citing the high risk he might pose to other children as the reason for imposing what was effectively an indefinite term of imprisonment.

'Which led to the immediate question for the prison service of where to put him. An adult prison was out of the question for a child of his age. In the light of the judge's comments he was considered too dangerous for most children's institutions, mental hospitals weren't equipped to take him either, and no one in their right minds thought for a moment that Broadmoor was the answer.

'So, as with other children convicted of killings in the UK, during his time as a juvenile he was held at the St Helens Lancashire secured unit of Red Bank where there were specialist facilities for dealing with the education and treatment of significant child offenders with teams of child psychologists to work with him.

'And you knew, wherever he was sent, the other inmates knew who he was, and what he'd done, what he was capable of if provoked, so they left him well alone, gave him respect even. After all, how many of them were inside for killing someone? In terms of the local totem pole based on what you were away for, it had to put him right at the top of whatever ranking there was inside. In fact, for the first time probably in his life, his reputation gave him status, made him sought after, popular even, with his contemporaries.

'He was inside, but it was on his terms, on which he was successful.

'As I heard it, he never had any trouble with bullying again.

'Peter Bath had sorted that problem for him, a lesson well learnt.

'For the first time in his life everyone around him, from other kids to the staff, treated him with respect and as a result he was a model inmate, quiet, peaceful, a bit of a loner still but one that people gave space to.

'He could keep himself to himself as much as he wanted, see the other guys inside when he liked, read his books, study, do what he wanted really, other than walk out freely. There was a workshop there for occupational therapy and vocational training and much to his and everyone else's surprise it seems one of the projects that he really got involved with was spannering a bike. The Young Offenders Institution he was at then had bought a couple of knackered trail bikes and he and some of the lads stripped them down and rebuilt them nut by nut into great little runners. One of the screws taught them to ride and they had a great time burning round the edge of the recreation ground. The Governor was a bit worried by all accounts when he found out. I think he had visions of Jim and his mates doing a Steve McQueen style *Great Escape* impression or something over the wire but Jim went to him with a delegation to explain what they were about, invited him down to have a look and gave him a demo of what they were doing. Organised his first bike show, he joked afterwards, but it was notable he led the group. It showed how much he had come out of his shell by that time.

'He had made his own world.

'All of which seemed to ring true, since as Bomber had told Iain in one of his interviews, "All I ever wanted was peace, to be left alone to get on and do my own things."

'Once he'd turned 18, he was transferred to an adult prison where he served the remainder of his time without incident until finally being recommended for release at the age of 24. Even at the time there were those who questioned the decision to release him, questioning whether the psychopathic tendencies some of the psychiatrists had diagnosed could really have been cured, or whether it was just another symptom of the manipulative killer that some saw beneath the surface, playing the game and putting on the act that he knew those in charge would be looking to see in order to judge him fit for release.

'Again, as with others who had been convicted of killing whilst children, part of his resettlement programme involved relocating him to a new area under an order granting him permanent anonymity and a new identity, in the hope that this could help him start his life again. In time, the court protection of his identity was then also extended to his daughter.

'And so in the end, when he was in his early twenties, a model prisoner cum patient with good exam results, Grade As in science all the way at A level, they gave him a new name and let him back out into the world to make his own way again.

'Poor sodding guy.

'He walked out the door with no one and nothing to meet him other than an envelope of fuck off and don't bother us again money from one or other of his parents, and a choice of which way his probation officers wanted him to go.

'Then he walked straight into the first bike shop he found.

'North, east, south, or west.

'And that was how a young lad with a Manchester accent called Jim Pickering eventually appeared as a man in his early twenties starting a new life in Edinburgh as John Harris, soon to be known to those around him as Bomber.

'He was out, and being settled in a new location with a new name to give him a new start. But without the reputation of his old name that meant we was back to being a nobody and he'd come to be used to being a somebody in his world.

'So I think once he was out, he was just lost again, on his own, in a strange city. He had no structure to form his life around, no family to relate to, no old friends to hang around with. He was somebody looking for something to join, to give his life meaning.

'The one thing he did have was his love of bikes and that was what led him to a party.

'And that's where he found what the club offered him, the chance at last of a family he never really had to belong to.

'That's why Maggie was such a big hit with him.

'He was just out of jail. He'd always been shy, awkward even, that's what had got him in there in the first place when you think about it, and in his early twenties having grown up inside, Christ, I bet he'd never actually seen a girl until he got out, let alone talked to one.'

There was silence in the room after he'd finished as we tried to take in what we'd just heard, until eventually our managing director blurted out a shocked, 'Christ! And he never told anyone?'

'No,' said DI Chambers as he stood up to leave. 'He never told anyone and what's more, no one ever knew. All his juvenile files were sealed as part of his rehabilitation process and there was a Court Order protecting his identity until the day he died.'

'No one?'

'No one,' he said firmly, 'until now of course.'

'Now?' we asked, 'why now?'

'Because he's dead,' he said simply, closing the file on the desk and sliding it towards us.

Author's note: fiction, respect, and thanks

All characters, events, and in particular the clubs named in this book, any patches described, and any documents quoted or referred to are all entirely fictional and any resemblance to actual places, events, clubs, patches, documents or persons, living or dead, is purely coincidental. None of the views expressed are those of the author.

The Osman Warning guidelines are invented but are based on a number of documents which have been released by various police forces under Freedom of Information requests.

As ever, for all of my inventions I apologise to the one-percenters in the areas mentioned, and any clubs with similar names or patches; and in particular I'd refer readers back to my notes at the end of *Operation Bourbon, The First Chapter* concerning The Blue Angels MC in Scotland and The Rebels MC. No disrespect is meant; just what I hope is an enjoyable story.

And finally:

Dear Reader

I just wanted to take this opportunity to say thank you for reading *DILLIGAF*, I hope you enjoyed reading it as much as I enjoyed writing it.

I'd love your feedback so please do leave a review on Amazon, whether you loved it or hated it, just let me know.

Reader reviews are the lifeblood of any writer's career, they help tell us what's working so we can give you more of it, and what isn't so we can change it; and they're also vitally important for getting our books noticed whether it's by readers browsing online or by being able to submit books on advertising services.

So every review means a lot to me - and I'd like to take the opportunity to give something back such as the free further reading guides below. So, if you're not already part of my readers' group and getting news of my upcoming books as well as my offers and giveaways, please do head over to my website at www.bad-press.co.uk and join in by requesting my current free offer.

Thanks and ride safe.

Iain

FREE EBOOK GUIDES
Want To Know More? 25 Key Books

Your free guides to essential reading about the biker life and gangland.

Request your free guides today and join Iain Parke's reader group for news of new books, special offers and great giveaways.

Available in 3 easy to use formats:

Visit: http://bad-press.co.uk/free-reading-guides/

Also available by Iain Parke
from bad-press.co.uk

Heavy Duty People

Heavy Duty Attitude

Heavy Duty Trouble

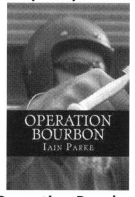

Operation Bourbon

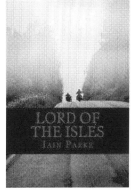

Lord Of The Isles

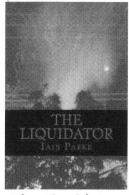

The Liquidator

20743717R00150

Printed in Great Britain
by Amazon